Content Editing by Melissa Bourbon

The Book's Savant Talent

Editorial Assessment by Leoneh Charmell

Cover Art by Elvins Acurero

Interior Design by Avril Acurero

https://thebookssavant.com

THIRD EDITION

To my husband,
Who put up with all the late nights and crazy hours while I worked
on this project.
Who always supports and believes in me no matter what, and who
always picks up the extra slack when I can't.
Thank you for all of it...

To my son,
You are the inspiration behind everything I do.

The Twelve Realms

A DIARY OF A DEITY NOVEL

THE BURNING

LORYN MOORE

TABLE OF CONTENTS

PROLOGUE

Gabryel

Gabryel's heart pounded as the flow of blood settled in his ringing ears.

Thrum, thrum, thrum.

He could barely think over the deafening boom of it, and only a single question managed to break through the panic: *Where was she?*

The possibilities, none of them good, raced through his mind as he plowed through the destruction that surrounded him. Broken glass littered the ballroom floor, along with the burning shards of ribbons and flowers—

frivolous, useless décor. It didn't matter. All that mattered was her.

He kicked aside any chairs that still stood, looking for his granddaughter, his heir. An image of her coffee-colored eyes swimming with tears and terror flashed in his minds-eye. He moved faster, scanning every inch of the ballroom as he searched.

"Dad! Where are you?" His daughter's voice, full of authority, cut through the dust. A cloud of debris seemed to cling to every molecule, and he struggled not to choke on the thick, musty scent of it. He turned to find her standing behind him near a large crack in the glass wall; blood matted her hair and ran down her neck. His stomach dropped.

"Mack!" he kicked aside discarded hats and shoes as he ran to her. When he drew closer, he could see that blood stained the shattered glass wall and realized that it was her blood. She'd been blown back into it. His throat constricted as he skidded to a halt in front of her.

Though she was a goddess grown with two adult daughters of her own, he still saw the girl she'd once been. His only child, and she was hurt badly. He could tell that she didn't want him to see how much pain she was in, but she couldn't fool him; he knew her too well.

He swallowed, fighting to control his reaction to the sight of her injury as he laid a tentative hand on her shoulder. "Are you OK?"

She ran her fingers over the back of her head and winced when they came away bloody. "I'm fine. Nothing a night in stasis sleep can't fix. But Bekka—" She peered over his shoulder, to the singed archway where her daughter had been only moments before. She was gone. "Where is she?" Mack asked, her voice as wobbly as a drunken sailor.

It flashed through his mind again—the screaming, the panic, the fear. He scrubbed a hand over his eyes, and at the same moment, a cough sounded nearby. Killian, his son-in-law, kicked a cello and some discarded violins aside while he struggled to his feet, and without thinking, they hurried to help him.

His arm hung at an impossible angle. Dislocated shoulder and fractured ribs, judging by the way he clutched his side with his good arm. Gabryel made the diagnosis instantly. He'd seen the wounds before, in his youth, back when the gods had tried to kill each other for sport.

He grabbed Killian's arm, and they locked eyes as an understanding passed between them. Better now than later. He took the useless appendage and popped it back into its socket in a smooth, practiced motion. Killian gasped and then let out a relieved sigh.

Deities they might be, but what had just happened qualified as a killing event, and that was something that hadn't occurred in nearly a millennium. His jaw flexed as frustration and guilt swelled within him. This was his fault, his responsibility. They'd been unprepared. They'd been complacent. *No*, he thought, *we've been arrogant.*

Shaking his head, his gaze tracked his surroundings once more. The dust had begun to settle, and he could make out dozens of unconscious gods and goddesses that laid sprawled around the edges of the room, alive but unmoving. All of them had already succumbed to stasis sleep. He knew that he needed to get the healers here right away to ensure that everyone was accounted for and safe before he could see to his own injuries.

Footsteps crunched, and all three of their heads snapped up. Remi's hands shook and her eyes were wide as she approached them. A pang of concern quickly overshadowed the relief he felt at the sight of his second granddaughter when he noticed that she limped forward, one leg dragging as she shuffled closer. He promptly scanned her body and found the problem—a large shard of glass protruded from her thigh. The skin around it was already bruising while thick, glossy blood slithered down her leg, visible beneath the burnt fabric of her wedding gown.

She stumbled forward, moaning in pain as Gabryel lunged to catch her elbows. He held her steady, careful not to touch the burns, cuts, and gouges that covered her body. He knew they would heal soon enough, but the sight of them on her pale flesh threatened to undo him.

When he'd gotten her steady once more, she turned her wild eyes, swimming with tears, up to him. "What happened? Thayne's unconscious. I think he's OK, but I don't understand. I—" She looked around, her complexion whitening with each passing moment as she fought against her injuries to stay alert. "Is everyone OK?"

"I—" he began but was cut off as Remi realized what the rest of them already knew.

"Wait, where's Bekka? Where's my sister?" The question echoed off the towering, glass ceiling of the ballroom, and before he could formulate an answer, Remi's eyes glazed over as she lost the battle to stay conscious. Her legs went slack, and she slumped into his arms, stasis sleep pulling her under without her permission. It didn't surprise him, given the extent of her injuries and the blood loss she'd endured. She needed at least a few hours to heal and restore her strength.

He locked eyes with his daughter and son-in-law; they were the last three deities conscious in the ballroom now. An unspoken thought passed between them—an understanding.

Something that they'd agreed never to speak of again, unless absolutely necessary.

Mack licked her dry, cracking lips. Her hands trembled, "The prophecy." She stared at them, her eyes wide with terror. "It's begun."

CHAPTER 1

It's all Just Fine

A *n hour earlier...*

I raced down the halls of the Valerian palace I called home. My ankles wobbled above my four-inch heels as I gained speed. *The things we sacrifice for beauty,* I mused, as I swung around the corner, lost my balance, and smacked into a white-washed wall. The stone plaster cracked from the impact of my body, but I couldn't be bothered by that now.

I needed to hurry. If I didn't get to my sister's wedding soon, she was liable to burn my hair off. "An angry fire goddess could have such devastating consequences," I murmured, and my urgency ramped up a notch. "Bald is not a good look for me."

I turned another corner, kept my balance, and broke out into a sprint. The spiral staircase that led to the glass globe of the Palladio Ballroom stood just ahead of me. I gripped the intricate, iron railing and hauled myself upwards, taking two stairs at a time, and when I reached the over-sized balcony that served as a landing, I skidded to a halt. My body buzzed from the pleasant rush of adrenaline coursing through my veins.

I surveyed the area, noted that the ballroom doors were still closed, and breathed a sigh of relief. It seemed I was still in the window of acceptability since three of my immediate family members spared me no more than a fleeting glance before they ignored me. The exception was my grandpa, Gabryel, the ruler of the Valerian Realm and the last creation deity left in the multiverse.

The golden metal of his battle armor clinked as he stepped forward and leveled a steely gaze on me. While the intricately carved armor was only used for ceremonial purposes these days, it made me think of all the bloody battles fought over 900 godly years ago in The War of the Nefarals. We'd learned about it in school growing up, and with each powerful step my grandpa took in my direction, an image flashed in my minds-eye.

Step. Grandpa Gabryel and his armies, casting spells and wielding their charmed weapons as they conquered the Twelve Realms and ended the terrible reign of the darkly powered deities we call Nefarals, thus bringing the once dominant Nefaric Pillar of Power to heel.

Step. My grandpa resplendent in his golden armor after his victory, appointing himself as Peacekeeper rather than Supreme Leader, as so many had feared he would.

Step.

My gaze moved from the intimidating armor and up to the warm, kind face that I knew so well. All thoughts of heroic victories dissipated as quickly as they'd come.

His booming baritone teased, "Nice of you to join us, Bekka." He surveyed my flushed face and disheveled appearance. "Everything OK?"

Wispy, blonde fly-aways danced in my peripheral vision and tickled the back of my neck. I tucked them into my chignon as best as I could without a mirror and then waved a hand in dismissal. "Minor issues. All solved. We're good now."

He shook his head at me, clearly amused, as he dusted some white, stone plaster from my bare arm. "You're sure it's nothing I should be concerned about?"

"I just got a little too confident in these heels. It's nothing I can't fix first thing tomorrow."

He gave me a thoughtful look. "You know, your grandmother put her fist through a wall on our wedding day."

"I bet you never sassed her again."

He laughed, the sound rolling out of him. "Actually, she tripped on her gown on her way out the ballroom before her fist ended up there." He gave a brief pause, and I waited for him to continue. I never tired of hearing stories about Grandma Gilliyana. Though she'd ascended long ago, her celestial soul leaving our world centuries before my birth, I'd always felt a kind of kinship with her.

When he spoke again, his gravelly voice was filled with the fondness of her memory, "She never did like wearing gowns or heels. She preferred silk trousers and flats, or battle leathers. Never armor, though. Times were different all those years ago, but then you know that; I've told you about how it was back in those days more times than you can count."

I grinned. "Don't worry, I like your stories, and I like hearing about her."

His eyes grew distant and somber. "I know we don't have much of her left in this palace, as so much of that was destroyed during the war. But trust me when I say, you have her spirit. And her smile."

I reached for his hand and squeezed it to draw him back to me. His eyes cleared, and the shadow of her memory seemed to pass. I sighed, "I wish I could have met her."

"Me too, Bekka. Me too."

It pained me to know that he still mourned her loss so acutely over nine centuries later. I'd always wished there was something I could do to mend it, but all the matchmaking in the world couldn't fix what that final war had cost him. His victory had saved countless lives and improved so many worlds, both human and godly, but the price had been his beloved wife's life.

He cleared his throat and gestured toward the opposite end of the balcony, eager to change the subject and if I had to guess, to get a little time alone. "You should check in with Remi and your mother before the ceremony starts. Can you do me a favor?"

I nodded automatically.

He leaned closer. "Take care of your sister today. I know she'll want to lean on you, so make sure you let her."

I slid my gaze in Remi's direction and caught the high color in her alabaster cheeks—a sure sign of the nerves buried beneath her otherwise composed surface. My twin sister could bluff with the best of 'em, so it surprised me to see any sign of distress in her at all.

"You got it, Gramps."

"Thanks, Trouble," he said and winked at me. He was the only person I allowed to continue calling me by my childhood nickname. When other people said it, it irked me, but with him, it made me feel warm, known in some way. I liked it.

I offered him a salute in acknowledgment before he turned his back to me, striding over to the floor-to-ceiling window to peer out into the capital city that surrounded us. Doriad was beautiful, as was our entire home planet of Vyngale. A cool breeze fluttered through the balcony, and I realized that he'd left it open; I could smell a floral perfume from the gardens below and a bite of sea-salt from the nearby ocean. I spared one glance out into the bustling, golden city I loved so much, with its tiled rooftops shining in the waning sunlight, before I turned my attention to my sister.

Moving toward her, I eased past my dad, Killian, and saw the tiny, white glow of a comm device pressed onto his temple. He listened as it translated tiny vibrations into sounds that only the wearer could hear. His expression grew dour, downright angry, and I did my best not to interrupt him. My guess was that whatever he'd just heard had something to do with the Prophecy Aversion Branch (PAB) of our godly government, the one he and my mom, Mackayla, both ran. The PAB worked in concert with many of the Pillars of Power in our godly government, but the branch reported directly to the Time & Dimensional Pillar.

As I drew closer to the stunning bride-to-be and my mom, I gave them a tentative finger wave.

Remi's lips twitched at my sheepish approach. "Glad you finally decided to make an appearance. Good thing too, or else I would have had to make good on my promise to burn your hair off if you let me down today."

I wiped a dramatic hand over my brow. "Crisis averted. But speaking of crises, what's going on there?" I hitched a thumb over my shoulder in our dad's direction.

My mom chewed on her lip as she looked at him. "Just a blip the PAB's algorithm picked up." The PAB had thousands of concurrent algorithms running to detect the onset of any potentially disastrous prophecies predicted by our seers if they hadn't already come to fruition. "There are some inconsistencies that we're trying to work out."

I looked at my dad, who'd now taken to pacing along the opposite side of the balcony. He was far enough away that I only made out a curt, "No, that's not good enough," followed by a "we need more information before we—" He strode further away from us and out of hearing range.

I chewed on a lip as my belly knotted with concern. Prophecies were serious business, and we did not mess around with them because, in our world, getting the future right was a matter of life or death. "Anything we should worry about?" I asked.

My mom opened her mouth to reply, but my dad's voice echoed from the tall ceilings, "Mack!" He waved a hand, urging her to him. She held a finger up to Remi and me before she pressed her own comm device onto her temple and hurried to join him. As she did, my dad slid his hand to the small of her back and moved further away.

Remi pursed her lips as she surveyed them. "I think they're holding out on us."

I shrugged my shoulders in a hapless gesture, "Nothing we can do. If they wanted our help, they'd ask." Remi and I had worked for each pillar of our godly government, along with all of the major sub-branches, since we had come of age four years earlier. This included a stint at the PAB. It was the perfect crash course in how to run a universe, which made sense because one day we would be expected to do just that.

Remi tapped a finger to her chin, "I don't know. It seems fishy to me." After a pause where we both mean-mugged the parents who'd given us life, she shook her head and changed the subject. "So, any luck with the other thing today?"

I crinkled my brows, struggling to shift gears.

When I met her inquiry with confused silence, she elaborated, "You know, the other thing." She widened her eyes, and after a moment of befuddlement, her meaning clicked into place.

I wagged a finger. "Oh no, we're not starting this again."

Remi urged, "Oh, come on! Consider it a wedding gift."

"I already got you a gift, and it's a good one too. So, can we just drop it? I've come to terms with the fact that I'm defective, and that's totally fine. I don't need powers to be complete. I can live without them. Granted, it won't be for long since I'll age and die like a human if they never come, but it's all just *fine*." I tried to infuse indifference into my voice, but the truth was that none of it was fine. At 22 years-old, my powers were years overdue, and I wanted them more than the very air I breathed.

She crossed her arms over her chest and assessed me. "Liar."

I caved. "I never said it would be a happy life."

"Can you stop being such a wet rag and do it? I think I've earned two presents. I'm the one who's about to walk into an arranged marriage that will force me to live in another realm for the rest of my life."

She had a point. Each realm operated independently, with its own laws and governing body. Nothing linked us except the Peacekeeper's core tenants, which all realms upheld without question. But due to this individuality, the most common way we shared our resources was through royal unions, i.e. arranged marriages. I imagined that the only royal deities who remained unphased by this terrifying eventuality had ice-water running through their veins.

I gaped at her, adopting my best impression of outrage, and pointed my finger to my chest. I mouthed, *"Wet rag? Me?"*

"Stop pretending like you're offended. We both know you're not. You owe me one last try, for old times' sake."

After a brief stare-down that I lost, I shrugged, "Fine, but I'm telling you, it won't work."

She waved an impatient hand at me to proceed anyway.

I spared her a final, exasperated look before I closed my eyes, concentrated, and snapped my fingers. As I opened my mouth to confirm that nothing had happened, I felt something—a buzzing? Or a zing? Astonished, I tried to grab onto it. My heart galloped with excitement, and adrenaline pumped through my system, but before I could latch onto it, the sensation dissipated. My emotions whiplashed as disappointment clawed out from the depths of my belly. I kept my eyes closed and tried not to let it show.

Remi whispered, "Anything?"

I paused and took a moment to compose myself. I waited for a few more heartbeats, hoping that I would feel something again, but when I didn't, I opened my eyes and shook my head. "Sorry to disappoint, but nothing happened."

Frustration coursed through me and the back of my head began to throb, a sign of the tension headache that I was certain my future held. Not that I was a seer or anything, but I got these headaches often enough to know the signs of impending agony.

I rubbed a hand over my neck to soothe it as Remi surveyed me. "You sure? I could have sworn I saw…" As she trailed off, she squinted at me as though trying to see into the depths of my soul. It was disconcerting.

"I'm not a specimen, Rem. You can stop examining me now."

She shook her head as though to clear it. "Sorry, right. I just thought I saw something." She leaned closer. "You're sure nothing happened?"

I shook my head. "I don't think so. I thought maybe, for a second, but then nothing."

Before we could debate the subject further, my dad rested his hand on my shoulder. Remi and I turned to face him in unison, each surprised to see him there and off his comm device. A good indicator that they'd been able to sort out that pesky blip.

He opened his mouth to say something, but then closed it; his eyes drifted from me to Remi and softened as they took in my sister. I followed his lead and had to admit that she looked beautiful in the golden laced wedding gown, adorned with metal armbands and a golden chest plate.

The ceremonial armor held a symbolic promise that she would be ready to fight for her new realm's prosperity and for her new husband, a place called Bicaidia and a god named Thayne.

Our mom and grandpa joined us then, the same sad expressions as our dad's on their faces, and I knew that mine mirrored theirs. How could it not? Remi was my best friend, my partner in crime, and my twin. We shared everything, even a womb, and now she would be whisked off to become a princess in another realm.

It didn't help that the only way I would be able to visit her was if I arranged diplomatic travel with the Bicaidian royals and my grandpa—not the simplest process ever conceived. The idea of life without her ever-present company hurt more than I cared to admit.

For a long moment, we all stood in a circle, each looping an arm around the other's waist, holding on tight to each other this one last time before everything changed.

At last, our grandpa rested his hand on Remi's shoulder. She looked up at him, into his ice-blue eyes framed by snow-white hair. At 2,500 godly years-old, which equated to roughly 25,000 years on the mortal timeline, he was middle-aged for a deity. He looked good for his age, despite having gone gray earlier than most gods. His eyes crinkled at the corners, a sad smile in them. "It's time." Those two words held more resignation in them than I would have expected.

Before any of us could say or do more, a symphony of harps, violins, and cellos sounded through closed double doors to the Palladio. The ceremony would start any second now, so we all hurried to our places. My mom rushed to gather the two bouquets sitting in vases near the window and handed the smaller one to me and the larger one to Remi; her silver gown flowing like mercury in the rustling breeze.

I took one last opportunity to squeeze Remi's arm as she passed by me to the end of our succession. "You ready, sis?" I whispered.

Her coffee-colored eyes, the only feature we had in common, settled on me. "No turning back now." Her words were as stiff as her shoulders and as empty as her stare, completely emotionless. I understood her sentiment all too well, there was a lot at stake here, and we all knew it. Bicaidia's deities and resources filled a plethora of power gaps in our world. We had a duty to uphold and, when it came down to it, neither of us would ever let our people down.

With that as the final word, I moved to my place behind my grandpa. I adjusted my own fitted, silver gown, untied the rings from the thin, satin ribbon attached to my bouquet, and clasped my hands in front of me. A second passed, and the ornately carved doors opened. I watched as my grandpa prowled down the aisle, his ceremonial armor eliciting stares and whispers from everyone in the crowd. Once he reached his spot as officiant, I entered the ballroom, my heels clicking against the floor.

The glass globe of the Palladio hung over a cliff, halfway down a spectacular waterfall. This ballroom could go anywhere we wanted it to in the mortal or immortal realms. It provided us with protection or invisibility wherever we chose. This location damn near took my breath away, the perfect spot for a wedding. A soft green forest swelled around us, alive with singing birds, rustling trees, and millions of fireflies. They winked in the low light of sunset, and my heart throbbed at the beauty of it all.

My mom cleared her throat behind me, and I realized that I had hesitated, overwhelmed by emotion, so I took my cue and made my way down the aisle again.

The guests sat in silver leaf chairs with iridescent gold ribbons and deep, red roses in vases. The chairs were arranged in a large circle around an arch, made of ivy that bloomed with white, star-shaped flowers. Shimmers of twinkling light within the branches matched the glow of fireflies outside.

All 150 deities in attendance turned in their seats as I walked, and nerves pricked up my spine when I realized that their eyes had fixed on me now. Only close friends and family from Bicaidia and Valeria were invited to attend in person. However, a small subset of reporters had permission to broadcast the royal wedding live to all the uninvited deities in both realms. This knowledge had me squaring my shoulders and tilting my chin high.

I drew closer to the archway and saw Thayne standing there. His black hair and handsome, angular face gleamed in the low-light. His expression grew stern as he waited for Remi to make her entrance. *No ice-water in his veins either*, I thought, sensing the tension that rolled off him in waves. Lucky for him, he was marrying the best goddess in the multiverse, not that I was biased or anything. I hoped that one day he would come to appreciate that fact.

At last, I arrived at the archway and took my position on the bride's side of the wedding party, my grandpa standing front and center. The music shifted, and the chords transformed into a melody that seemed to embody the beauty of love and devotion; a goal I hoped my sister and her soon-to-be husband would one day achieve.

I dragged my gaze away from the musicians and back toward the end of the aisle. Remi stood there now, her arm intertwined with our father's on one side and our mother's on the other. Her golden-laced gown fit her slim body like a glove, and her scarlet waves tumbled over her shoulders. I stole a glance at Thayne and saw that his mouth hung open, an expression of pure awe and gratitude on his face. Pleasure overwhelmed me, and I beamed while I watched my sister float down the aisle, as graceful as a dancer.

As I watched Remi approach, I felt it—that strange buzzing sensation from earlier, like a quickening deep inside my body. I began to hum like a bowstring strung too tight. My skin heated, and my breath rasped while my muscles tingled. As I tried to fight the scalding heat that burned inside me, Remi appeared by my side. She handed her bouquet to me, and I took it, shocked that it didn't erupt into flames on contact with my fingertips. The energy coursing through me grew so vivid that it stung every pore in my body.

I bit the inside of my lip and tasted the metallic tang of blood on my tongue. Something was very wrong, but I was standing in front of 150 guests at a wedding. *My sister's wedding,* so I couldn't very well excuse myself from the proceedings. What would everyone think? What would Remi think? *She will definitely set my hair on fire if I abandon her now.* My thoughts raced as my body grew hotter and hotter.

I tried, but I just couldn't seem to focus. My grandpa was saying something important about commitment, and was it duty? But I couldn't make it out. My eyes darted around the room as I handed Remi her rings. Time sped up, and next to me, Remi and Thayne clasped their hands, their magic swirling up each other's wrists in a binding promise of unity. The cementing of their union unleashed a roar of applause that flooded my eardrums. Yet somehow, the world remained fuzzy and unfocused.

I looked down and saw that my fingertips shone a fluorescent blue in the dim lighting. Without warning, the glow traveled up my hands and onto my wrists. The progression was slow at first, and then it happened faster and faster as it spread up my arms and onto my chest. I choked.

Remi broke her connection with Thayne and turned to look at me, "Bekka, what's wrong?" Her words wobbled in my mind as I tried to grasp their meaning. I couldn't speak. I shook my head, tears pricking the corners of my eyes. Terror raged through me.

And then the energy inside of me erupted.

It showered the room with an explosion of nuclear heat in all directions. The force of the blast cracked the walls of the Palladio, spider webs crinkling into the glass dome. The pulse of energy blew through the guests. Gods and goddesses flew across the room, and others lay sprawled on the ground. The blaze incinerated every rose along with each shimmery ribbon; it melted the chairs into glossy puddles on the floor.

I reached for my grandpa, but he'd been blown back by the blast as well. I heard him shout something indiscernible and my eyes followed the sound of his voice. He ran toward me, jumping over scrabbling limbs and melted plastic to get to me. Desperate, I held out my hand.

And then, just as quickly as the energy had exploded out from me, it reversed—my body became a vacuum, the energy being sucked back toward me. A small glowing ball floated before me, so hot that I felt the hair on my arms singe, sizzle, and burn away. The orb grew, slowly at first, and then it got bigger in rapid succession, doubling in size in seconds, then tripling. Winds roared around us and whipped my hair into my face so hard that it broke my skin. Our guests screamed, scrambling back to their feet as they attempted to flee.

I collapsed onto my knees and fought for a foothold in my mind. Something that would help me *focus* the power. But there was nothing for me to use. I didn't know how to leash it. "Help!" I shouted. "Please, someone. I can't control it!"

"Bekka!" My grandpa's voice pierced through the mayhem around me. His body glowed blue with power now; he was getting closer. It flowed around him like a cloak, and I prayed that he could stop me.

The now blue ball of flame roared in front of me, fifty feet tall, the promise of a fledgling sun, and I was powerless to stop it. The terror I felt at the prospect of a star forming in such close proximity was indescribable. Few things could kill a god or goddess, but creating a sun on top of one's self and one's loved ones was on that list.

As my grandpa fought to get to me, his approach slowed by the force of the solar winds whipping around me; my eyes burned from the heat and my helpless tears. "Please, Grandpa!" Desperation and panic overtook me.

After what felt like an eternity, he reached the fledgling sun and placed one glowing hand on the hundred-foot, molten sphere. The heat evaporated, and it fell to the glass floor, the glowing orb nothing more than a dead rock. The heat inside me had stopped as well, and my breath now came in ragged gasps.

I crumpled into a boneless heap on the floor; my hair was soaked from my own sweat, and my dress had been burned clean away. When I looked up, I saw my sister—my amazing, beautiful sister, whose face was streaked with tears. There was an angry, red cut knifing a jagged line along her jaw, and the lace of her perfect dress had burned away in patches. The shock on her face was reflected by every single person still left in the room.

But before I could say or do anything to apologize, a swirling dark mist appeared, enveloping me in black and blocking me from the view of the people I loved most. Was this my grandpa? Was he protecting them from me?

Then, a man stepped out of it with a dazzling smile on his perfectly formed face. He was beautiful. The stuff of dreams or maybe erotic fantasies. Definitely *not* my grandpa. When he spoke, his voice was rich as chocolate, "I've been waiting a long time for you." He knelt beside me, lifted me from the floor, and walked back through the mist.

My last thought as we left behind every person I'd ever loved was, *"Holy crap, I'm naked!"*

Then everything went black.

CHAPTER 2

Enemy Territory

"Bekka?"

I heard someone calling me, but I turned away from the voice, not wanting to wake up. My head was fuzzy, and I had a vague recollection that something terrible had happened. I didn't know what, but I was certain that I would get chewed out for it. I concentrated a little harder, my head throbbing as I tried, but all I got were flashes—my grandpa looking determined, black mist, and heat. The heat was so intense that I couldn't place its source. *Probably just a bad dream,* I decided, trying to fall back asleep.

"Is she ever going to wake up? She's been asleep for hours," a voice I didn't recognize whispered. It sounded like a kid, perhaps a little girl? It was hard to tell around that pre-puberty age.

I groaned in response. "No… Must. Sleep. Longer."

"How about you sleep later?" a deep, male voice suggested. "I have coffee, donuts, and a proposition for you instead."

The voice brought a niggle of recognition to the back of my mind, and I said the first word that popped into my muffled brain, "Grandpa?"

A deep laugh reverberated in my psyche. "Well, that's a first. No one's ever called me Grandpa before. Do I look that old to you?"

The girl giggled and said in an exaggerated tone, "You sure do, graaandpa." Then the surface I was on began to jostle and bounce—a bed. I could barely hear myself think through the peals of laughter. He must have been tickling the girl. Only a tickle-fest could elicit such a response from a kid, and I couldn't help but grin.

I cracked open my eyes and saw a chiseled jaw and dark hair obscuring the rest of his face. Beneath him, getting tickled to within an inch of her life, was a small blond girl, no older than ten. It was safe to say that neither of them was my grandpa; must have been my addled brain grasping at straws.

The guy pointed with one hand and continued to tickle the girl with the other. "Coffee and donuts are over there, as promised."

I looked to my right, picked up the mug, and took a deep swig, then I grabbed a glistening sugar donut and bit into the fluffy dough. The scent was heaven, and the crunchy sugar sent my taste buds into overdrive. I glanced around me and noted that I was in a bedroom. The bed was soft, and the floor was warm and marbled; the décor was lavishly adorned. Nothing specific in the room looked familiar to me, but the theme felt homey, like a room in the Valerian palace that I just hadn't seen yet. Which made sense since there were hundreds of them, most of which belonged to palace appointees and lower caste servants, similar to the two embroiled in the nearby tickle fest.

Settling into the pillows, I gulped down more coffee, hoping the haze that enveloped my brain would clear soon, and then, *maybe,* I could remember how I'd gotten here in the first place. I must admit that I was quite confused. Mostly because no one seemed to be mad at me, and for some reason I couldn't pinpoint, I felt certain that people should have been berating me.

As I licked the remaining grains of sugar off my fingers, my palms started to glow a fluorescent blue before they winked out. Then, like having a vat of cold water dumped over my head, the memories bombarded me in rapid succession and no discernible order.

My sister's wedding, the fledgling sun, everyone fleeing and screaming. *Wait a minute, was I naked in front of all my friends and family?* I shuddered in horror and then snuck a peek beneath the covers to check. I slapped a hand to my forehead in relief. At least now I had clothes on. I didn't allow myself to consider who might have dressed me; after all, I had to deal with one indignity at a time or else I'd explode.

"Oh, gods, the wedding," I groaned aloud, covering my eyes and sinking deeper into the cushions of the bed, not wanting to face the reality of what I'd done. "I ruined my sister's wedding."

The guy and the little girl stopped rustling the bed and the gales of laughter ceased. I splayed my fingers and peaked out through them. As I suspected, they had stopped with the tickle battle and now surveyed me with concern. The little girl was freckled and in that awkward baby doe age where limbs and bodies don't quite fit like they're supposed to.

My gaze traveled from her and fixed on the guy. Now that his hair no longer obscured his face, I could honestly say he was the most beautiful male I'd ever seen—strong jaw, straight nose, full mouth, and his eyes. His eyes were unlike any I'd looked into before. They were a vivid, moss green, wide with dark lashes, and just a bit tilted at the ends. He was the kind of good looking that would make a girl want to shower, do her hair, and wear full makeup if there was even a chance she might be in his presence.

I looked down at my boxer shorts and white T-shirt and crossed my arms self-consciously over my chest. Whoever had dressed me hadn't bothered with a bra, so this was not my finest moment. Another blast of recollection hit me, and I knew where I'd heard his voice and seen his face before.

I scrambled out from beneath the covers and leaped to my feet, the braless state quickly forgotten. I pointed an accusing finger in his direction and gaped at him. "Wait a minute! You kidnapped me!"

I turned a circle around the room, seeing the lavish comfort differently in the wake of this new revelation. All the doors were shut, and the windows were closed while the curtains were drawn together. But before I could light into him, another much more terrible memory hit me—Remi's battered face and body; all those deities fleeing and injured. Were they OK? My head ached, and my stomach churned. What had I done?

I whispered now, too scared to voice my worst fear any louder than necessary, "Did I kill my sister? My family?"

My mind reeled with too much information to process all at once.

My kidnapper rose slowly from the bed like I was a wild animal that he shouldn't make any sudden moves around. He used both hands to press the air down beneath them. "Rebekkah, calm down."

Apparently, he had never met a female before because those two words were like gasoline and a match for any goddess who was as upset as I was at this current juncture. I exploded. "Calm down? How am I supposed to calm down? I think I might have killed my entire family! Or at the very least, I ruined the wedding. Remi is never going to forgive me, especially not if she's dead! Maybe my grandpa can explain what happened because I—well, I have no idea what happened. And just who the hell are you anyway, and why did you kidnap me?" My rambling rant faded away, and I turned on him with anger, panic, and fear fighting for dominance in my racing mind.

He hadn't hurt me yet, but he'd taken me away from everyone who mattered in my life without my permission. And now that I was awake, who knew what he had planned for me? He stepped forward and I automatically stepped backward, not willing to let him anywhere near me. The little girl bit her lip, worry lining her face as she surveyed my wide, panic-stricken eyes.

He didn't take another step forward but stayed right where he was, leaving a safe distance between us. He slipped his hands into his pockets. "Your sister and your family, along with everyone at the wedding, are fine. Your grandfather stopped the star before it gathered enough mass to become deadly, so any injuries sustained will heal with a few hours in stasis sleep."

My legs wobbled with relief at his words. I wanted to believe him because the other option was too terrible for me to accept, but just in case, I asked, "I'm supposed to just trust your word on that?"

His gaze never wavered from mine, a good sign that he wasn't lying. Still, I didn't know him, and I couldn't be sure of that. "Try to remember. Then you'll see that I'm telling the truth," he suggested.

I cut my eyes between them, weighing my options. I pointed a warning finger at each of them, "Don't move." I waited until they both agreed with a nod before I closed my eyes and tried to concentrate on what had happened.

At first, everything was chaotic and hazy; the events were tumbling around in no meaningful order. However, after a few moments, my thoughts cleared, reordered, and I saw how it had ended. My grandfather had stopped the star before it was too big to control, just as my kidnapper had said. Then there was my sister; she had been crouching over Thayne, and he'd been unconscious but alive. But then I remembered her eyes, open and staring with terror as she'd looked at me. I cringed at the memory but took comfort in the knowledge that she'd been alive when I'd last seen her. As for my mom and dad, I strained to see them in my mind's eye; then I remembered that they'd been knocked far away from the forming supernova. So, if Remi had been safe, then surely they must be too.

I let out a shaky breath of relief, and my knees almost buckled with it as I opened my eyes. Neither the young goddess nor the god had moved an inch. They just watched and waited for me to finish.

"I remember," I breathed, the sheer relief of it overwhelming. Regaining my composure, I drew myself to my full height. "What do you want with me? Why am I here?"

His jaw flexed, and his expression grew serious as he considered my inquiry. When he replied, it wasn't what I expected. "Your help."

His answer shocked me, and a little of the fear I felt ebbed; not fully abated, but it diminished. If he needed my help, then odds were that he wasn't planning to kill me. Unfortunately, I reminded myself, killing me wasn't the only terrible thing that could happen, so I couldn't let my guard down.

I eyed him from beneath my lashes. "Am I a prisoner?"

"A guest."

"If that's true, then who are you and where am I?"

I glanced from side-to-side surveying the possible exit points—no good options. I would have to outrun both the girl and my kidnapper to get anywhere near them. I thought I could take the kid, but the guy, not so much. He looked like a resting wildcat, his muscles coiled and strong. My instincts told me that he would snatch me off my feet before I made a single step out of the room. So, I decided to bide my time and wait for a better opportunity.

He gestured toward the girl, who smiled at me and bounced from foot-to-foot, "This is my sister, Lilja."

She held out a hand. "It's nice to meet you, Rebekkah. We've been waiting for you for a long time."

The words struck a familiar chord, and I made the connection in my mind. It was what my kidnapper had said just before he pulled me through the black mist. I had no idea what they meant by it. We had never laid eyes on each other before, so why would they be waiting for me?

I shook the girl's hand, feeling a little dumbfounded, "Um, it's nice to meet you too, Lilja." This had to be the most cordial kidnapping in the history of kidnappings. It was creepy.

When we finished, the guy stepped forward. "My name is Arrick." He paused for a beat to let that settle. Something about it sounded familiar, and I waited for it to sink in, scanning my memory, but everything came up blank. To be fair, I was still a bit fuzzy after everything that had happened.

Rather than answer him or offer him a hand in greeting, I arched a brow. "So, where am I exactly?" I knew I wasn't in Valeria anymore, but that left a dozen of other universes as possibilities.

He looked at me with an expression of disbelief as he answered, "You're in Moldize, of course."

Instantly, it all clicked into place.

That was where I'd heard the name before. We'd learned about the ruling family of Moldize, but little was known about them other than their names. Arrick was a Moldizean prince, and his existence was shrouded in even more mystery than the rest of his family. The hairs on the back of my neck stood on end. *This is so much worse than I could have imagined*, I reflected. I worked to control the tremor in my voice and whispered, "Well, that's unfortunate. Since we're enemies."

He chuckled, the sound genuine and rich. "Are we? I hadn't realized."

I withdrew further away from him, sweat prickling my hairline. "You're kidding, right?" He couldn't be serious. The Moldizeans were not just exiled from the Twelve Realms; they were enemies of the peace and prosperity we fought to maintain. My grandpa had described them as beasts too wild and malicious to be tamed. Their human wards were reputed to be no better than the gods who ruled them.

Simple contact with any Moldizean carried a steep price—imprisonment for a minimum of 1,000 years.

Harboring them or allowing them to enter the Twelve Realms carried an even steeper punishment. Death. My grandpa had enshrined these policies into law once he'd become Peacekeeper.

"I know your grandfather, Gabryel, hates us," he replied as if he had read my mind. He pointed a finger from him to me. "But why does that make *us* enemies?"

I hid my fear behind bravado, propping my hands on my hips, and cocking my head at him. "Because you're evil."

Again with the chuckle. "Do I look evil to you?"

I tilted my chin up in defiance. "Evil doesn't *look* like anything." Apparently, I was suicidal. Why else would I argue with my evil kidnapper?

"Does Lilja look evil to you?" His eyes glittered with what I considered to be an inappropriate level of amusement. Strangely though, his offhanded attitude calmed me and strengthened my bravado.

I narrowed my eyes at him, "Are you screwing with me?" I was less frightened now, and more annoyed. I had become fed up with the who-does-or-does-not-look-evil argument. I wanted answers, dammit, and he had yet to give me any straight ones.

"Certainly not. But I am asking you to question everything you've heard about us. I'm asking you to see with your own eyes and tell me whether you *really* think we are evil. If that's what you believe, then I'll take you home right now."

I didn't miss a beat, "OK, please take me home." One tickle fight, a little banter, and a cute kid did not equal good guys, at least not in my book. Besides, how could I possibly know whether they were evil or not? He was hot, but I couldn't trust that as a character reference. What I could count on was that he'd kidnapped me and brought me here without my permission. As a rule, good guys didn't run around kidnapping people.

"What would you say if I told you that if you leave, this entire solar system, and most importantly, our home planet of Myzhrele will cease to exist in less than a week? Myzhrele is home to all mortal life in Moldize, and if it dies, then millions die with it. That's mothers, children, husbands, babies, and not to mention all the animals left in the mortal realm. Would that change your mind?"

My heart skipped a beat. He just told me I could go, and now he dropped this on my lap? I stammered. "W-what are you t-talking about? And what does that have to do with me?"

"It has everything to do with you," the little girl said, her eyes filled with hope—and perhaps a little hero worship. "You're our savior."

"Come again?" I asked, genuine confusion now taking hold. I was not anyone's savior. I just came into my powers and, as a result, had almost killed everyone I had ever loved. That in and of itself should make me unqualified to be anyone's savior.

Arrick stepped forward and rested a gentle hand on the girl's shoulder. "Lilja, let's take it a little slower, OK? We don't want to overwhelm her."

She looked down at the floor, "Sorry." Her expression was sheepish and shy. He had a point; she didn't look evil.

Arrick slipped his hands back into his pockets, a casual gesture, but I could feel the tension rolling off him in waves. "We've been waiting for you to come into your powers. We've needed a creation deity on our side for a long, long time. Sadly, there's been a shortage, and it's down to the wire now."

"So, you thought you'd kidnap me? And, I'm sorry, but did you say *creation deity?*" I asked, stunned. For some reason, this hadn't registered with me before now. But of course, he was right. No other deity could create a star, and I had done just that without even thinking.

My mind rebelled against this realization, hoping for another explanation. There had only been thirteen other creation deities since the beginning of time. They had each created their own realm, thus the origin of the multiverse, and now *I was one of them?*

The responsibilities that came along with this title were immense and terrifying. As a creator, I would be my grandpa's heir apparent and the future Peacekeeper of the Twelve Realms. I felt nauseated by the prospect. *Whoever thought it would be a good idea to give me this kind of power deserved a serious talking to... or maybe a bitch slap.*

He gave me a side-eyed look of suspicion. "Yes, creation deity. It's what you've been destined to be since the day you were born."

My mind reeled at his words. "What do you mean *destined?*" Destined was a strong word. In our world, it implied the existence of a prophecy, and that was impossible. My parents knew about all the prophecies in Valeria and never once mentioned one about me. *They wouldn't keep something like that from me, would they?*

Lilja stared at me with a bewildered expression on her face. Before my mind could travel further down the rabbit hole, her voice interrupted, "Is she serious?"

Arrick stared at me, his expression cold as ice. He studied me harder. "You mean, you don't know?"

"I have no idea what you're talking about."

"You're the creation goddess who is destined to save Moldize from destruction, to right the wrongs committed by Afryel, and to usher the multiverse into a new era." When I just stared at him with a blank expression, my mouth going dry, he continued, "You're *She Who Was Sent...*

the most powerful creator to ever exist. From the prophecy." When I continued to stare at him, speechless, he narrowed his eyes. "Does any of this sound even remotely familiar to you?"

My thoughts tumbled like tiny hyperactive gymnasts from all the information he'd just thrown at me. This was a lot to take in all at once. First my sister's wedding, then my kidnapping, and now I was a creation deity destined to help my family's sworn enemy?

"How is that even possible?" I blurted, all the bravado I had mustered flowing out of me like seawater at low tide. This was too much. I couldn't think straight. "Are you sure you have the right goddess?"

It was a question grounded in the hope that maybe they had it all wrong; maybe I wasn't who they thought I was. Because if I was, then the implications that came along with it were too much for me to handle.

It meant that millions of lives relied on my abilities, which were brand new and untrained. It also meant that my family had known about this, for however long, and that they had chosen to keep it from me. Their betrayal stung even as I tried to cling to the comfort of denial.

His expression showed zero trace of uncertainty, "We don't have the wrong girl. We've known about the prophecy for a long time, and we knew it was linked to your family. Once your sister came into her powers, we knew it had to be you. Since then, we've had you under surveillance, waiting for the right moment to intervene. When you created that sun yesterday, we knew the prophecy had been set in motion. I saw an opportunity amid the chaos to bring you back with me, so I took it."

There was so much wrong with everything he'd just said that I couldn't even begin to unpack it all. It implied that my family had plenty of time to tell me and chose not to. I thought of how my parents had turned their backs on Remi and me before the wedding, trying to shut us out of their PAB business. Was that blip they mentioned connected to this whole mess? I had no way of knowing, but something in my gut told me it was.

Because they weren't here for me to rage at, I focused my anger on him. "You've had me under surveillance for years?" I asked, my mind fixating on that detail. I didn't know what was worse. The kidnapping or that they had been watching me without my knowledge. The invasion of privacy alone made my skin crawl. "Stalking me is not a good way to convince me to help you."

"We weren't stalking." He pinched the bridge of his nose in frustration. "This is not how I expected this to go," he muttered, speaking to no one in particular; then, he fixed his gaze back on me. "You really don't know anything about your destiny? Your parents and your grandfather never told you anything?"

Rather than answer him aloud, I shook my head.

He let out a cold laugh as he turned from me. "How can they hate us so much, even as our home and all mortal life in our realm is on the brink of destruction?" His words were edged with untamed passion and bone-deep despair.

The raw show of emotion from him disarmed me, so I answered him honestly, "They believe you're evil."

Lilja brightened with anger, her fists bunching at her sides, "We aren't evil. Afryel, our great uncle and the original creation deity of Moldize, was evil. But he isn't here anymore."

Arrick finished his sister's sentiment, "She's right. He left years ago, and since then, we've tried to right the wrongs he committed. But we'll never get the opportunity if you don't help us. You're the last hope for our people. You're the only one who can save them."

The weight of their expectations was the last straw, and my mind rebelled, "Please, just give me a minute." Millions of lives, Arrick had said, and they all relied on me. Tiny black spots danced across my vision, so I sat down heavily on the bed, putting my head between my knees. *How could my family do this to me? They all knew that I would become a creation deity. How could they have let me believe I was defective?* Not to mention the fact that they'd left me untrained and unprepared to handle all of this. Anger and frustration flooded my veins and tears threatened to overflow.

This was too much.

I pushed back to my feet and rushed to the largest of the windows, "I need some air."

They could try to stop me if they wanted to, but no matter what, I was getting out of this room. I threw the curtains open to discover glass doors that led out to a large balcony. I unlocked and flung them wide, rushing outside. I hit the railing, doubled over, and sucked in ragged breaths.

I looked down at my hands as though they didn't belong to me. I saw a faint blue glowing beneath the skin and felt tears slide down my cheeks. I wiped them away with the heel of my palm as the betrayal I felt cut through me like a knife. *How could my family have kept this from me? If this was meant to be my destiny, then shouldn't I have had the opportunity to decide for myself? To prepare?*

I clenched my fingers into a fist as anger began to overtake the sense of betrayal. Deep down, I knew the answer, and it infuriated me—they didn't trust me to make this decision for myself. Maybe they wanted to protect me, but I knew, just as well as they did, that destiny had a funny way of intervening when a prophecy was involved.

On an impulse that I didn't allow myself to question, I turned back toward the doors. Arrick and Lilja had followed me, but they were careful to keep a good distance between us. This was my chance to make up my own mind. There was no one here to shelter or choose for me, which meant that I could decide whether to help these people all on my own.

My lashes were still damp with tears when I croaked, "I don't even know how to use my power. Even if I wanted to, I don't know how I could help."

Arrick moved onto the patio to stand beside me. He planted his hands next to mine and stared out past the railing. I followed his gaze and realized that there was a small town just over a sand-colored wall. Heat assaulted me, and I squinted as an over-bright sun beat down on us. After a few moments of silence, he answered, "That doesn't matter right now. All we need to know is this: Will you help us or not?" His eyes bore into mine, and there was naked hope in their depths.

I paused, waiting for inspiration to come or maybe a sign of what the right thing to do would be. I still didn't trust either of them. Old habits died hard, and we had only been talking for a millisecond in the grand scheme of things. If I said yes right now, how could I be sure I was helping the right people? Would I be putting my freedom, or maybe even my life, on the line by breaking the Peacekeeper's law? Besides, there could be something else to this prophecy that they didn't want me to know about. But, if I said no, could I live with condemning all those souls to death?

I decided to answer his question with one of my own, "What does saving this galaxy entail, exactly?"

"We'll get to that soon. But first, does that mean you'll stay?"

I hedged, letting the silence linger. Something tugged at me, deep in my belly. I didn't want to be the cause of needless death. But I wanted to know what was going on, and I wanted more information before I made any decisions.

At last, I answered, "It means I'll hear you out, and then I'll decide for myself what to do next."

He smiled, "That's a good first step. I'm hoping we can convince you to take more. But for now, we don't have a lot of time. So, get dressed and make it quick. Clothes are in the armoire. Meet me outside when you're ready."

Before I could protest, change my mind or say anything else, he walked through a shroud of black mist, Lilja following in his wake. Alone on the balcony, it left me wondering, what the hell had I just gotten myself into?

CHAPTER 3

The Burning

Two minutes later, I was clad in jeans, a light hoodie, and a pair of canvas shoes comfortable enough for walking. I didn't know what he had planned, and I wanted to be ready for anything. I pushed open the bedroom doors to find Arrick there alone, waiting for me.

He turned on his heel. "Let's go." I jumped to follow him as he led me through a massive room.

I looked over my shoulder in either direction and leveled a confused look on him. "Where's Lilja?" For some reason, her unassuming presence made me feel more comfortable; without her as a social lubricant, I felt edgy and nervous.

"She has lessons today. But don't worry, you'll see her again soon."

Before I could get too disappointed, I took in my surroundings, and my mouth gaped open in amazement. "Whoa. Where are we?"

We were in a grand atrium with 40-foot tall, painted ceilings. The obsidian and jade walls displayed intricately carved, white statues. The color contrast was exquisite, and the black marble floor was so glossy that I could see my reflection in it.

"This is our home. Castle Molo."

"Oh," I breathed, trying to hide my surprise at its beauty.

"What? Expecting an evil lair?"

"Ha, ha, ha," I intoned, the words dripping with sarcasm, but the truth was, I *had* been expecting something more sinister. Perhaps cavernous with undertones of evil? But I guess I should have remembered that evil can look like anything. It can hide in plain sight or in pretty castles for that matter. "Doesn't prove anything," I muttered. They said they were not evil, but gods and goddesses said a lot of things, not all of which were true. I needed to remember that it was their people I had agreed to consider helping, not necessarily them.

He gave me a cocky grin. "Not going to take our word for it, are you?"

"I hate to break it to you, but centuries of bad relations with Moldize are working against you."

He scoffed, then opened a door to let me through. "And whose fault do you think that is?"

"Excuse me? What is that supposed to mean?"

He shut the door behind me and then turned on me, walking me backward. I came up short, my back pressing against a wall. His body was so close I could feel the heat of it as anger flashed in his eyes. "Your grandfather is a bigoted prick who won't get over an eternity's old grudge, no matter the cost."

My mouth hung open and my face heated with outrage on behalf of my grandpa. Sure, I was pissed at every single person in my family right now, but he was my grandpa, and no one criticized my family but me.

"*He's* a prick? You kidnapped me from my sister's wedding, and now you're holding me here, manipulating me through some story about a prophecy and how millions of lives hang in the balance. Don't think I haven't noticed that little point because I have. So, what makes you so much better than him?"

"If my enemies asked me for help to save their only life-sustaining planet, then begged me for mercy, I guarantee you that I would listen. I wouldn't turn my back on them and then let all of their people die. *That's* what makes me better than Gabryel." He spat the name as though it disgusted him before he turned and strode down the hall so fast that I had to jog to keep up with him.

"I'm sorry. What did you just say? You asked my grandpa for help?"

"We did. Before we knew about the prophecy, we requested aid from Valeria and from him. He's known about our imminent demise for decades now. He just doesn't give a damn." His comment before, about the hatred that Valeria directed toward Moldize, took on a whole new meaning. I thought that my grandpa had refused to open communication with them at all. I assumed that he had never heard their appeal for help. I did not realize that he had heard it and then chosen to ignore it. This revelation disturbed me.

I asked the obvious question, "Well, if he won't help you, what do you expect me to do?"

"You're *She Who Was Sent.*"

I mentally added the "duh" that should have followed, judging by his tone. Apparently, that was a title, not just something he had said earlier that sounded cool.

He reached for the doorknob to my immediate left. "This is it." He moved to turn it, but I darted my hand out to stop him.

"Wait!" I said, my nerves getting the better of me. "What's in there?"

He gave me a confused look, "My family. More specifically, my parents."

"Oh," I said, and then feeling foolish, I shuffled my feet awkwardly before asking, "What are your parents' names again?"

"Seriously?" If I didn't know any better, I would swear that he was offended. "Don't you learn anything about us in Valeria?"

"Sure, but the information we have is somewhat limited. And besides, it's been a while, and I never really thought it would be applicable. My plan was to avoid Moldize at all costs so that I would never have to meet any of you."

"Brilliant plan. How'd that work out for you?"

"Not so great."

"Damion and Erykha," Arrick said.

"What?"

"My parents. Their names are Damion and Erykha."

"And they're the gods of what exactly?"

He ground his teeth, "The Hunt and Physics. They are both leaders of their Pillars of Power in Moldize," he ran a hand through his hair before he muttered, "Or at least what's left of them." He shook his head and cleared his throat before he refocused on me, this time speaking with more purpose, "Erykha runs the Science & Technology Pillar and Damion runs the Mortal & Godly Affairs Pillar."

I absorbed that, realizing that this made them upper-caste and high-powered deities. Given this new information, I would need to tread somewhat lightly in their presence. But then something seemed to niggle at the back of my mind as I took in his other comment and wondered what he meant by 'what's left of them?'

I wanted to ask for more details but decided against it. He seemed to vibrate with impatience and there was something else I wanted to know more. So, I asked the question that I knew would irritate him the most. If I was honest, it gave me a little pang of pleasure to do it, "And what are you the god of again?"

To my surprise, his expression shifted from irritated to smug and maybe a touch secretive, "We can discuss that later."

I glared at him, "Sorry that I don't know every little thing about every single person in your family. You don't need to get so touchy about it."

"It just goes to show how little your family cares about us."

I had no comeback. It was a fair assessment since we spent minimal time worrying over the state of Moldize and more time taking care of ourselves and our allies. At my lack of smartass retort, he pulled on the handle and opened the door for me to walk through. It took everything in my power not to gasp at the beauty in front of me. The hall was open to the daytime sky—a dusty blue—and frothy clouds danced overhead, a blood orange sun streaming its light inside.

Columns that stood fifty feet tall flanked the main hallway while paintings and sculptures flanked the side corridors. The statues were etched in white marble and beautiful beyond measure. There were mermaids and animals, the details sculpted to a level of perfection that made me want to study them for hours.

I recovered my wits, pulled my eyes forward, and saw a slight, small woman striding toward me. Her thick, chestnut hair formed a cape around her shoulders as she beamed at me.

"Rebekkah!" she exclaimed, the glossy white of her smile taking up most of her face. Green eyes, the mirror of her son's, twinkled from under thick lashes. She spread her arms wide and embraced me. Her head came up to about my shoulder, and I restrained myself from the urge to pat the top of it. When she pulled back to look at me, her long, purple dress flowed around her like water, an intricate, gold bracelet winking at her wrist. "Welcome to Moldize! I'm Erykha, lady of this universe and Arrick's mother. I can't believe you're finally here. He's told us so much about you."

I waved a hand. "Oh, I'm sure he doesn't have much to tell. We've only just met." But then I remembered that they'd had me under surveillance. For years. So, I could assume that he knew more about me than what could be gleaned from the prophecy alone. Again, it was creepy.

She shared a look with her son, and her expression turned serious, "Thank you for agreeing to meet with us. We are so grateful to have you here." The warmth and sincerity in her voice surprised me.

A male voice interrupted, coming from the door we had just entered through, "Sorry I'm late." A tall god with sandy, blonde hair, a deep tan, and a powerful build that matched Arrick's strode toward us. He had a compound bow slung over his back and a hunting knife at his side. "I see you've met my wife and my son. I'm Damion, Lord of Moldize." He held out a hand to shake, and I reached out hesitantly to meet it. He shook, beaming at me in obvious pleasure.

Despite myself, I had to admit that so far this didn't seem like the hellfire and brimstone place that I had expected. Sure, I hadn't been to the mortal realm or seen them interact with their mortal subjects, but I had a hard time picturing them as cruel. I just needed to remember that they wanted something from me and until I knew exactly what that entailed, I couldn't make any snap judgments either way. I needed to see things for myself.

Damion gestured to a small, round table a few paces away with four chairs arranged around it, "Let's sit down. It will be more comfortable for what we need to discuss."

We followed his lead and settled ourselves into the seats. Arrick was positioned across from me, and Erykha and Damion were on either side. Once we were seated, I decided it was time to get down to business, "I'm sorry to be curt, but Arrick told me that this solar system is faced with imminent destruction." The abruptness of my tone caused all three of them to frown at me. "It seemed like you guys had something specific in mind that I could do to help. I mean, Arrick did kidnap me to get me here, and he told me that I'm *She Who Was Sent.* But I'm still missing *exactly* what it is you want me to *do.*"

Instead of answering my question, they shouted in unison at Arrick, "You did *what?!*" The look of total outrage and betrayal he threw my way was worth the price of admission. The vehemence of their reaction surprised me, though. They weren't all in on the kidnapping plan? They actually expected me to believe he'd acted without their knowledge?

Apparently, that was the case because when Arrick spoke, it was to defend his actions, "I saw my opening and I took it. You know Gabryel would never let his beloved granddaughter out of his sight, especially now that the prophecy is unfolding." He appealed to his parents. "No one saw me except for her, I swear it."

Damion's eyes turned to marble. "But they'll be looking for her. And who do you think they'll suspect first?"

"Then let them suspect. They have no proof, and we have protections in place."

Damion pinched the bridge of his nose. "Gabryel is not an enemy we want to agitate, and you know those protections won't hold for long against him."

"One problem at a time," Arrick said in a calm voice. "First, we'll help her fulfill the prophecy, and then we'll deal with Gabryel."

Erykha ran her fingers through her long hair and shook her head, as though biting back a retort. Damion just looked up at the ceiling and frowned.

I decided it was time to interrupt the family feud that I had started. "So, I told Arrick that I would hear you out. I guess what I want to know is why is this entire solar system slated for doom?" As deities, our sworn duty was to use our considerable powers to keep the mortal and immortal planes disaster-free and habitable. Many things could cause a catastrophe, such as they described. But all of them were easily avoidable if we did our duty to prevent them.

Obviously, something had gone very wrong here. The extent to which they needed my help would hinge on what exactly that thing was.

Damion's expression darkened. "You haven't shown her the mortal realm yet, have you, son?"

Arrick shook his head before replying, "No, I thought it would be best to explain first. Otherwise, she might mistake it for something we can control." Everyone seemed to agree that this was for the best, and that had me even more concerned. If apocalyptic effects were being felt in the mortal realm, then that was a bad sign.

Damion looked at Erykha, who sighed, splaying her fingers on the table, and said, "Since we're pressed for time, I'll go with the short version. Our solar system is dying, and along with it, Myzhrele, the only planet in our realm that harbors mortal life. Our sun here is a red supergiant, and it's become increasingly unstable over the past five years. Based on our calculations, we don't have long before it turns into a supernova and blows our mortals' home planet off the map, killing all life here." This revelation stunned me, and I struggled to listen through my shock as Arrick continued the story.

"Until recently, we've been able to use technology and the gravitational pull of passing asteroids to keep Myzhrele just inside the habitable zone. But the size of the sun and the weakening of the planet's atmosphere have wreaked havoc on its surface conditions. Fresh food and water have become scarce as temperatures, and radiation sickness are on a steady rise."

I clasped my hands together. My knuckles whitened under the pressure I exerted as I struggled to think. This was a huge problem. The human scientists in Valeria believed that stars had billions of years of hydrogen fuel to support their main stage life cycle, but that was only true if the gods bothered to maintain it. My grandpa did that for all twelve of our allied realms. But clearly, that had not been done for a long time in Moldize. "There are still habitable zones for mortals and animals to live?" I asked, concern for the humans and the animals pushing its way to the forefront of my mind.

Arrick answered, "Yes, but because of the sun's increased luminosity and size, the planet is now in a runaway greenhouse effect. Meaning—"

"It can no longer sustain liquid on the surface," I interrupted. "But people are still living there, so surely there must be water."

"Most of the seas, rivers, and lakes have already evaporated. No matter how much water we try to create, the sun takes it." Erykha's eyes were full of pain. "Right now, our people are moving south as that is where the atmosphere is least damaged. There is still groundwater and minimal surface water there, but that won't last for long."

"You can't just move the planet again using the asteroids as you have done before? Or what about evacuating the people to another planet in your universe?" I asked, trying to think of anything that might help.

Erykha bit her lip and shook her head. "To answer your first question, there are other uninhabitable planets that are too close in the outer orbits. We're concerned that if we move our life-sustaining planet any further away from the sun, the opposing gravitational pulls could have adverse effects."

Damion stepped in to answer the second question, "We've been preparing for this outcome for a while. We have a planet ready in another, more stable solar system for the deities who live here. It's not ideal, but we can manage. We've already started evacuating them there to get them out of the blast zone. But as far as the humans are concerned, we don't have any other planets that come close to what we'd need to sustain mortal life in our universe. Afryel vanished before he could make more solar systems like this one." He spread his arms wide. "Myzhrele is all we've got."

Arrick locked his gaze onto mine, "What we really need is to fix our sun."

Suddenly, it all made sense.

The reason behind the kidnapping and why my powers were the key to helping them—only a creation deity can build or destroy planets and suns. "So, you need someone to push your sun back into the main stage of its life cycle. Then, once the sun is fixed, we'd need to regrow the vegetation, eliminate the radiation, repopulate the planet with animals, and refill the water sources."

"Exactly!" Damion's eyes were full of hope. It seemed like he thought that because I understood the problem and what should be done about it, that there was something I could *do*. Unfortunately, he was sorely mistaken.

"You need my grandpa, not me. Just let me go back to him so I can explain everything to him. I know he's said no before, but if he hears it from me, he might change his mind."

All three of them shook their heads at my response, with tight-lipped expressions and somber eyes. It was Erykha who spoke this time, her hand reaching out to touch mine, "Your grandfather has made his position clear. There is little chance he'll change his mind. We can't risk sending you back there to ask for his assistance. If we do, we may never get you back, and we would lose any hope we have left. Either you accept our request for aid, or we prepare for the worst."

"No, you're wrong. He must not realize how serious this is."

Damion shook his head, "He knows. But he'd rather let it all come crashing down than help us."

"But why?" I asked, trying to see what I might be missing. Why did my grandpa hate these deities so much? There had to be something they weren't telling me.

Erykha continued, "He believes we are evil and that we cause nothing but pain and misery to our mortal wards.

Then that they, in turn, reap nothing but pain and misery on each other."

My head ached. This was all wrong. "But you're not Afryel. Surely, he can be convinced that things have changed if that's the case. I don't see why he wouldn't listen."

Damion sighed and rubbed his neck in discomfort, "You don't understand. In the early days of Moldize, the founding family enjoyed tormenting their creations. Horrified by the conditions in the mortal realm here, Gabryel tried to conquer us, along with the other eleven realms during the war. But the problem was that, unlike those other realms, we still had a creation deity here: Afryel. Along with him, we also had a good population of high powered, upper-caste deities, most of them Nefarals. Gabryel attacked us once, and it didn't go well for him. So, instead of risking his entire campaign striking against us a second time, he took a different approach—he cut us off completely from any other universe, destroying all comms lines and all open portals. Then, when he appointed himself as Peacekeeper, he officially banned us from all multiversal relations under pain of death or imprisonment. We've been isolated ever since. He even punished the people who helped us send a plea to him for aid. We never heard from them again."

My eyes were wide as I took in the full meaning of Damion's explanation. The banishment and punishment he described were not a surprise to me; after all, that was the law, and my grandpa upheld it without question. Though, seeing it from this perspective, I couldn't help but empathize with them.

But one part of his story threw me. According to Damion, my grandpa had lost a battle in Moldize during the War of the Nefarals. That was not part of what the historians taught us growing up. I couldn't help but wonder, why? And what had that battle cost him that made him so vindictive even now, over 900 years later?

My head spun as I tried to wrap my mind around everything they'd told me so far, but before I could process this further, Erykha continued the story, "Years later, Afryel disappeared out of the blue. He took all the founding deities with him, except for three: his sister, her husband, and me, their daughter. I was an infant at the time, and my parents refused to speak about what happened. After everyone deserted us, it took us decades to rebuild our numbers, though we never really recovered. We lack the resources of power here that you have in Valeria and the other eleven realms. Our population consists primarily of lower caste deities with weaker powers, and because of that, our Pillars of Power are weak. So, we have been slow to fix what was wrong with the mortal realm. By the time we managed to establish peaceful governments and provide better technology to our people, the sun had started to deteriorate. Soon after, the Moldizean mortals began to realize that there was something seriously wrong and all our hard work began to unravel. It was slow at first, and the human rulers managed to keep people calm in the early days of The Burning."

"The Burning?" I interrupted.

Arrick replied, "It's what the mortals call this crisis. It makes sense, too. The sun is burning every habitable inch of their planet and turning it into a wasteland."

I absorbed this information, unable to picture what this would look like on a planet. "You said in the early days, but they're what? Fifty years into this crisis on the mortal timeline? What's the situation down there now?"

Erykha winced and shook her head. "It's not good. When resources grew too scarce, and cases of radiation sickness began cropping up all over the northern hemisphere, chaos ensued. Governments, infrastructure, and the electrical energy that powered their world collapsed. The survivors live by scavenging what remains of the old world and hunting or growing what they can. The problem is that the supplies they need to stay alive are insufficient to support the number of people left. They're desperate, and they fight amongst themselves for the scraps that remain."

After a long pause, I unclasped my hands and stared at Arrick. "I'm sorry, but I don't know what to say. No one ever prepared me for any of this." I waved my hand, encompassing the whole story they had relayed to me and my role in this insane prophecy. "Even if I wanted to, I don't think I can help you."

"But you're a creation deity, and you're *She Who Was Sent*," Erykha said, as though that were all the explanation required.

"But we don't know that the prophecy is still valid. My family never even told me about it. That fact alone may have altered it entirely," I argued. "Besides, the only thing I've ever created was horrifying and dangerous."

"Bekka, you created a sun," Arrick said, eyes filled with amazement. "Surely you can fix a dying one."

"That was an accident. You were there. Did it look like I had any clue what I was doing? That's like saying that one plus one equals eight thousand."

Arrick's eyes glittered with determination. "Only a creator can do what needs to be done. So, you're still the best chance we have to fix this before it all blows up in our faces. Literally."

"If I'm your best chance, you're doomed."

They all looked at me, imploring me with their eyes. "We have faith in you," he said.

I shook my head in denial. "That faith is misplaced. I don't trust myself to do anything with a failing star. I'd be as likely to blow it up as to fix it."

"Then we're no worse off than we are now. Please Bekka," Erykha begged. "We're desperate."

My mind scrambled to think of more reasons this could never work. "I'd have to learn to harness and control my power. Who's going to teach me? The only creation deity I know is my grandpa, and you insist he won't help us."

Arrick's lips twitched upward in a cocky grin. "I'll teach you. Let's just say I know a little something about having too much power too soon."

Well, *now* I was curious. *What was he the god of again?* I racked my brain, trying to remember if it was common knowledge, but I got nothing for my efforts. "But you're not a creation deity? How can you teach me?"

He shrugged. "Power is power. You just need to know how to access it, focus it, and bend it to your will. That's harder to do when you have more of it, which is why *I'll* show you."

I opened my mouth to ask him about his own gifts, but Damion spoke before I got the chance, "We are pressed for time and, honestly, we have nothing to lose. Either you fix it or you don't. If you blow it up, the outcome is the same as it would be if we did nothing." I pursed my lips, not mentioning that the only difference would be that the death of millions of sentient beings would be my fault. Oh yeah, and I'd be dead too.

I considered myself to be good at reading people. I could tell that they genuinely needed my help, but three main concerns kept me from agreeing to their plea immediately.

The first was that I had no idea what I was doing when it came to my power. Yes, I was a creation deity. But I didn't know how much of using that power was instinctive and how much needed to be taught and honed. If it was the latter, then I didn't have much time to learn.

The second issue was Moldize, and by extension, Myzhrele itself. I didn't know if saving a place rife with human atrocity was the right thing to do. Some of the stories I had heard about this place made my skin crawl. And if even half of them were true, did I really want to perpetuate that?

The third—though lesser—issue concerned the council law. Since I was not in the Twelve Realms, I didn't think that the banishment laws regarding Moldize applied. But how would my grandpa react if he learned that I was complicit in saving a sworn enemy of the Twelve Realms? Filled with deities he believed to be little better than savages?

As though sensing one source of my hesitation, Erykha cupped my hands in hers, "Before you make up your mind, give us one day to show you the mortal realm of Myzhrele and its people. You have our word that you will be safe for that day. Then you can decide."

I pushed up from my chair, and it screeched behind me as I moved away from them and began to pace. Movement was essential for my decision-making process, and I needed to think. Time moved differently in the mortal realm—one day there was equal to 2.4 hours in the immortal one, so the downside, if I agreed, would be minimal.

The sticking point was that I had this sneaking suspicion that what they showed me in the mortal realm was going to sway me in their favor. And once I came back, I would have no choice but to help them, morally speaking.

Otherwise, if there was nothing worth saving, why would she suggest that I go?

As I paced, I tried to talk myself into leaving right now, knowing that going any further with these deities would likely cross me over the point of no return. But before I could logic my way into going home, I turned to them and said, "OK, one day." I held up a single digit for emphasis. "Show me."

CHAPTER 4

Living by the Rules

After more displays of gratitude from Erykha and Damion than I felt comfortable with, Arrick led me away from his parents and out into a long hallway. My heart hammered in time with my footsteps. I couldn't believe that I just agreed to go to the mortal realm of Moldize, the enemy of the Twelve Realms. *I must have taken crazy pills when I woke up today.* I debated walking back into that room and telling them, *'never mind.'* But then I looked at Arrick's determined gaze and the words stuck in my throat.

If I took a moment to reflect on why I'd agreed to this, I had to admit that there was something internal tugging me in this direction. It sought to pull me into their crisis and drove me to help them.

The only thing that made sense was the prophecy.

In my experience, destiny was a powerful force. Once anyone came face-to-face with theirs, you had to move mountains to stray them from it. I needed to make sure that I kept a clear head and didn't let that force overtake my own sensibilities, difficult as that may be.

Arrick's words broke the silence between us, "Before we go to the mortal realm, there is a lot you need to know, but we don't have much time. I'll have to give you the condensed version. Moldize is nothing like Valeria. Your experience in the mortal dimension will be much different."

This didn't surprise me. It sounded like it was going to be a radioactive wasteland, except for the southern hemisphere. But who knew if that would be much better? "All of the Valerian worlds are peaceful and thriving cities. I'm expecting the polar-opposite of that."

"You're not wrong. But there's more to it than that." We reached an intersection of four hallways and he stopped, turning to face me head-on.

"What do you mean?"

"There are rules that must be followed while we're there. If we don't stick to them—to the letter—then we could end up stranded. The only way to get back to this realm would be… *unpleasant.*" The way he said *'unpleasant'* raised the hairs on my forearms, so I decided not to press him for details. I would simply follow the rules like he said. Then I would never have to find out what he meant.

"Every mortal realm has rules. I know my way around them pretty well."

The corner of his mouth quirked up, "You don't know your way around Moldize." I opened my mouth to argue, but he continued before I could. "The first thing you need to know is that no mortal can be shown evidence of divinity. They may have their suspicions, but they cannot witness a divine act. If they do, then we would be stuck there until we resolved the issue."

This stunned me. "Why?"

In Valeria, our mortal charges believed in the gods, and they worshipped us. But they had no accurate likenesses, which allowed us to operate freely in their world. We also exercised a certain amount of discretion while we were there, mostly because we didn't want our faces splashed all over the mortal news feeds. But if a mortal happened to witness us using our magic, they counted themselves lucky, and we all moved on with our lives.

"The mortal realm is designed to ensure that they don't know about us. They believe in one omnipotent god there: Afryel. He's the only deity to ever appear to the mortals and display his power. He was also an egomaniac. He wanted to be the only one they worshipped, so he made the rules in accordance with this desire."

"Your grandpa sounds like he was a real peach."

"Great uncle," he corrected.

"Whatever."

His responding grin made my toes curl in my boots. The word smolder came to mind, and I took a moment to recompose my thoughts as he continued his explanation. "The most important thing you need to know is that the portal we cross through will alter you physically. You'll need to appear human while we're there."

This wasn't exactly news to me. All portals that provided access to the mortal realm had a built-in dimmer switch. It disguised the bright light of our godly essence and allowed us to blend in with the humans. "We do the same thing in Valeria."

He drew his brows together in confusion. "I hadn't realized that you altered yourselves physically."

I looked at him like he was one knife short of a set. "Of course we do." We couldn't go walking around looking like giant bug zappers, now could we?

"OK, that should be an easy transition for you then. I was concerned that you would object."

"No objections here."

He took a sharp right down one of the adjoining hallways. "OK, good. Let's keep moving."

I followed him, taking three steps for each one of his as we walked. There were dozens of wooden doors lining either side of the hall and we breezed by them without a second glance. He made another sudden stop and I almost tripped over my feet to follow suit.

Arrick turned to face me and rubbed a hand over the back of his neck. "Before we go, there is one other thing we need to think about. But it has nothing to do with Moldize."

I furrowed my brows as I tried to decipher his meaning. "What other thing?"

"Your grandfather will be looking for you. Now that you've come into your powers, it's only a matter of time before he starts looking at us. The prophecy will point him in our direction sooner rather than later. Gabryel is not known for diplomacy with his enemies, so we'll need to make sure you're here when he arrives. Otherwise, I'm concerned that there won't be anything left of Moldize to save."

"You don't think he'd—"

"Raise our universe to the metaphorical ground?" he asked, brows raised. "I think he would in a heartbeat if he thought we'd hurt you." Arrick stepped closer, his stance powerful and predatory. Despite my rapid heartbeat at his nearness, I held my ground. He continued, his words deathly serious, "Don't you see? You're your grandfather's heir. They would never let you risk yourself to save another universe's solar system. Especially not one that's in Moldize. You're Valeria's future."

I allowed his words to sink in and tried to picture my grandpa through his eyes. I found that it wasn't as hard as I thought it would be. That disturbed me because he was right. Now that my powers had appeared, I would be groomed to take my grandpa's place. It chafed to realize that my parents and my grandpa had known I would be a creation deity and thus his heir all along, thanks to that prophecy. I wished for the hundredth time that they would have let me in on the secret rather than let me believe I was defective for four damned years.

Dread washed through me as I calculated just how much training would be involved, given the massive shoes I would have to fill. "How much time do you think we have before he figures out that I'm here? You mentioned earlier that there were protections in place, right?"

Arrick's eyes flickered as though calculating the odds in the back of his mind. "I'd say we have a day before he realizes we have you. Then a few more hours, at most, for him to break through the protections. They're strong. But if Gabryel wants into our realm, then he'll get in. It's only a matter of time."

I could feel pressure building behind my eyes. Arrick was right, but he was missing another critical piece to the puzzle. He thought I needed to be here to deter my grandpa from destroying Moldize, and while that was true, there was more to it than that. He seemed to be operating under the misguided notion that I had any control over my grandpa's actions, but the truth was, I didn't. Especially not where his enemies were concerned. The prejudice he harbored toward this place ran too deep.

If I chose to help them and my grandpa arrived in Moldize before their sun was fixed, he would drag me back home kicking and screaming before he let me lift a finger for them. And once I was back in our realm, there was no open portal between Moldize and Valeria. So even if I wanted to come back and save their people, it would be impossible.

My family would double down on security after the breach at the wedding. They probably already had. They would make sure that no one got in or out again without their permission. So, we needed to fix the sun before my grandpa breached those protections. That was the only way this could work… if I decided to help, that is.

Rather than voice my concerns aloud, I decided to keep this information to myself. My intuition told me that this new knowledge might change Arrick's strategy. I didn't want him to force me to make a go or no-go decision right now. I wasn't ready to do that. Not yet. I still had this picture in my mind of all the terrible people in the Moldizean mortal realm. If the stories were true, then did I really want to risk my neck to save a planet chock-full of rapists and murderers? I had to be sure that helping them was the right thing to do before I agreed to it.

"Well, then," I decided, "We better hurry up." I took a few purposeful strides in the same direction we had been walking before. Arrick cleared his throat, and I turned at the sound of it, realizing that he hadn't followed me.

"What are you doing?" he asked, amusement evident in his expression.

I injected as much vinegar into my voice as I could manage, "Heading to the mortal realm... obviously." When he just stood still, I crossed my arms over my chest. "Are you going to impart any more revelations or dire warnings before we go? There is only so much I can take in 24 hours, you know. Any more and my brain will explode."

"No, I think we've hit our quota of those for today. You're just going the wrong way."

"Oh, right." I began walking in the other direction, breezing past him and toward an adjacent hall. Before I could get more than a step away, he locked his hands on my shoulders and gently turned me to the right. There was a door right there helpfully labeled, *'Exit.'*

"Seems a little out of place if you ask me."

He chose to ignore me as he opened the door.

CHAPTER 5

Stripped Bare

he door to a hell dimension, I thought immediately. *Or at least, something resembling hell.* Hot air scorched my skin as Arrick nudged me into the intense red sunlight and whipping winds. My body convulsed in discomfort as my throat, nose, and eyes dried to the consistency of sandpaper.

I shielded my eyes with my hands and squinted, trying to see through the granules of sand pelting me. From where I stood, it looked like there was nothing for miles but mounds of hot sand. No water or trees or shelter of any kind. There was no doubt in my mind that a regular life-form could not survive in these conditions. The only reason I was still standing was because of my godly status.

Turning on my heels to go back through the door to Castle Molo, I ran smack into Arrick's chest. Off-balance, I tilted sideways. I would have teetered over, but he caught my forearms and held me upright. My legs felt shaky, as if they weren't quite working right, and when I finally regained my footing, Arrick let go of my arms. I risked a glance beyond him, instantly noticing that the door we walked through only moments before was gone.

I had to shout to be heard over the dull roar of the wind. "What happened to the door?"

"Why?" he asked, raising a brow in challenge. "You want to go back already?"

I cleared my throat and straightened my spine, "No. I just wanted to make sure we still have an exit strategy."

He held out his wrist and ran it over where the doorway had been moments before. The air wobbled like a mirage, and then the door snapped back into focus. "The exits are hidden to protect us from detection, but they are always there," he shouted. Then he slid the sleeve of his black hoodie up and showed me a symbol tattooed on his wrist.

"What's that?" I asked. The symbol itself was written in a sort of black inked calligraphy.

"It's our all-access pass," he said, leaning toward me so that he no longer had to yell. "Just stick by me and you'll be fine." His body was close to mine now and his nearness both unnerved and thrilled me. That, and he smelled good. *Really* good. He pushed the sleeve of his sweatshirt down and stepped out of my space bubble.

"This might be a stupid question, but where are we? We can't be in the southern hemisphere. There's no way this place could support life."

"We're in what used to be known as Lionelle. We never enter the mortal realm in the populated zones. It helps us avoid detection. This is the quickest and safest route to get to where we need to go since it's just north of the habitable area and the radiation here isn't too intense yet."

I could feel my skin begin to crack from the dry, hot conditions, but I chanced one more question. "What happened to the people who used to live here?"

"You mean, did they make it out?" His gaze grew distant and somber as he pressed his lips together into a tight line. "Some did. Some didn't."

He didn't bother to elaborate and I didn't press him any further; I saw too much pain and regret in him, and it suddenly seemed too personal. We barely knew each other, after all. What right did I have to make him revisit his past pain? He used his hand as a visor and looked beyond me, into the distance. "We need to get moving. Are you ready?"

I nodded and we began to trek through the desert. I sunk at least a few inches with every step, and after only fifteen minutes of walking, my legs shook beneath me. After a few more steps, I stumbled, falling to the ground. A puff of dust swirled around me and I coughed. I wiped my mouth and gasped for breath through my burning lungs.

Arrick turned and spotted me on the ground. He covered the short distance between us and offered a hand to help me up. I took it, and he hauled me to my feet. "Something's not right," I said to him, my legs trembling beneath me. "My body feels strange."

He drew his brows together in confusion. "Of course it does. It's part of the effects of the portal. I thought you said that you did the same thing in Valeria."

Alarm bells rang dimly in my exhausted brain as I replayed the conversation we'd had in the hallway before we went through the portal. "What are the effects of the portals in Moldize, exactly?" I asked, my voice monotone.

"They strip you of all your godly powers, including your creation gift, our light, and our inherent strength. The only power you'll maintain is your ability to heal. Though, it's been slowed down significantly to mimic a mortal's healing time."

I spoke too soon before.

It never occurred to me that my powers would be stripped; I had been thinking only of my light. If I had known the true extent of what I would give up to come here… he was right. I would have objected.

"Are you fucking kidding me?!" My voice would have been a shrill shriek if I had any power left to put behind it. As it was, it had been thoroughly sapped, and no wonder. I was trekking through piles of sandblasted hell at one-thousandth of the strength that I was used to having.

"See, this is the reaction I expected earlier," he observed, shaking his finger at me to emphasize his point. When I only glared at him in response, he rested his hands on his hips and looked out past me into the desert. When he refocused on me, his captivating eyes were filled with resignation. "If you've never had your powers stripped before, it can be disorienting. So, if you don't want to do this anymore, I won't force you to. I'll take you back right now. Just say the word."

I held his gaze as I debated the merits of accepting his offer. I was many things, but a coward wasn't one of them. So, I shook my head and said, "No, I'll stay." It wasn't as though I were in any real danger. We still maintained our ability to heal, and it wasn't like I could die. Or at least, I didn't think so. "Wait a minute; I can't die, can I? You said we still heal, right?" Might as well make extra certain I knew what I was getting into.

"No, you can't die. Our accelerated healing is just slower, not gone."

"OK then, let's keep going," I said, nodding more assertively this time. "I've got this."

He spared me a skeptical glance before he pointed to a large dune about fifty feet away, "Good. We don't have much further to go. We just need to make it there." We both pulled our hoods up to protect against the pelts of sand that blew around us. I pulled my drawstring as tight as it would go and still allow a peephole for me to see through. Then I followed Arrick toward our destination.

When we reached the dune, Arrick used his wrist to access another doorway. It slid open automatically, revealing what I could only describe as a reinforced bunker—food, packs, water, clothes, and weapons lined the metal walls and were piled high on shelves in the dimly lit room. Crates were stacked at odd intervals and made the space tighter than was fully comfortable with both of us inside.

"You'll need to change before we go any further," he explained. "We'll need to blend in where we're going." He strode toward the shelves that housed clothing and began to rifle through them.

"And where exactly is that?" I questioned as he threw a pair of lightweight cargo pants and some lace-up hiking boots to me. He then tossed a thin, tan t-shirt and a lightweight cargo jacket to match as well. Next came the undergarments, thick, black, granny panties and a black sports bra. I may not have the gift of foresight, but I had a vision of a very large wedgie in my future. I cleared my throat meaningfully since he seemed to have missed my question regarding our destination altogether.

"I'll explain once we're on the road. But first, you'll want those."

"Isn't it a little warm for pants and a jacket?" I questioned, holding the clothes hesitantly to my nose to sniff them. To my relief, they smelled freshly laundered.

"You need protection from the sun, wind, and sand, but it needs to be thin enough that it breathes for the heat," he said, and I nodded my understanding before surveying the space to find somewhere private where I could change.

I was still blinking the sand out of my eyes and saw no immediate option for privacy. When I turned back, Arrick had already stripped off his hoodie and his undershirt. The muscles of his abs rippled as he unfolded a thin shirt from a locker and slid it over his head. My girl parts tingled without my permission; I couldn't help it, and when he unbuttoned his pants, I nearly had a heart attack. Before he could slide them down his heavily muscled legs, I let out a strangled protest. I had to stop him before he got completely naked and ruined me for all other guys because, based on what I could see of his body so far, that was a real concern.

My awkward interruption worked. He stopped what he was doing and looked at me in confusion, probably wondering what that strange noise was all about. Then he took in my flushed appearance and apparent embarrassment. He rolled his eyes and let out a low laugh, "Right, I forgot. You Valerians are such prudes."

"Well, that's rude," I retorted, flushing bright pink. "And how would you know anyway?"

"Everyone knows that. It's common knowledge."

I thought about it and shrugged, deciding not to argue. There were worse things we could be known for. "So, I'm not the kind of girl who wants to see a guy she barely knows naked. Sue me."

"Then we'll have to make sure we fix that." His look intensified, and I felt a flutter low in my belly. For a moment, I could have sworn I saw a flash of interest in his expression that had nothing to do with my ability to save this planet. But before I could be sure, it passed, and he clarified his statement. "It will be important that you trust me where we are going. That will be easier if we know more about each other."

"Oh, right," I agreed, not sure if I was disappointed or relieved that he hadn't meant that sexually. I decided on relieved as I scanned the room once more, looking for a nook or cranny I could use for privacy.

He caught on to what I was doing and gestured over his shoulder, "There's a bathroom back there." He was pointing to an area of the room obscured by a large stack of crates. "Knock yourself out. Oh, and if you don't want an eyeful of some guy you barely know, it would be a good idea to let me know when you're coming. I'll be sure to cover my more impressive body parts."

No matter how dire the circumstances, guys just couldn't seem to resist a good old-fashioned penis joke. I deadpanned him, "Oh my gosh. You're hilarious,"

He gave me a look that could have melted all the panties in Valeria, "I wasn't kidding."

I was almost certain that he was messing with me. So, rather than reply and encourage him further, I tucked the clothes under my arms and made my way to the bathroom.

Once inside, I pulled on the clothes. I was impressed at the fit of them and by how comfortable they were. There was no mirror, so I executed a quick pat-down to ensure that everything was zipped and secured. Then I pulled my hair back into a tight ponytail and braided it. When I finished, I ran my fingers over it to check for any major fly-aways. No way I was going around in that wind with loose tresses any longer than necessary. If I did, it would be better just to shave it off and start from scratch than to try to untangle it.

I walked out of the tiny bathroom and asked, "Are you decent?"

Rather than answer me, Arrick appeared, fully clothed, from around the stack of crates and handed me a pack. It was heavy and filled with supplies. It buckled in the front for support and had a camelback for water. Very handy. He then grabbed a colorful knit scarf from a hook behind him and unwrapped it.

"This goes around your head and face. Protection for your skin. The sand can be pretty brutal," he explained. Oh, how well I knew that already. My eyes were still gritty, and sand burns stung along my cheeks.

He slid the purple and green garment around my neck and pulled it over my head. He then buttoned a flap around my mouth. He grabbed a similarly colored one of his own and performed this ritual on himself. Then he slung a bigger pack over his shoulder, a tent and sleeping bag attached to it.

"Why are there so many different colored headscarves?" I asked, noting the vast array that hung on hooks by the door.

"Different tribes mark their affiliations by color," he explained. "We're going to the Itorian tribe. We want them to welcome us, so we wear their colors. They are one of the most peaceful tribes, and I feel safer taking you there than to any of the others. It's where I spend most of my time while I'm here."

I knew that Moldize was a dangerous place, but what he said concerned me. There was a difference between *most peaceful* and just plain peaceful. Not missing a beat, he passed me a pair of thick-lensed, black sunglasses with a rubber band that looped around the back of my head. I settled them into place around my neck and let them hang there for now.

"Should I be worried?" I asked, fingers fidgeting with anxiety.

His hand lingered on the door, ready to push it open into that vast wilderness, "About what?"

"The Itorian tribe."

He slid his own glasses into place and grimaced. "Not worried exactly. But once we're with them, you'll have to try to blend in. They are the *most* peaceful, but they are not pacifists. You'll have to be mindful of how what you say and do impacts the tribe. They'll order corporal punishment without hesitation if your actions put anyone in their tribe at risk, whether it's intentional or not. Do you understand?"

I gulped, "But it's not like they can really kill me. And corporal punishment isn't the same as capital punishment."

"That's true. But with your powers stripped, they can hurt you, Bekka. And badly. Something tells me that you've never been hurt before, at least not physically or purposely. Don't let this be the first time."

I nodded, and he must have sensed my anxiety, noted the stiffness of my spine. He placed both hands on my shoulders and said, "I'll do everything in my power to keep you safe. But it's important that you understand that I must obey the rules of the mortal realm. If it comes down to you feeling some pain or our exposure as deities, I'll have no choice." He showed me his palms, as if in helplessness. His next words were quiet, and I could tell that he hated to say them, "You can still change your mind. If you want to go back now, you can. I won't stop you."

He was giving me another chance to turn back. It both warmed and insulted me. Kind of him to offer but infuriating that he thought I would run away at the mere possibility of a little pain. It seemed to me that this was a risk that the humans faced here every day. It was only fitting that I experienced it too. He was right about one thing, though—no one had ever hurt me before, not physically. But these people needed my help. Plus, he wouldn't bother to show me his world if there was nothing left worth saving, right? I needed to believe that there was a reason I was here, a reason that I was chosen to be *She Who Was Sent*.

I nodded my head to reassure myself. "No, I can do this. I offered him a sly smile. "I'll blend, and I won't mouth off to anyone but you. And I'll do it quietly, I promise."

Though the scarf covered his lips, I could see his sharp cheekbones rise beneath it and crinkle his eyes in a grin. "Something tells me that that's the best I'm going to get, so I'll take it. Are you ready?"

I swallowed hard and blinked rapidly, trying to work up some moisture in my eyes before they got sandblasted again. My legs still felt wobbly, so I pulled a foot up behind me and stretched. I repeated the treatment for my other leg, then I bent over and touched my toes. It was a routine I had seen human athletes do a hundred times. I never understood why until this moment.

Arrick gestured to my thigh, "The more we walk, the more they'll loosen up."

"Good to know." I lifted one leg and shook it, then the other. "OK, go ahead and open the door. I'm ready."

As his hand pushed open the door, I braced myself in expectation of the scalding winds and biting sand. But when they hit me, I found that the clothes took a lot of that bite out of them. We stepped outside of the bunker, and Arrick closed the door behind us.

He pointed toward another large dune in the distance, one taller than the rest, "That's our next stop. It's not speed travel, but it's a shortcut that will get us to our destination faster."

I squinted, groaning inwardly. "How far away is that?"

"About a mile."

I nodded, feeling a little encouraged. That was nothing. I could totally handle that.

Maybe this wouldn't be so bad after all.

CHAPTER 6

The Last Thing You'll Ever Do

Twenty-five minutes later, my calves burned, and my throat blistered. It may have only been a mile, but without my godly powers, it felt like I was walking with three fifty-pound weights attached to my body. When we, at last, came to a stop before the massive dune, I fell forward onto its soft, sandy exterior and hugged it. I would have tongued it too, so profound was my gratitude, but I didn't want to get sand in my mouth.

"Thank the ascended! We made it!" I cheered, fist-pumping and executing a minor victory dance. My energy was too sapped for an all-out boogie. Arrick just shook his head and laughed, or at least I think he did. I could barely make out any sounds over the howling winds. He pulled up the sleeves of the cargo jacket he wore to expose the tattoo on his arm. He waved it across the front of the dune. I heard a chime and another invisible door slid open.

This was not a bunker; it was a tunnel that split into three different directions. Each were helpfully labeled with their destinations and the distance required to get there, along with an ETA. He turned toward the tunnel on his right and gestured for me to go first. I did, and my relief at being on solid ground once again was so heady that there were simply no words. Based on the flashing ETA, we had thirty minutes of walking to go 250 miles. He was right. This wasn't exactly as awesome as speed travel, but it was still way better than traveling 250 miles the mortal way.

"We don't have anything like this in Valeria," I observed, wiping sweat from my brow. We had domiciles, or luxury hovercrafts, that flowed through a network of tube-shaped tunnels. They were powered by the natural magnetization of the planet and pumped up with a little godly magic. As a result, they traveled at the speed of light and were invisible to the mortal eye. "How does it work?"

"They're spelled to translate our walking speed into a much faster rate outside of the tunnel," he explained, dusting the sand off him. It fell into a grainy pile on the ground and he continued. "It's the precursor to speed travel via domicile. That's probably the reason you don't have them in Valeria. Unfortunately, Afryel and our upper-caste founders vanished before they could upgrade our full network. As a result, we only have access to domiciles in certain areas and for long-distance journeys in the mortal realm. These spelled tunnels are the primary way we get around here."

I frowned, pursing my lips together in thought. "I'm surprised Afryel would have allowed it to be upgraded at all. You said he wanted his people to worship only him, so why bother letting other deities into the mortal realm? At least, outside of the normal upkeep process?" I asked, my natural curiosity getting the better of me. Afryel could have exerted complete control over the access to this realm with his power as a creator. So why allow a public transit system that all deities could use at random if his goal was to be viewed as a single, omnipotent god?

Arrick shrugged a shoulder. "Erykha and Damion disagree with me, but from what I can tell, I don't think Afryel started out evil. When he first created Moldize, there's evidence that he genuinely wanted to build something good. But somewhere along the line, something went wrong, and things started to change."

"You don't know what happened? What went wrong?" I asked, eyebrows drawing together in a combination of confusion and interest.

He chewed on his lip as though deciding something. I wasn't sure if it was deliberation on how much to tell me or if he honestly wasn't sure how to explain. "No, we don't. Mostly, we've had to piece the history of our universe together from mortal records. But those records are inherently flawed because they are missing a large swath of time and various details."

"You mean to tell me that you have no records of your own?" I asked, brows raised in surprise. "How is that even possible?" We kept extensive records in Valeria, as did every immortal realm in the multiverse. They were critical to the work we did to keep everything running smoothly.

His response stunned me. "All of our records were destroyed on the day Afryel disappeared, and the founding family vanished."

Questions swirled through my mind in rapid succession. "What about the non-royals? The other families who lived here? Surely they knew something?"

He shook his head, "Back then, there was only the founding family. It was a large, extended family that included hundreds of upper-caste deities, but it was still only the royal family. Afryel's sister, Erykha's mother, was the one who opened our borders after everyone vanished. It's how we rebuilt our numbers."

My mind struggled to process how something like this could possibly happen. "Don't you have any seers? Or gods and goddesses of time who have come here since then? Can't they help?"

He shook his head again, "Most of the deities who live here now are lower caste gods and goddesses from other universes. They wanted to get away from their home worlds. We don't offer much here, but our universe is free of the archaic caste system that binds them in most other realms. As a result, none of them have gifts powerful enough to get us back to the time when it all happened."

That made sense. Lower caste deities played a more supporting role in keeping the multiverse running. They often worked for the top caste deity with their equivalent power to carry out the grunt work. Additionally, time gifts were inherently flawed when used in the immortal realm for even the most powerful deity. For anyone with a weak gift, they wouldn't be able to get back very far. Maybe a few years at most.

"One more question," I said, though that wasn't entirely true. I had a million of them. I just didn't think he would have the answers. According to him, there was a giant black hole in Moldizean history, and all the people who had any answers were gone. "You said that the mortals only had Afryel's likeness. But if your records were destroyed, then how can you know what he looked like? How do you know that the mortal renderings were of him and not someone else? Did Erykha's mother tell you that?"

He stopped walking and turned to face me. He crossed his arms over his broad chest and eyed me thoughtfully. "No, she didn't. She didn't talk much about the past, so I suppose we don't know for certain. It's just an assumption based on what we've been able to piece together."

"But other gods and goddesses in the royal family had access," I argued. "So, what makes you sure it's him at all?"

"I guess we aren't," he allowed, picking his pace back up. "We just assumed that it was him because of how the rules that govern the mortal realm are structured. They make it so any deity, other than him presumably, can't access their powers."

I thought through everything I'd learned since I got here. Maybe they were right, and the mortal renderings were of Afryel. But then, this nagging suspicion in my gut told me that an essential piece of this story was missing. "You're making a lot of assumptions," I observed. "And you know what they say about assumptions."

"Are you calling me an ass?" he asked, trying to deflect my curiosity with humor. But I would not be deterred.

I shrugged, not addressing the question directly. "Look, call it an outsider's perspective. But it seems to me that there are more holes in this story than a sea sponge. It feels like you're missing something important."

He stayed silent for a few beats, and I could tell that he was contemplating what I said.

I interrupted his thoughts with one final question. "If you have no records, then how do you know what happened with my grandpa and the war?"

He shrugged. "A little from my grandmother and a little from some Valerian deities who came to live here later on. Some of them had firsthand knowledge that they shared with us. Though it was limited."

My eyes widened in surprise at the mention of Valerian deities in Moldize. "Wait a minute; how did they even get there?"

Arrick's lips spread into a sly smile. "The same way you did. We have our methods."

I stared at him as I considered pressing him for more details. But a few seconds passed, and I decided to let it go. My guess was that it had to do with his power, and he had been more evasive than a cat in the bathtub any time I asked about that. Instead, I continued with our earlier conversation, "OK, but for the record, I still feel like something is missing."

His eyes searched mine as he suggested, "Maybe, once we finish saving the world, you can help me figure out exactly what that something is."

I twisted my lips to the side and then replied with a casual, "We'll see."

We walked a while in contemplative silence, and I started to take a more pointed interest in my surroundings. There had been pictures hanging from the walls since we started down this tunnel, but I hadn't paid them much attention. They were scattered every 10 to 20 feet, and I was far too absorbed in the mystery that was Moldize's history to notice what they housed.

Now that I took note of them, I wished I hadn't. They functioned much how the pictures in the Valerian palace halls did. They showed what the mortals outside of these walls were doing, but that was where the similarities stopped. In Valeria, we watched major scientific achievements in space travel and medicine transpire before our eyes.

But here in Moldize, I watched as people lay starving in no more than lean-to shelters, while violence and theft seemed to be a predominant way of life. I watched as tribes raided other tribes for barrels of food and jugs of water. I had to turn my face away as I witnessed a man hanged for stealing food, the stern faces of his accusers unflinching in their certainty that this was justice.

"This is what we are walking into?" I asked, gooseflesh prickling up my arms. Why would they have bothered to send me here at all if this is what I would see?

"It's not all like this," he explained. "There's good, bad, and endless shades of gray out there."

I stared at a picture of three men shooting an unarmed woman for the supplies on her back. "This doesn't look very gray to me. This looks like evil."

He sighed and said, "Look at me, Bekka." Hesitantly, I turned away from the horror show and stared into his depthless eyes. "It isn't all this way. But you must understand, the end of days does things to people. It makes them desperate. It makes them do things they wouldn't otherwise do in a normal world."

"If you're trying to tell me that desperation breeds crime, I already know that. It's just that it looks to me like they're enjoying this," I argued, referring to a particularly disturbing image of a mass execution by shooting. The men wore red and yellow scarves and showed no signs of remorse as they lined people up and shot them to death. I didn't bother to hide the disgust and horror I felt at the sight.

Arrick looked at the picture behind him and frowned, his jaw flexing with anger. "Those are Lorus's men," he explained, and I could see hatred and repulsion in his eyes. "Some people just have evil inside of them. It burrows and waits for the right moment to be released. These conditions, this world, gives them free rein to unleash it. But look," he said, pointing to another picture frame. I turned my sickened gaze away and looked at what he wanted me to see. "There's still goodness here, despite all of the atrocities."

There were two women, injured and starving, huddled together in a makeshift shelter. The view panned out, and I saw a party of four men wearing brown scarves and handmade leathers standing outside of the hut. I tensed as the scene unfolded. But they didn't set fire to the hut or try to steal whatever goods these women had left. Instead, two of them laid down their weapons and entered the shelter.

They still carried their packs and the women both shied away from them, obviously terrified. With great care, the men opened their bags and set down two corked jugs and two cans of something that looked like food. I could see their mouths move, but no sound traveled through the moving pictures.

The women stared at the offering as though they couldn't believe their eyes. Then, one of the men said something that must have been important because both women's eyes grew wide, and they nodded their agreement. He approached them, carrying a smaller bag, and then he began to examine each of their bodies. As he did, checking their injuries and wrapping their wounds, I realized that he had to be a human healer. When he finished, he grabbed the jug from behind him and handed it to the ladies. The other man had kept watch the entire time, making sure that they were all safe.

When the healer finished helping them, he picked up his pack and rejoined his team. They pointed into the distance and continued down the path in front of them.

Before I could say anything, Arrick beat me to it, "Then there are those who will always seek to help and to heal, no matter how terrible things get. There are two sides to every coin and endless shades of gray in between. This is why I'd risk everything to save this place. There is nothing I wouldn't do, no price I wouldn't pay if it meant I could save them."

I stared at him as I took in the intensity of his body language, the forceful fervor of his words. This was the raw truth I wanted to see from him, the naked motivation for why he wanted me here. There were no manipulations, no games, and no lies. This was his truth, and now that it was laid bare to me, I was unnerved. He was desperate to succeed, and I would need to be wary of that because cornered animals were often the most dangerous.

"There's truly nothing you wouldn't sacrifice? You would even kill to save them?" I asked, seeking to understand the depth of his commitment to this mission. Sweat sprung up on the back of my neck as he moved closer. I took a step backward and found myself pressed against a bare space on the wall.

He raised a hand and leveled it above my head on that same wall. Then he leaned down and whispered in my ear as though it were a secret. "In a heartbeat. I'd give my very soul if it offered them salvation."

I stared up at him, into those electric eyes that moved with emotion. It was as though he were pleading with me to understand, but I didn't. Not fully. How could I? I didn't know these people. I hadn't lived with their slow demise for years, as he and his family had. But knowing the lengths he was willing to go to save them had me unsettled. "You should be careful."

He pulled back a little and looked down at me. "What do you mean?"

"That kind of desperation is dangerous. It could cloud your judgment."

He shrugged one broad shoulder and moved away from me. "I'll take that under advisement." Then he turned and walked down the hall toward our destination, leaving me frozen in place. I sucked in a deep breath. Now that his body was further away from me, I could think clearly again. I followed behind, in no hurry to catch up.

While his honesty was refreshing, the full meaning of his words was disconcerting. He might be willing to go that far to save his world, but I was not. I did not believe in trading one life for another. If I had to choose between the lesser of two evils, I would move mountains to create a third option.

I took a few moments to compose myself and then I jogged to catch him up, "How much longer?" I asked, artfully changing the subject.

He looked at the utility watch on his wrist, "About five minutes until we hit the end of this tunnel. Then we'll need to hike a few miles to get to the Itorian village. We should be there before sunset." We fell back into silence, each burdened with our own thoughts, the click of our boots on metal the only sound in the hallway. I did my best to ignore the pictures on the walls, having already gotten my fill of horrors for the day.

I already knew that there were three tribes that I would take great pains to avoid: the red and yellow, grey and white, and black and orange. Those three seemed to be the most violent. They enjoyed the kill and thrilled in stealing what others had and taking it for themselves. Everything was a possession to be owned by the most powerful. In this case, that meant the most bloodthirsty and brutal. Even women were a commodity, a means to grow the tribe's ranks and for the pleasure of men. Nothing more. I never wished I had a penis more in my life than when we approached the end of the tunnel and Arrick held his wrist up to the door.

I put my hand on his before he could swing it open, "Should we have considered disguising me as a man? Being a woman here seems like it might be unpleasant."

"Sweetheart, there is no disguising what you've got as man parts." His eyes traveled the length of my slender body, lingering on the girls for just a heartbeat longer than necessary.

I cleared my throat and pointed to my face. "Eyes up here, buddy."

He grinned devilishly. "Look, you're still a god. You're as strong and fast as a very strong man is here, though you're on equal terms with them rather than stronger. You can't die, and we should be able to take anyone down who is stupid enough to attack us." He patted the massive hunting knife buckled to the side of his pant leg. It was weird how I hadn't noticed that before. He finished with an earnest, "You have my word that I've got your back if it comes to a fight." I nodded in understanding and felt my shoulders relax. "Now, let's go. We are wasting precious time. We only have 21 hours left." I did the math in my head and knew that that was just a little over two hours in the immortal realm. That should give us plenty of time to figure out a plan to stay a step ahead of my grandpa once we returned, should I decide to help.

Arrick pushed open the door and a blast of wind and sand hit me once more. The heat had dialed back quite a bit, and I could see that we were at the base of a lush, forested mountain, having just exited from a cleverly disguised cavern. This region was much more of the living variety than the one we'd previously inhabited. At the lower elevations, where we were now, there were low-lying shrubs with cacti sprinkling the hills. Rocks, gravel, and sand were everywhere. This was the high desert, and I smiled at the sheer loveliness of it. The wind was much softer here, and

Arrick unbuttoned the mouthpiece of his head wrap and pulled it down so that it looked more like a scarf now. I followed his lead.

The heat was still intense but much more manageable, and there was an unpaved path ahead of us. He checked to see if I was ready, and with my confirmation, we began walking along the path that led up the mountain. The trail maintained a gradual incline the whole way. I suppressed a groan as we trudged through the gravelly dirt toward our destination.

Gusts of wind still shot through the hilly terrain at regular intervals. It made me wonder why we bothered to remove our face protection if we were just going to get pelted with rocky sand every twenty minutes. But somehow, I refrained from commenting.

With every passing moment we climbed, the terrain changed, and the weather cooled. The sun grew heavy in the sky while grass started to pop up gradually along our path. Soon, trees shot up, growing taller as we ascended, indicating that a water source was nearby. Or at least that regular rainfall occurred in this area. We had moved from a high desert into a forest, and I was amazed by how quickly the landscape transitioned.

Without warning, Arrick stopped, propping himself up on a rock and pulling out a canteen. His pack was not equipped with the same camelback feature I had. I grabbed the tube from my shoulder and sucked, dragging my tired body up on the rock with him.

Once I'd settled, I said, "It's really beautiful here." I used my hand as a visor against the low-lying sun and surveyed the scenery. It was rugged and unforgiving, true. But there was something lovely about the wild, untamed nature of it.

He offered me an appreciative grin as he poured a little water down his neck. It may have been cooler than the first region we had been in, but it was still hot. The heat seemed to permeate us no matter how high we ascended, and I guessed that this was probably due to the expanding sun.

He took the knife out of its sheath and used the sharp tip to clean under his nails. "I love this trail. My dad used to take me hunting here before the animal population dwindled. He taught me how to fight, hunt, and clean my prey. He believed in living amongst humans for a while so that I understood what it meant to be mortal. He believes that gods tend to forget what life is like for their creations. Then they become too aloof to really care."

I watched as the metal of the knife caught the remaining sunlight. "I've never thought of it like that before. So, then you've lived out here with a tribe before?"

"Yes."

I recalled what he'd said about how he spent most of his time with the Itorians, "The one we are going to now?"

He nodded, "Actually, they know me pretty well. I'm one of the village leaders."

I raised my brows, wondering why he hadn't mentioned that before. "Really?"

He nodded. "Itoriah is where I live when I'm in the mortal realm. My role as a head scavenger within the group allows me the freedom to come and go as I please. I just need to make sure I bring back plenty of loot when I return. It's the only way I can really help them. I resupply the camp from the stores we have in the immortal realm. I'd bring them everything we have if I could find a way to transport it back. That's why my pack is twice the size of yours." He softly kicked the massive pack at his feet.

"I was wondering why that was so big." I chewed on my straw absently as I considered what he'd said earlier in a new light. "So, all that stuff about them ordering me to be corporally punished was bull then?"

He tilted his head back and forth as though considering my question, "You'll be under my protection. But I wouldn't press my luck if I were you. Being my wife will only get you so far in the tribe. If you piss off the wrong person—"

"Excuse me? Did you say wife?"

A smooth, arrogant grin slid into place, "You caught that, huh?"

"You think? Explain, please."

"The status of wife offers you certain freedoms and protections that you wouldn't otherwise have while we're there."

"I think I can handle myself." I wasn't sure how I felt about going undercover as man and wife. On the one hand, it gave me an inappropriate thrill. On the other, it seemed like a level of forced intimacy that I wasn't sure I was comfortable with.

He shook his head decidedly. "Not if you want to blend in. The women here aren't like you. They have protectors, husbands and sons who will fight to keep them alive should anyone challenge them. They are loved and respected in this tribe, but they are never single past the age of 16."

"Are you saying that I'm a spinster?"

His lips twitched with amusement as he looked at me, "Yes."

I let out a bark of laughter before I covered my mouth, stunned at how well the sound traveled through the hills.

"Sorry," I whispered. "I didn't mean to..." But a loud crack echoed through the woods before I could finish, and Arrick fell to the side, his head slumping into my lap. My breath caught in my throat as something wet, warm, and sticky soaked through my pant leg. When I looked down at him, I saw an entrance wound in his temple, which meant that the sticky substance warming my legs had to be his blood.

I let out a heart-wrenching scream as I shook him, trying to wake his lifeless body. *He couldn't be killed!* My mind shouted at me. *He couldn't be killed!* "Arrick?" My heart thrummed in my ears when I heard the sound of boots on gravel.

My gaze shot up and locked onto a man who had a large gun pointed right at me. I couldn't help it. I gasped and scrambled up from the rock and onto my feet. I heard Arrick's body fall to the ground with a thud. The sound reverberated through me and left my body like a ringing bell.

The man leered at me. "Hello, Beautiful."

He wore a red and yellow scarf, and my guts roiled in response to it. While the language was unfamiliar, it appeared that I still had the godly ability to understand any language spoken to me.

The words, said in the tribe's tongue, came to me effortlessly, "What do you want?" I asked, eyes locked onto the gun. I heard more crunching footsteps behind me and turned to find another man, this one holding a knife. I tried to flee, but he grabbed my arm and wrenched me back to him. I struggled against his hold, fighting for all I was worth to pull free of his grasp, but he wrapped an arm around my neck, and I felt the cool metal of his knife against my throat. I froze.

"Try to run, and I'll cut your throat where you stand," he breathed. I tried not to cringe at the scent of him. Clearly, hygiene was not a priority to these people.

A third guy came from my left then and began to pat me down. "She's clean. No weapons." Why in the hell didn't I have any weapons? My mind asked frantically.

When I snuck a glance to my left, Arrick had landed in a way that obscured his pack, and the third attacker kicked him to the side for easier access to its pockets. I cringed at the sound of his boot hitting flesh. Tears budded at the corners of my eyes. How was it possible that he was dead? He said we couldn't die! My mind reeled and I shook with rage and terror, feeling powerless as the man with the knife to my throat shoved me forward.

The knifeman sneered, "She'll be a nice prize for Lorus." His bronzed skin and black hair shone in the sun, and his mouth pulled back in a smile to reveal yellow, rotted teeth. "She's still soft."

The one with the gun licked his lips, finger trained on the trigger, "We should give her a try then, just to make sure she's really worth giving to him. Don't you think?"

I didn't miss the lust in his eyes as they traveled the length of my body. My skin crawled in horror. I was a god. There was no way this mortal twerp was going to rape me. No fucking way.

I rose to my full height and snarled, "Touch me, and it'll be the last thing you ever do." I was pleased to find that my voice remained dead calm, despite the terror bucking inside me.

"You hear that?" the knifeman said. "Such threats from a helpless woman."

Before I knew what he was doing, he grabbed my jacket and ripped it down the front, the buttons scattering across the ground. Then he tripped me and fell to the ground on top of me. I was kind enough to break his fall, and the breath went out of me in a whoosh.

I recovered quickly and fought for all I was worth, thrashing and kicking as the gunman came from behind and dragged my arms above my head to keep them still. "She's strong," he said, appreciation evident in his tone. He was enjoying the fight, the challenge. But it couldn't be helped. I'd either fight or be taken right there in the dirt. And that was not an option.

The third one came over to my legs and began to yank off my pants and boots. I bucked and squirmed as I felt the air touch the naked skin of my legs, the only protection left between me and the ground was the granny panties I wore. I snarled and snapped, managed to get my hand free, and raked my nails across the cheek of the gunman who held my arms. He yelped in surprise, and I proceeded to use my newly freed arm for leverage. Then I twisted, my legs finding purchase, and I knocked the third guy who held them off balance. Then I lashed out at the knife guy with my heels. He dodged my blow and then lunged forward to help his friend get my legs secured once more.

Before he could get to me, I kicked out again and he jumped backward in surprise, "Hold her down!" he roared. Then his head jerked unnaturally to the side as a loud crack issued from his body. His eyes went blank just before he fell to the side. Before anyone could react, a massive hunting knife slipped across the throat of the third guy. Blood spurted as he sputtered and reached to his throat to stop it. But it was useless; he was already dead.

The gunman released my arms and scrambled back as fast as he could. I twisted to face him. Arrick advanced on him, his gait predatory, his knife dripping black with arterial blood.

His eyes grew wide with disbelief as he stared at Arrick's unmarred flesh. "But y-you're dead! I shot you in the head. I saw the bullet hit your skull!"

"You're right, you did," he said softly, no more than a whisper. Then he leaned down and grabbed the man by the shirt front, pulling him to his feet and looking into his eyes. Then, louder, he said, "Maybe you should think twice before you try to kill the god of death. Oh, and she was right; trying to rape her is the last thing you'll ever do." With that, he plunged the knife into the man's temple. I saw the life drain from his eyes as Arrick ripped out his knife and chucked his body aside like a rag doll.

I stared, mouth agape as souls fled the men's bodies, sheer as mist. They swirled and slithered along the ground, winding around Arrick's legs and then absorbing into his body. He shuddered for a moment, shoulders rising and falling as his breath heaved. Then he settled, turned to me, and all hardness evaporated from his expression as he rushed to my side. "Bekka, are you all right?" He put his hands on either side of my face and turned it, looking me over to see for himself if I was OK. He wrapped his arms around me and hugged me to him.

I kept my cheek pressed against his chest for a long moment and listened to the rapid beat of his heart. My body was trembling with a mixture of fear and adrenaline as my mind reeled. Not just from everything that had happened, but from what he'd said. That comment earlier about having too much power too soon… Now it made sense. He was the Moldizean god of death—a Nefaral with a gift equal in power and rarity to my own. I'd never met a death god, and I'd never seen their power in action. At least, not until a moment ago. But I knew that they held dominion over the soul, the internal essence that powered all life.

When I finally stopped shaking, I said, "I'm OK; they didn't hurt me." He held me so tightly that I could barely breathe. It was like he was trying to assure himself that I was still there, still in one piece.

"This is my fault. I never should have let my guard down. What they almost did to you—" He broke off and held me at arms-length, his eyes searching mine. "You're really okay?"

"I am. You stopped them before they did any real damage." I felt a breeze whip through the forest and had a realization. I was yet again in a state of undress. Granny's panties were not adequate clothing, and rocky sand pelted my skin from the wind. Breaking myself away from him, I moved to grab my pants and shoes from the ground. My hands trembled from the adrenaline dump while I struggled to get my clothing back into place.

I'd just tied my last boot when Arrick strode toward the bodies and stared down at them. "We'll need to hide them. They're Puhari, and if Lorus finds that his men are dead this close to the border..." He trailed off, and it was clear that if this happened, it would not bode well for us. I swallowed hard and did my best not to look at what was left of our attackers. He'd killed them so quickly, so efficiently. But then again, he was the god of death, and wasn't this what death deities were known for?

Rather than let my mind scurry down that rabbit hole, I asked, "What border?"

"Many years ago, there was a war that ended with a truce that divided up the land between the Puhari and the Itorians. They stay on their side and we stay on ours. This location is close enough that it's disputable which side of it we're on, so if Lorus decides that these men were killed in his territory—" He shook his head in thought. "There's no telling what he'd do."

I let that sink in as I tried to picture the possibilities. Mass shooting? Hanging? Burning? None of them seemed like good alternatives to me.

I glanced over to the men from the corner of my eye and looked away quickly. I tried to control my gag reflex at the prospect of what Arrick wanted me to do. There was blood everywhere, and their lifeless eyes stared into the sky, empty as glass.

"Well, then," I said, mustering as much bravado as I could manage and swallowing back bile. "I guess we should hurry."

We worked silently, Arrick taking the legs and me the arms. We were careful to move them as far away from the Puhari lands as we could manage. That would decrease the likelihood of discovery by their Puhari comrades. And if they were discovered, it would appear as though they had broken the truce. Or at least, that was our aim.

We carried the bodies of all three men to an area thick with underbrush and trees. Unfortunately, we didn't have shovels. So, we were forced to conceal them under a multitude of loose branches and leaves. When we agreed that we'd done the job well enough, we sucked down about a gallon of water and gathered our packs. My body shook all over, and I couldn't be sure if it was from the terror of the attack or the horror of what I'd just done. My best guess was that it was from both.

Arrick said, "The village isn't too far from here. Just another hour of hiking." When he pointed toward our path, and I saw that it was uphill again, I did a mental grimace. All I wanted was a bed, a shower, and a metal scrub brush. I wanted to scour the blood, dirt, and grime off my skin until it was pink and raw. I imagined that this was the only way that I could wash away the events of the last hour as if they'd never happened.

Arrick asked me if I was ready, and after I nodded, we started back along the path. I fell into step just behind him. My body was exhausted, my brain was numb; I felt tingly yet dull, and I couldn't pinpoint one prevailing emotion. If I were honest, I wasn't sure I wanted to. Then, after a few minutes of silence, I dimly realized that there was one thing left, something important that I needed to know.

"Why didn't you just tell me that you're a death deity?" I asked, my voice quiet and exhausted. It was clear from our conversation in the godly realm that he'd intentionally kept his power a secret.

He rubbed his hand over his neck in thought. "You know why."

"That doesn't answer my question."

His jaw flexed. "Because if I had, then you would have run for the hills before we even got the chance to talk to you." He stopped and turned to look at me. I ran smack into his chest again, bracing my hands against his abdomen to steady myself. His hands grasped my shoulders, and he stared intently into my eyes. My belly jumped at his piercing gaze, making it almost impossible to concentrate on his words. "Do you deny it?" he asked, searching my face for an answer.

I thought back to the moment when I realized that I'd been kidnapped. It had only been Lilja's presence that had soothed me and the fact that Arrick had seemed desperate for my help. But if I'd known his true nature, that he was a Nefaral, right away, would I have stayed? I shrugged helplessly in response.

"Death deities are not exactly welcomed with open arms across the multiverse," he explained, releasing his grip on me and slipping his hands into his pockets. "There's a reason why there are only two of us left."

To his point, death deities did have a sordid past within the godly ranks, even among the Nefarals themselves. Most of them were driven insane by the demands of their gifts. Once that happened, they were eventually executed for any number of gory crimes against humanity or other gods.

I bit my lip, unsure of what to say. From what I'd seen of Arrick so far, he was both compassionate and caring. But he could also be brutal when the occasion called for it. I reminded myself that we barely knew each other, and he had a right to keep his own counsel. So, my response was measured, "From what I understand, it's not an easy gift to live with."

"You're right. It isn't." He stared out past my shoulder now, and his eyes had a faraway quality that struck a chord within me—*sympathy*. Without thinking, I reached out my hand and brushed his forearm with my fingertips to comfort him. He looked down his arm, surprised, and then he ran a hand through his hair and continued, "Human death frees the soul from the confines of its body. Once the soul is free, it finds me. I'm like a beacon for them, and if I'm close to them when they die, they're drawn to me like moths to the flame. I can't escape them, even with my powers stripped in this realm. The souls of the nearby departed always find me. And when they do, they meld into my being and become a part of me. I'm forced to bear witness to all the good and the terrible things they did in their lifetimes. Then I must decide where to send them. Heaven, hell, or reincarnation."

I remembered how he'd shuddered and how his breathing had been labored just moments before when the souls of those evil men had melded to him. Chills ran the length of my spine before I found the right words to say to him, "I'm sorry; I can't imagine what that would be like." I slipped my hands into my own pockets, feeling guilty for all that I was coaxing him to divulge.

He continued, "Heaven and reincarnation, those are easier choices since I'm not condemning a human soul to an eternity of suffering."

"What about tonight? What did you do with those men?" I asked.

His eyes narrowed with anger. "Hell isn't always a difficult decision. Those bastards deserved to suffer for a long time. But other people," he sighed. "Things aren't always so clear. Hell is a terrible place, so I have to be certain that I only send the most deserving down to its depths." I could see how making those kinds of decisions all the time would weigh heavily on someone with a strong moral compass. And I was starting to suspect that Arrick had a code nearly as strict as my own.

"Did you create the afterlife here?" I asked. Death deities were the only gods, aside from creators, who could build habitable dimensions. The only difference was that their inhabitants were dead. Heaven and hell were their domain, and they created the beings that ruled over both. As gods, we rarely visited these dimensions. Most death deities created wardens, spirit guides, like demons and angels, who kept order and doled out punishments or rewards. So thankfully, I had never been to a hell dimension. But I had read enough about them and seen enough renderings to understand his reluctance to condemn people to it.

He shook his head. "Not exactly. Hell and reincarnation were already here when I was born. I built our heavenly dimension as soon as I came of age."

I pursed my lips in question, "Who built hell and reincarnation then?" It couldn't have been Afryel. Creators held no sway in the metaphysical world. We could see it and visit it, just as all deities could, but we couldn't *create* it.

Arrick shrugged. *Ah, right,* I thought. *The black hole in history.* "We have no real way of knowing what happened," he explained. "Maybe a long lost relative? Or an ally?"

I ran a hand down my braid in thought. Then shifting the conversation away from Moldizean history, I said, "You know, we don't have a death deity in Valeria right now."

"I know," he said, and his tone was curt. He must have been wondering what my point was.

I got right to it, "Without someone like you, the souls of the dead just walk the world aimlessly, unable to connect with anyone. The worst part is that there is nothing we can do about it. I guess what I'm saying is that we all serve a purpose. Just because yours isn't all puppies and unicorns doesn't make it any less vital."

His lips twitched at the visual I provided. "So, you're not afraid of me?"

I extended my fingers, intending to touch his face, but then hesitated. It felt a little too familiar, a little too intimate. I let my hand fall back to my side and said simply, with my gaze locked onto his, "No, I'm not. I think I'm starting to see who you really are. You don't scare me, Arrick."

He looked down at the hand I'd dropped and brushed his fingertips across it gently. His touch electrified me, lit me up from the inside out. There was something about him that drew me to him. A passion or intensity, perhaps? It made him feel familiar to me in a way that I couldn't quite explain. My heart fluttered in response to this knowledge, and I looked down at my hand. For a moment, I could have sworn I saw a faint blue glow where his fingers had connected with my skin. But I blinked and it was gone.

CHAPTER 7

Itoriah

We spent the rest of the hike in silence, each lost in our own thoughts. As for me, my brain was working overtime to stop replaying the attack. Results were mixed, and every so often, I felt the ghost of a blade against my neck. Despite this, I pressed forward. I kept close to Arrick and prayed to the ascended that we wouldn't encounter any more Puhari raiders.

It was at least an hour before I noticed signs of habitation in the forest around us. I heard voices and saw flickering firelight bouncing off the leaves. Then we stepped into a clearing and I saw an armed guard. He pointed his gun right at my head. Before I could pass out in a puddle of my own piss, which was a real concern, I caught sight of the scarf—purple and green. The menacing face split into a wide grin, and he started laughing, the sound low and genial. The man lowered the weapon and moved to embrace Arrick, his strides long and purposeful.

"Arrick!" he exclaimed as he slapped the death god's back companionably. "Where the hell you been, man?"

"Kaleb!" Arrick replied, slapping his back in turn, issuing a loud thumping noise. As they embraced, I took in my surroundings. In either direction, as far as the eye could see, was a perimeter. Every five feet, torches stood, fire flickering brightly from their tips; guards patrolled near them, all carrying assault weapons. About ten feet away was a large bell. I wondered what it was for. A warning mechanism, perhaps?

Arrick cleared his throat, and I spun around at the sound. I looked down and saw that he held out his hand to me. I stared at it for a beat, brows knitted in confusion. Then I remembered we had to pretend to be married here. Recovering my wits, I reached out to him, grasping his fingers and stepping to his side. Kaleb gasped as the flickering fire settled onto our bodies and lit us fully. He could now see the blood caking our clothes and staining our skin.

"What the hell happened to *you?*" His voice had an edge to it. I couldn't pinpoint whether it was concern for his friend or something else. He jerked his chin in my direction, "and who's she?"

Arrick replied, "This is Bekka, my wife. And we ran into trouble on the way in."

Kaleb's eyes widened fractionally in surprise as he stared at me. Then his gaze flicked back to Arrick. "Wait," he shook his head as though to clear it. "What kind of trouble?"

"Puhari raiders along the border."

"Shit," Kaleb cursed, rubbing a hand through his shiny, black hair. His handsome face hardened as he demanded, "Tell me what happened." His tone brooked no argument, and from his manner, I could tell that he was a leader of some kind here. He expected to be answered.

Arrick obliged, filling him in on the rest of the story. He explained the entire situation, minus how he was shot and had then resurrected. "I did what I had to do to keep her safe," Arrick finished, defending his actions.

"I would have done the same," Kaleb assured us, nodding in approval. "But you've been gone a long time, man. Things have gotten tense with the Puhari over the past few months." He mussed his hair, a worried expression lining his face. "If they find those bodies…" He trailed off, staring into the darkening forest. "There's no telling what they'll do. Lorus has lost whatever mind he had left. He's erratic now. Unpredictable." Kaleb turned to me then, and his eyes suddenly softened with empathy. "I know Arrick said you weren't injured, but are you sure you're OK?"

He was looking at me as though he could see into the inner workings of my mind, so I shifted uncomfortably. I cleared my throat. "Yeah, I'm fine."

He squinted one eye as though he didn't quite believe me. "You sure about that?"

I nodded, making sure that my posture was straight and my demeanor was confident. This seemed to satisfy him, and he turned his attention to Arrick, "You know we need to tell Niko about this, right?"

"I do. I just need to get Bekka settled with Mariah and Jarrod first. Meet me there in thirty?"

Kaleb nodded, "Sure. I'll trade shifts with Caden. Shouldn't be a problem." Then Kaleb gave me one long once over and shook his head, smiling once more. He turned to Arrick, "I can't believe you're fucking married, man. My sister is going to be pissed."

Arrick let out a low laugh, his eyes sparkling with amusement, "Which one?"

"All of 'em," Kaleb said, grinning too. "Syl most, though." Then he hitched his finger in Arrick's direction as he spoke to me, "Good luck with this one. He's a total pain in the ass."

Arrick rolled his eyes and shook his head, smiling as well, "Thanks, man. I appreciate that."

"You know it," Kaleb said, still grinning as Arrick led me beyond the perimeter and into Itoriah.

"Friend of yours?" I asked, my lips twitching upwards despite myself.

"How'd you guess?" Arrick asked facetiously and I shrugged in response as we entered a large clearing.

The village itself was different than I expected. There was a large main street lined with shop booths and tents. The shops all seemed to work on the barter system since there were no prices. From my observations, it looked like the people used their skills for the good of the group and traded based on what they needed most.

At the center of town was a community supply booth, which housed all kinds of useful items. Mostly, it looked like the essentials of what someone would need for a good, solid raid. Then there were overnight goodies that would be helpful in case anyone forgot a toothbrush, for instance.

As we made our way deeper into the belly of Itoriah, Arrick's face split into a heart-stopping grin while he greeted everyone he came across. They returned his smiles with their own; some of them even stopped to offer him a hug or a handshake and welcomed him home.

The warmth I felt from these people toward Arrick amazed me. They all seemed to adore him. Even more, I was shocked that he seemed to care deeply for them. He was a god, for goodness sake. We cared for our people, but not at an individual level per se; it was more of an arms-length, greater-good kind of caring.

It left me wondering just how wrong we'd gotten it all these years. Maybe the Moldizean deities didn't abhor humans and seek to torment them. If this were any indication, they cared for them. Even treated them like family.

As we strode further into town, Arrick took the opportunity to introduce me to his friends, and by the time we broke away from the crowd, my cheeks hurt from all the smiling. The general reaction to the news that Arrick was married was pure astonishment combined with a healthy dose of disbelief. I was pretty sure that some disappointment was thrown in there for good measure. But they were all too polite to show it.

As we continued through the shopping square, the number of people began to thin. A few moments later, we hit a gap in shop fronts and entered a more residential area. There were lean-tos with tents and tarps draped around hobbled-together wooden frames, air mattresses lining the grounds.

I couldn't help but notice that almost everything was mobile and could be packed at a moment's notice. The only permanent structures were the wooden pillars that provided support for the tarps. Not critical by any stretch of the imagination. I guessed that they would be left behind without a second thought.

As we passed the makeshift homes, I saw small groups of people clustered around fires. The golden glow made everything look mystical and just a bit eerie. A group of young girls cast furtive glances from beneath their lashes at Arrick as we strode past them. He seemed oblivious, but when they realized I was with him, they shot eye daggers at me. If looks could kill, I would be a sizzling pile of ash right now. But then again, did ash sizzle? Okay then, a smoking pile of ash.

Arrick stopped in front of me, and I ran smack into his broad back. I sucked in a surprised breath, gulping air like a fish out of water. "Ow," I wheezed. I was still adjusting to this pseudo-mortal existence, and I was learning quickly that everything hurt without exception.

"Sorry," he said, eyes fixed on a set of residential tents in front of us. "But we have another small problem."

I groaned, "Oh no, you don't. There are too many problems already. I'm crying uncle on the addition of more problems. No new problems allowed, okay?"

"If that's true, then I don't think we'll have anything left to talk about," he replied, his tone light and teasing. "Besides, this is just a small one." He held up his thumb and his forefinger to demonstrate just how tiny it was.

I rolled my eyes, "Alright then. Fine. Hit me with it."

"You're about to meet my parents."

I scrunched up my nose, confused, "Your parents? I don't get it? I thought I already met them."

"My other parents," he clarified before he launched into a more in-depth explanation. "This village believes that I am an orphan. They 'found' me a while back. They adopted me into the tribe and assigned me to a family, as they do with any new tribe member under the age of 25. We are standing outside the door to my foster family's home right now."

Interesting. What a tangled web he had woven. "How long have you been here with them?"

"About fifteen years in mortal time. Give or take." I looked him over and tried to place his actual age. Definitely late 20s to early 30s, if I had to guess. The appearance of our magic slowed our aging process to a crawl in the immortal realm. But here, we aged on the human timeline, godly power or no.

And if he'd been here since before he was 25, then… "You must spend a lot of time here." It was the only thing that made any sense. Otherwise, he would have aged less than two years since his early twenties.

He shrugged and slid a hand through his hair, "They needed me." He said the words simply, as though it were no big deal. But the truth was that most deities avoided taking prolonged trips to their mortal realms to avoid the faster aging rate. Time here decreased our life spans, and that was something most gods didn't want to contend with, whether they were needed or not.

"OK." I eyed him curiously. "And how is meeting your parents a problem exactly?"

"Well, I've never brought a woman home before. They might be a little… excited. Especially since we'll introduce you as my wife, not just a friend."

It seemed wrong to me, lying to his other family. But then, how else were we going to explain my presence here and why I needed to stick close to Arrick? We had talked about this earlier, but now that we were about to meet *his family,* I felt guilty. What would they think when I just disappeared? That is if we managed to save the planet and I went home to Valeria. "This feels wrong to me," I said, voicing my concerns. "If they're going to be that excited, then you should wait to introduce them to your real wife."

He shook his head. "We've already told too many people in the village. Besides, I have no plans to marry anyone here. Or back in the godly realm, for that matter. So, why not give them a little happiness *and* make sure you have a stronger position within the community? Will you trust me when I say that this is for the best?"

I chewed on a lip and looked for any sign that he wasn't being completely honest with me. When his serious expression didn't waver, I said, "Fine, I trust you."

"Good." His lips tilted upwards at my response. He continued. "My mother's name is Mariah, and my father's name is Jarrod. I think you'll like them."

"OK, then after we meet them, are we going to see that Niko guy?"

"*We* aren't going. Niko is excitable, and I don't know how he'll react to what I'm going to tell him. So, *you* will stay here while *I* go talk to him. Mariah will get you set up for the night in my room. This is us." He pointed at the flap of canvas to my right.

I paused for a moment as he held open the tarp, the meaning of what he'd said hitting me. "I'm sorry, but did you say *your* room?" Now that he mentioned it, this should have been obvious to me before this moment. Unfortunately, I hadn't thought that far ahead. Deciding to deflect my discomfort, I put one hand on my hip and angled myself toward him, giving him the evil eye and a devilish grin. "Now, you're not trying to get into my pants, are you?"

His eyes twinkled with amusement. "Would it work if I said yes?"

I dropped my hand and ditched the coy smile. "Sure wouldn't."

"Then, no. But if you don't stay with me, there will be others who *will* try to get in your pants."

I made a show of thinking the prospect over really hard, "Alright, fine. I'll stay with you tonight. But I am making a blanket and pillow barricade."

He cocked a brow. "What? You don't trust me?"

"With my life, sure. With my virtue, though? Not so much." He did need me to save the planet, after all, so my life should be safe in his hands.

"I'm hurt."

"No, you're not."

"You're right. I'm not." He gestured for me to enter through the open doorway. When I did, I was immediately hit with a blast of warmth, light, and sound. The tarps were lined with thick, colorful quilts that appeared to act as both décor and sound barriers between the family's homes, which were separated only by their fabric.

Two folding chairs stood arranged around a folding carding table. Unlabeled glass bottles sat in the center of it, along with a deck of cards. Kitchenware and a small camp stove sat on another folding table while two people stood over it. They bickered over whose turn it was to wash the dishes, and though they argued, I sensed it was of the light-hearted, teasing variety. Arrick set his pack on the ground and I followed suit, listening to the banter and grinning.

Arrick interrupted, "Why don't you leave the dishes to me? I'll do them later."

They both turned to see who had interrupted their melee. When their eyes fixed on Arrick, they beamed. "Oh my goodness!" shouted the older woman, who I assumed was Mariah. She had a golden tan and inky, black hair streaked with gray. She wore it in a braid down her back, and it swung back and forth as she rushed toward her adopted son. When she reached him, he wrapped her into an embrace, swinging her around as she laughed.

"Mariah, did you get more beautiful since I last saw you, or is it just me?" Arrick asked, beaming back at her.

He set her down, and she swatted him playfully, "No, only older. You see these wrinkles? You're responsible for them. You were gone much too long this time. You had us all worried."

The man, Jarrod, I presumed, stepped forward now. He had light curly hair piled into a ponytail atop his head and a good-natured smile. "We're glad to see that you made it back to us in one piece. You are OK, right?" His canny gaze took in the smears of blood on Arrick's face and his shirt.

"It's not mine," Arrick lied smoothly. "Just a run-in with some Puhari. They attacked us. Unfortunately, I have to report the altercation with Niko soon." Mariah's eyes went wide and she pressed her hands to her mouth. Arrick rested a reassuring hand on her shoulder. "We're okay, though."

She squeezed Arrick's hand, her knuckles whitening. "Thank God for that."

Arrick squeezed back. "I'm sorry for worrying you. I hadn't meant to be gone so long, but resources have grown scarcer, and I have to travel farther to find anything useful." The lie rolled smoothly off his tongue, and I thought again about that tangled web his life must be here.

The fact that if they ever learned the truth about him, then he could be trapped here indefinitely had to weigh on him.

The woman's eyes grew somber as she stroked his cheek, "I'm just happy you're home, my son."

"Me, too." As I watched their interactions, I saw real love there. They might not be his biological parents, but he had genuine affection for them, and I could tell that the feeling was mutual.

I cleared my throat, feeling like I had been lost in all the homecoming excitement. I waved tentatively, "Hi."

Mariah's eyes sparkled with welcome, "Who is this you've brought home with you, Arrick?"

"This is Rebekkah, my wife," Arrick said while he held out a hand to me, and I took it, all part of the charade once more. Both Jarrod and Mariah gasped as wide grins spread across their faces.

"I go by Bekka," I replied automatically, but Mariah saved me from having to say or do anything else. She pulled me right into a big, boney hug, "It's so lovely to meet you! I'm Mariah, and this is my husband, Jarrod. Arrick has never brought home a woman before. Now, just think, you're his wife. Oh! This is such blessed news. Are you going to have a ceremony? If so, you must have it here!"

"Mariah, let the girl breathe," Jarrod chastised. Mariah released me, and I offered Jarrod a grateful smile. I could see that his eyes also glowed with happiness as he took in my bedraggled appearance. I suddenly became painfully aware of how I looked.

My jacket was open and buttonless, my shirt beneath filthy, and my pants soaked with both Arrick's and Puhari blood. I didn't even want to think about how my hair looked. They might not be my actual in-laws, but I wished I'd had the chance to take a shower before I met them.

But before I could get too insecure, Jarrod pulled me into a quick embrace and then held me at arms-length to look me over. "I can't believe that our son has finally chosen to take a wife. We never thought we'd see the day."

When he let go of me, he found his wife, and flung an arm around her shoulders. Her hand looped around Jarrod's waist as she inched closer to him. The affection between them was easy and natural, and I felt Arrick move closer to me in response.

He rested a hand on the small of my back, tentatively, as though asking for permission. I stepped closer to him, giving my consent, and he slipped his arm around my waist. I felt goosebumps rise where his hand touched my body, and I leaned into him, resting a hand on his chest. Though we were just playing the part of newly-weds, I had to admit that I didn't hate this. In fact, it felt good. Maybe even a little too good.

Unnerved by my own reaction to his body, I turned my attention back to Mariah and Jarrod and away from Arrick's hand on my waist. "It's wonderful to meet you both. Your son is-" I turned my head up to look at him. His lovely, emerald eyes locked onto mine, and my knees wobbled. "The bravest and most complicated person I've ever met. He would do anything for the people he loves." We were supposed to be acting, but something about our locked eyes and our linked bodies had pulled the truth out from deep inside of me. My words seemed to surprise both Arrick and me, but Mariah and Jarrod nodded their agreement with enthusiasm.

"Without Arrick," Mariah explained, "We would have either starved or been overrun by raiders a decade ago. We are fortunate that he came to Itoriah when he did."

Arrick rubbed the back of his neck, and I'd be damned if he didn't blush at her praise. "Niko is the one who keeps everyone safe and fed. You know that he runs the show around here."

"Yes, but who is his most trusted adviser? Who leads our defenses in battle when raiders attack? And who is the one who brings home ten times more supplies than all the other scavengers combined? That's you, my son," Mariah argued, pushing a finger into his chest for emphasis.

"Kaleb and I are both responsible for the defenses here," he corrected. Then he shrugged uncomfortably, and

I realized that he had left out the full extent of his importance to this tribe. He'd said he was *a* lead scavenger, as though there were many of them. But he was *the* lead scavenger, advisor to the leader here, and one of two generals who defended them in battle. My perspective on him shifted for the hundredth time today, and I wondered if I would ever get the full picture of who he was. Or if he would continue to surprise me, no matter how long I knew him.

I squinted as I looked him over once again. "You never mentioned any of that."

Jarrod laughed and shook his head. "He wouldn't. He tends to downplay his contributions here. None of us understand why."

"An overactive sense of modesty," Mariah observed, rolling her eyes. "But enough about that. Please, come sit and tell us, where did you two meet?" We moved to the small folding table when Mariah arranged two extra folding chairs around it. We sat, and Arrick pulled my hand into his, winding his fingers through mine. His fingers were smooth, long, and just a bit callused. As he brushed his thumb over my knuckles in mock affection, I realized that I didn't hate this either.

I answered Mariah's question, "At my sister's wedding. He kidnapped me." I leaned closer to my faux in-laws and widened my eyes. "It was terrifying."

Both Mariah and Jarrod cast confused glances at Arrick. His lips twitched at my candor, and he added his own spin to the events, "She means that I swept her off her feet. She was having a bad day, so I stepped in to help. We decided from then on that we'd stick together." That was an interesting version of events, but still technically true.

"Well, that's a, um, lovely story," Mariah answered, clearly unsure of how to respond. Jarrod just looked from Arrick to me, obviously wondering if I was kidding.

"It really is," I replied, beaming like I hadn't a care in the world, and they both relaxed and smiled.

We heard rustling, and not even a second later, Kaleb's head popped into view from the canvas entryway. "Yo, Arrick." He offered Mariah and Jarrod a quick grin of acknowledgment before he focused back on my faux hubby. "I saw Niko on the way over here. I told him about Bekka, and he wants you to bring her along. He says that he has to meet the woman who finally tied you down. He thinks I'm lying, man."

Arrick frowned. "I would rather she stay here so that Mariah can get her set up for the night."

Kaleb shook his head somberly. "He thought you might say that. So, he told me to tell you that it's an order."

"Don't worry," Mariah assured, resting a hand on her son's shoulder. "I'll get her a sleeping bag and any supplies she'll need that aren't in her pack."

I smiled. "Thank you. This is so nice of you. I really do appreciate it."

She shook her head. "Not a problem at all, my dear."

"You will have to tell us more about yourself when you get back from meeting Niko. We'd love to hear where you were from before you came here," Jarrod observed, gesturing in a way that I assumed encompassed their home in Itoriah. Arrick retrieved his pack from the doorway and I followed close on his heels.

"You wouldn't believe me if I told you," I muttered under my breath as we marched back from the direction we entered, Kaleb following a few paces behind us.

His voice carried easily as he relayed his conversation with Itoriah's leader, "Along with the Puhari situation, Niko wants to talk about The Burning. He wants to know what you saw out there while you were scavenging. He's hoping you might have some good news."

Arrick nodded and pressed his lips together. He didn't look pleased by this prospect and I couldn't blame him. He didn't have any good news to report on that front; he certainly couldn't tell them about me and the possibility that I might be able to help.

As we pushed out of the residential tents, we strode further down a rocky pathway toward a wooden long-house. The people were fewer and farther between this far from the village center, with mostly guards surrounding the home and very few pedestrians. We walked up a small flight of stairs, the wood creaking beneath our boots as we went.

Before we even had the chance to knock, the door swung open, and a short, wiry man with tawny muscles stood before us, "About damn time you came home! It's good to see you, Arrick."

Arrick stepped inside, Kaleb and I following his lead. Then he deposited his pack onto the floor just inside the threshold and grinned, "You too, Niko."

He reached out a hand to shake. Niko grabbed it, pulling Arrick into a hug and thumping his back. From what I gathered thus far, this was the traditional greeting amongst friends in Itoriah.

"You were gone far too long. And my nephew says you've brought home a wife this time?" Niko asked, peering around Arrick to survey me. His dark eyes were sharp and filled with intelligence as he looked me over. I cut my eyes to Kaleb and immediately saw the family resemblance, despite the age difference. Niko was older by ten, maybe fifteen years and a little shorter, but he had the same eyes as Kaleb. He stepped out of Arrick's grasp and moved closer to me. "Where did you find such a beautiful woman?"

Something about his approach sent the hairs skittering along the back of my neck. Danger, my senses seemed to call. But there was nothing about his stance that warranted such a reaction. "What's your name, girl?"

I swallowed hard, my throat bobbing with the effort to wet it, "Bekka."

Arrick slid to my side as his hand reached for mine. I felt his fingers encase my own, and I involuntarily relaxed at his touch. When he spoke, his voice was deep and serious. "As for how we met, it's a long story that can wait for another time. We have more important things to discuss."

"Alright then," Niko said, showing his palms. A white smile flashed across his face, and I sensed a viciousness in him tempered with intelligence and compassion. It was the strangest combination I had ever seen in a human, and I could see why the Itorians had made him their leader. He had a way about him, an essence of authority that surrounded him. He looked down at the pack and asked, "What did you bring us?"

"Mostly medicines, weapons, and tools. Some food too," Arrick replied.

"Good, we need everything we can get. Game is getting scarcer, and food is harder to grow. Water is a real problem, too; it seems like every day there is less of it. Then, if that weren't enough, we have the Lorus and his Puhari raiders breathing down our necks."

"That's actually why we're here. We ran into trouble with some Puhari on our way in," Arrick explained.

Niko nodded and eyed us dubiously. "Kaleb mentioned something about that. Come in and we'll talk." He turned and gestured for us to follow him deeper into his home. The entryway was dominated by a large staircase leading up to the second floor. To my immediate right was a hallway that provided access to the rest of the house. At the far end was a set of double doors, and Niko led us directly to them. As he walked, he explained the situation with the Puhari more thoroughly. "Lorus is just waiting for an excuse to break the treaty. From what our scouts tell us, his men are venturing closer and closer to our border every day. They're itching for a fight."

"Do you think he's low on resources?" Arrick asked. "And that's why they're getting so brazen?"

Niko opened the double doors and let out a cold laugh. "Who isn't low on resources these days? There's barely enough left for one tribe, and we're sharing everything between two."

We followed Niko into a comfortable sitting room. Arrick sat down on a three-seater couch across from two armchairs, and I sat down next to him. Kaleb took the chair furthest from the door, settling into the threadbare cushions.

Niko moved to a makeshift liquor cart and poured four glasses, filling each with a solid two fingers of golden liquid. He handed one to all of us and then sat in the leather armchair that Kaleb left empty, swirling his glass. He seemed to live awfully well for the end of times. His home was the only one in the entire city—or that I had observed anyway—that wasn't mobile, probably a reflection of his status within the group.

"Now," Niko said, taking a sip. "Tell me what happened."

Arrick launched into the story. By the time he was finished, Niko was leaning forward, elbows resting on his thighs, drink forgotten. His eyes glittered in the lamplight when he spoke. "Those fucking bastards," he snarled. "You're telling me they tried to take your wife on our side of the border?" It seemed his outrage was more because they crossed the border rather than that they'd tried to take me.

Arrick nodded calmly and leaned forward to match Niko's posture. "They did."

"Did anyone see you?" Niko asked, eyes cutting to the only window in the room. Hanging blankets were the only protection against the night air, and they ruffled, caught in a light breeze.

"I don't think so. Like I said, none of them lived to tell Lorus about it."

"Good," Niko spat, glaring down at his drink once more. "At first light, you and Kaleb will take three men of your choosing to where it happened. Then you'll bring those pigs back here and burn their bodies. Better not to leave any evidence."

Goosebumps crept along my arms, and I had to restrain myself from shivering. Arrick had mentioned that the Itorians were not pacifists, but the idea of burning bodies to cover up a murder made my skin crawl. Regardless of whether those Puhari men deserved to die, the idea of defiling their bodies after their deaths did not sit well with me.

Kaleb had remained silent through most of the exchange, allowing Arrick to explain what happened. When he spoke, his voice was clear and matter of fact. "It will be done. You have my word."

Niko nodded and then turned to me. "I'm sorry this happened to you on our land. Something will need to be done about Lorus. He's gone rabid."

"Nothing happened. Really, I'm fine," I lied, keeping my eyes steady on the commander.

Niko offered me an approving nod before refocusing on Arrick. "Now for the second order of business. Like I said earlier, conditions are getting worse. Our habitability tests look poor, so I wanted to know what you saw out there. Did you go further north?"

"I did."

He nodded thoughtfully, "Tell me what you saw."

Arrick took his first sip of the golden liquid and offered Niko a resigned grimace. "What do you want me to say? It isn't good. Only fifty miles away, it's already too hot for plant and animal life. Everything is dead and turning to dust. From what I can tell, it's getting closer. The Burning was a hundred miles away when I left ten months ago."

Ten months ago? My mind did a stutter-step, stunned that Arrick had been gone that long. Before, with Mariah and Jarrod, I'd thought they meant maybe a few weeks in mortal time when they greeted him at his family home. What had he been doing all that time? Searching for a way to save everyone? Searching for a way to get to me?

Niko ran a hand through his dark, wavy hair. "Shit," he cursed, swallowing the remainder of his drink in one swift gulp and rising to get another. I took a tentative sip and found the warm, caramel flavor soothing. "How long do you think we have before everything dies here?" he asked.

Arrick sighed again and rubbed his palms on his thighs, "It's hard to say."

"Say it anyway," Niko demanded.

"Based on what I've seen, a few weeks until it gets too hot for the plant life. Then maybe another week before all the surface water begins to boil and evaporate." He certainly didn't pull any punches. Adjusted for the time differential between the mortal and immortal realms, this was accurate. The only part he left out was that they had less than ten weeks before the sun went supernova and blew this planet to bits. But why bother mentioning it? No one would be alive to see it happen anyway.

"You're serious?" Kaleb asked, scrubbing a hand over his jaw, his eyes wide with shock. "It's that bad?"

"Yeah, it's that bad. I wish it were different, but all I can do is tell you what I see."

"Then we must make plans," Niko decided, pulling a rolled-up piece of paper off a bookshelf on the wall behind the liquor cart. He strode back to us and unfurled it onto the coffee table between all three seats. It was a map of Moldize. I looked at it. The words and places were completely foreign to me, but I tried to pretend like this was familiar. "Where do we need to go? How far will buy us six more months?" he asked.

Arrick rubbed his hands over his face and blew out a long breath. He looked Niko directly in his eyes, "There isn't a place that buys us six months anymore. I hate to say this, but we're at the end of times here. Let the people stay here with their families. Spend time with your family. Do whatever you need to do to prepare yourself because, without a miracle, there's nothing else we can do." The news seemed unnecessarily dire since I was prophesied to be that miracle. I could stop all of this from happening; I could save this planet. But then, how could Arrick explain any of that to these men without getting us marooned here? Also, what if I agreed to help and then I failed?

Niko's face went ashen and so did Kaleb's. They each finished the last swig of their liquor, and Niko chucked his glass into the far wall; it shattered, causing me to jump. Then he rose to his feet, calmer than I would have expected. Arrick and Kaleb didn't react to his outburst, and it made me wonder if this was something that he did often. Arrick had called him excitable before, and now, I thought the adjective suited him perfectly.

"It's even worse than I thought," he said, strolling back to the liquor bottle and grabbing yet another fresh glass. This time he poured four fingers.

"Aren't you just a ray of fucking sunshine?" Kaleb asked Arrick. "First the Puhari and now this?"

"Would you prefer I lie?" Arrick asked through gritted teeth.

"No," Niko replied in lieu of Kaleb. "The truth is always best. But what do we tell everyone? People will panic."

Kaleb leaned forward and rested his forearms on his knees. He shook his head in disagreement. "I don't think they will. Let's be honest here, we've all known that this was coming for a long time. All we can do is take advantage of what time we have left and keep everyone here. Together."

"He's right, Niko. People deserve to know what's coming. They deserve the chance to make these last few weeks count," Arrick agreed.

Niko slammed back his drink and poured one more. "Alright, then we tell everyone tomorrow."

"What can we do to help?" Arrick matched his body language to Kaleb's and leaned forward.

"We have a team of five scavengers heading out in the morning. I'll send word out tonight that they won't be going anywhere. After that, we'll need to have a town hall tomorrow to break the news to everyone. Bring Jarrod here in the morning and we can go over the details then. For now, let's have another drink." He walked over, carrying the bottle, and poured at least four fingers into each of our glasses.

Then he looked at me and offered me an apology. "I'm sorry you had to see that." He pointed to the shattered glass. "I hadn't expected the news to be so bad."

"Oh, no, not at all," I assured him, shaking my head. "If it were my house, I would have chucked my glass too."

He offered me a sad smile. "Go ahead."

"I'm sorry?" I asked, not sure what he meant.

"Throw the glass."

I looked at the glass in my hand and said, "Really? Are you sure?"

"It's been a shitty day, full of bad news. The least of my problems is another broken glass. So, go ahead. Throw it."

I hauled my arm back and chucked it against the same wall he had used. The glass shattered, glittering shards spraying out in all directions. "Thanks," I said, rolling my shoulders. "That was actually pretty satisfying."

"I'm glad. It was good to meet you, Bekka," Niko said. Then he turned to our other companions, "I think I'm going to turn in for the night. Talk to my wife and hold our daughter." My heart throbbed at his words and the expression of pain on his face.

Arrick and Kaleb nodded. Then Kaleb said, "We'll both be back here at 6 AM sharp with Jarrod. We can go over the details then."

Niko set his glass down. "Right. I'll see you guys tomorrow." He opened the double doors and gestured for us to leave. We said our goodbyes, and I followed Arrick and Kaleb back to the entrance of the longhouse.

After we stepped outside, Kaleb stopped and shook his head, his eyes haunted. "I knew it was bad; I mean, everyone does. But I let myself believe that maybe, just maybe, things would get better." He looked at Arrick, defeated.

Arrick rested his hand on his shoulder. "You know that's not possible, right, Kaleb?"

He nodded somberly. "I know. But I just keep thinking that something has to happen and that the world can't really be ending. How can God just let this happen?" He shook his head as though in disbelief. Then he waved his goodbye and turned to stalk away from us, back to his own family, I presumed.

I knew that the God he was referring to no longer existed here, but I understood the sentiment. All the most powerful Valerian deities spent most of their time preventing this exact disaster in our own universe. It seemed unfair that Moldize had no one to look out for its people in the same way. *Maybe now they would,* I thought. But had I seen enough to make my decision? Was I willing to leave right now and say yes to aid their cause? My mind weighed the pros and cons. Then I thought, *what could it hurt to stay the full 24 hours as promised? It would only cost us 2 hours in the immortal realm, and then I would have a lot more information to work with.*

I decided to bite my tongue and bide my time. After Kaleb was out of earshot, I turned to Arrick and asked, "Are you OK?"

His face was drawn, and he looked exhausted. He ran a hand through his filthy hair before answering, "Delivering that news to Niko and Kaleb was brutal. I just wish I could have told them that we have hope for that miracle, thanks to you. But they can't know who I am or who you are." He paused and braced his hands behind his neck. "But maybe that's for the best. Better for them to prepare for the worst and make the most of what time is left."

CHAPTER 8

Unbreakable Spirit

When we returned to Arrick's home, we took turns bathing. We used what little water was available and a powdered soap solution made by the Itorians. Once we had finished and changed clothes, Mariah was kind enough to loan me hers; we went back to the main sitting room. Mariah and Jarrod were playing cards at the table, amber glass bottles littered its surface and they each snorted with laughter.

"No, you see my finger?" Mariah asked. "It's below yours, so I win this round."

"But, you see?" Jarrod pointed. "My entire hand is on the stack of cards; it's just your *finger*. The game isn't called poke snatch. It's hand snatch for a reason." That caused additional flurries of giggles from Mariah, but neither moved their hand from the center of the table. It occurred to me that the news Arrick shared with Niko hadn't traveled into the rest of the camp yet. So, for now, they were spared from the worry and sadness that this information would bring to them.

I pushed up onto my tiptoes and whispered into Arrick's ear, "Should we tell them what we told Niko?" I wasn't sure what the best course of action would be in this situation. I didn't want to be the bearer of bad news or to ruin what had clearly been a night of carefree play, but at the same time, would they be angry if we didn't tell them what we knew right away?

He looked at his parents for a long moment, their smiling faces and jovial bickering causing his expression to soften. "Let's wait until tomorrow. Let them enjoy tonight."

Before I could say more, Arrick cleared his throat to announce our arrival. Mariah and Jarrod turned their heads in unison at the sound.

"Oh, good!" Jarrod exclaimed. "We could use a referee. Arrick, come tell your mother that I'm clearly the winner."

"Oh no, you don't," Arrick protested. "I'm not getting in the middle of this again. The last time I ruled against Mariah, she made me rebuild our market booth from scratch. I'm pretty sure she broke the old one on purpose."

She beamed, and I could clearly see mischief twinkling in her eyes. "Maybe I did, maybe I didn't. But do you really want to risk going against me again?"

Arrick laughed and shook his head, "Not a chance. How about we call it a draw, and you two deal us in instead?" Arrick moved deeper into the room and I followed him. He grabbed a toppled-over folding chair, righted it, and set it close to the table. He gestured for me to sit while he scooted the fourth chair into the spot to my right. But before sitting down himself, he strode to a rolling cooler and opened it. He grabbed two more of the glass bottles and came to join us. He unscrewed the top of one and handed it to me.

"What is it?" I asked, sniffing at the contents.

"Blackberry wine," Jarrod answered. "Mariah makes it. It's the best in the village."

"Oh, I don't know about all that," Mariah argued, waving away the compliment. "But we like it here. Besides, it seemed like a celebratory kind of night. We just learned that our boy is married, so we opened a few bottles."

I grinned at them as I took a sip. It was sweet, warm, and slightly pungent from the alcohol. I nodded enthusiastically, "It's really good."

"Don't let the flavor fool you," Arrick warned. "It's stronger than you think."

I eyed the bottle suspiciously and took another sip. "I think I can handle it."

Arrick's lips twitched. "Whatever you say." They spent a few minutes explaining the rules of the game to me, and when they finished, we played round after round. Drinking, laughing, and celebrating. About halfway through our eighth game, Kaleb walked through the flap that served as the front door. He was greeted with shouts of welcome and insistence that he join us. He pulled up a seat, grabbed a bottle of blackberry wine, and we dealt him in.

"Figured I'd come see what all this noise was about," he informed us, taking a long swig from his drink. "I'm glad I stopped by. This is way better than the night I was having." He blew out a meaningful breath.

Mariah beamed at him. "Is Syl on one again?"

Kaleb rolled his eyes. "When isn't she? I've gotta say, having four sisters under one roof with me is what I imagine living in the sixth circle of hell is like."

We all laughed at the comical expression of horror on his face. When we settled, Arrick reassured him. "I'll make sure I tell them that the next time I see them."

Kaleb narrowed his eyes at the death deity and pointed a finger at him. "Traitor. And if you do that, then I'll tell Bekka about that time with the—"

Arrick slapped Kaleb hard on the back, effectively stopping him from saying any more.

"About what time with the what?" I asked, curiosity piqued.

"Nothing," Arrick answered, giving Kaleb a warning glare that shut this topic of conversation down. Kaleb looked amused, and I debated pressing further but then decided to let it go. Something about the firm set to Arrick's mouth told me I wasn't going to get anywhere anyway.

Instead, Arrick dealt another hand, and then we all laughed when Mariah snorted at her cards and begged Jarrod to trade her. As we continued to play for what felt like hours, I couldn't help but relax into the ease and comfort of the people around me. The fate of this world rested in our hands, and yet we just sat, playing cards and doing our best to live in the moment. It seemed wrong, but at the same time, I imagined that this was what Erykha, Damion, and Arrick had wanted me to see in the first place. Before our journey here had been turned on its ear by the Puhari attack, they had just wanted me to spend time here.

To see that there were people left worth saving.

Amidst the play and amiable teasing, Kaleb, Mariah, and Jarrod told me about their village. They talked about how Kaleb's family founded it over two decades earlier, and they described all the people who made it home. There were not many of them, just under seventy-five in total. But they all worked together and used their strengths to make Itoriah as safe and prosperous as they could. They explained that the center of town was sandwiched between two residential areas, the eastern and western boroughs. It was fashioned after a famous market center that was once located in Lionelle before the world went to hell. Of course, they explained, it didn't quite hit the mark. But as far as they were concerned, the spirit of the market lived on in Itoriah.

The more we played, the more we drank and talked and laughed. I could feel myself letting go of the burden that had been placed on my shoulders since the moment I awoke in Moldize. I wasn't *She Who Was Sent* right now. I was just Bekka again, and it felt good. As we slapped at cards, missed, and laughed, I found that I was amazed at the unbreakable spirit that Kaleb, Mariah, and Jarrod possessed. Their world was slowly deteriorating and had been for years, but they still managed to find joy in their lives. It was as though they looked into the darkening void of imminent destruction and refused to give in to fear. They would live their lives to the fullest until it ended.

In the final round we played, I yawned broadly and cupped my hand over my mouth to stifle it. "Sorry," I mumbled. "It's been a long day." That was the understatement of the century if you asked me. The emotional whiplash from everything that had happened today was making me see double. Or maybe, that was the wine. Either way, I needed to rest.

"You're right. We should call it a night," Mariah agreed. "We'll have a long day tomorrow too. We need to plan that ceremony. We could use a little more cheer in this place, and I think that a wedding will do the trick nicely."

My body was warm, and my mind muddled from the wine, so I didn't have the energy or the desire to argue. As far as I was concerned, if they wanted a ceremony, then they could have a ceremony. All I had the energy to do right now was sleep. Arrick rose from the table and kissed his mother's cheek. I squatted between Mariah and Jarrod's chairs and dragged them into a group hug with either arm, squeezing their faces into mine. Then I slurred, "You guys are the best in-laws ever."

They laughed and patted my back amiably.

Then I moved to Kaleb and, on impulse, planted a smacking kiss on the top of his head. Leaning around his seat, I bent over and peered at him. "And just so you know," I wagged my finger for emphasis, "I *let* you win that last hand."

Kaleb laughed, "Sure, you did," he placated, still beaming. "You keep telling yourself that."

He winked at me, and before I could argue, Jarrod interrupted. His eyes fixed on Arrick as he suggested, "You should get her to bed. She's going to have one hell of a hangover in the morning."

I looked up at Arrick, my eyes going comically wide with concern. "That's not true, is it? I can't get hangovers, can I?"

Arrick shook his head at me, entertained. His lips quirked upward. "I warned you that stuff was strong. It sneaks up on you."

"ButI'mnotdrunk," I said drunkenly.

"Sure, you aren't," he said, but he didn't believe me. I could tell. "Now, let's get you to bed before you pass out and I have to carry you."

"I'm not gonnapassout," I murmured, my words blending. Arrick offered me his arm, and I walked, leaning heavily against him for support as shouts of goodnight from

Kaleb, Mariah, and Jarrod followed behind us. We made our way back to what could only be his room, an air mattress with a neatly made bed, an extra sleeping bag, and a pillow on the foot of it. *Perhaps he was right,* I thought as he settled me onto the foot of the mattress. *Perhaps I had overdone it tonight.* But who could blame me? I was still getting used to this semi-mortal body. Clearly, it had messed with my alcohol tolerance.

Besides, after everything I'd been through over the last few hours, I thought I deserved a drink. Or three. I hiccupped as Arrick passed me a large t-shirt and underwear, again of the granny variety. Up until this point, I'd had to go commando post bathing. I held up the undies for inspection. At least my virtue felt safe with this much fabric between us.

His lips twitched in amusement as I gaped at the underwear. He moved over to the bed and unlaced my boots. I set the panties down and watched as he slipped my shoes off my feet and then pulled my socks off as well.

"I can do that myself, you know," I protested, but only after he'd finished.

He looked up at me and grinned, "OK, then. I'm going to step out of the room for a minute to give you a chance to change." While he was gone, I slipped my clothes off and replaced them with the new ones. The shirt was long and provided plenty of coverage, falling almost to my knee. That and the broad fabric of the granny panties made me feel secure in my decision to go pants-less. I slipped under the covers and snuggled into the pillow. A few moments later and Arrick came back into the room. He was wearing a fitted t-shirt and a pair of boxers.

I tried not to stare as he moved toward me and sat down on the bed. His body was unlike any I'd ever seen before. Muscled and lithe, how I imagined a warrior's body would look. I may not have known him for long, but I had already seen so many different sides to him. I knew that we had a long way to go before our time together would be done. But I found myself wishing that I could have more of it. Realizing that my thoughts were heading into dangerous territory, I shut them down.

A teasing question from Arrick provided the perfect distraction. "No pillow fort tonight?"

"Nah," I said, yawning again. "I figure the granny panties are big enough to suffice."

I heard a low chuckle roll out of him as he leaned over to the lantern that sat an arm's length away from the bed and turned off the light.

"Hey Arrick," I whispered just a moment later.

"Yes?" He asked.

"I think that maybe you Moldizeans aren't so bad after all." A few minutes later, I heard Arrick's soft rhythmic breathing as he slept. A soft blue glow suffused the room, and I looked down, saw my hand, and smiled. Then I tumbled into the abyss of sleep.

CHAPTER 9

Unimaginable Power

I bolted awake, my body on full alert.

Something felt wrong, something I could not immediately place. It was pitch black without the light from the lantern, and I reached out a hand to search for Arrick. But no one was next to me.

My heart hammered in my chest, and I whispered, "Arrick, where are you?" I was answered by a burst of gunshots, all firing in rapid succession. The sound ripped through the silence of the night, and I heard a bellow of shouts and the ringing of a bell close on its heels. All at once, my mind registered that we must be under attack.

I scrambled out of the bed, tripped, and went down hard on all fours. I ducked my head for cover and threw my arms over it. I felt a hand on my back and nearly screamed, but Arrick's voice stopped me. "Raiders," he whispered. I looked up, trying to see into the dark. Then he pressed clothes into my arms and clicked on a headlamp as another chorus of shouts bellowed through the air. They were getting closer.

I tugged on my pants, working quickly, and yanked on my boots. I left the baggy shirt I wore on and tugged the Itorian scarf over my head. Arrick had moved across the room and now stood over a large chest. He quietly opened the lid and gestured for me to join him. I rushed to his side as he pulled out weapon after weapon. He pushed a shotgun into my hands and then gave me a strap filled with shells. I looped it around my shoulder, unsure how to use it. I had never fired a gun before in my life.

Then for himself, he slipped a holster holding two pistols over his shoulders and strapped twin blades onto his back. Then he pulled out two knives, plus a gun in an ankle holster. I had never seen so many weapons in one place before. The blood rushed out of my head as another cry sounded. Closer than before. People in our camp were starting to scream now. I heard air horns blare and responding gunshots from inside the village. The sounds were too close. They must have breached the Itorian borders. Through the myriad of sounds, I could still hear the bell ringing. Then it stopped abruptly.

I looked at the gun in my hands and my heart skittered in my chest. "I don't know how to—" I broke off, holding the gun out to Arrick, hating how helpless I felt.

He grabbed four shells from the strap and showed me how to load them. Then he racked it and said, "Just point at the bad guys and shoot."

He leaped to his feet and rushed toward the door; I followed close behind him. Before we made it out of the room, Jarrod and Mariah threw open the flap and stared in at us. Without missing a beat, Arrick hissed, "Jarrod, you're with us. Mariah, get the women and children on the west side of the village to safety. Move." He removed a gun from his holster and tossed it to Mariah. She nodded her head in affirmation and cocked the gun smoothly. Jarrod rushed to the chest, pulled out a rifle and a leather satchel that I guessed was full of bullets.

Then he followed us through the bedroom doorway, all four of us moving at a dead run. I heard more gunshots, followed by more screams. They were still getting closer. Our attackers were making their way deeper into the camp now. Adrenaline dumped into my system unlike anything I'd felt before. Part of the pseudo-mortal body that I was still fumbling to get used to. I fought through it and managed to keep a clear head as we hurried.

Arrick drew his pistol and one of the short blades at his back. He slowed to a stop as we reached the entrance to his family's borough. He slid his hand along the canvas and pulled back the tarp, looking out into the night. He pointed to his left and Mariah broke off from us, moving deeper into the residential part of the village. Arrick clicked off his headlamp and hurried toward the center of town.

Jarrod and I followed behind him, and the sound of clashing swords and deafening gunshots grew ever closer. We used the tents and the nearby trees for cover as we moved toward what sounded like a battle. Something whizzed past my face and planted into a tent behind me. I looked back, saw an arrow, and blanched.

Arrick feinted to the side and slipped behind a tent and into the darkness. Fires had broken out all over Itoriah, and the light from them cast shadows into long relief. As we moved to the next set of tent homes, I saw the bodies of two men just a few feet away. Their throats were slit, their purple and green scarves just visible in the flickering firelight.

My stomach roiled in reaction.

Arrick said to Jarrod, "Get to higher ground. The hill on the eastern side. Take cover and pick them off. Take Henry with you if you can find him. Go." Jarrod nodded and ran into the darkness without hesitation, his rifle trained across his chest.

When he was no longer in sight, Arrick looked at me, "This is going to get ugly." He pointed behind me and through a cluster of tents. They were tight together but could be navigated easily by someone smaller, like me. "Keep your head down and use those tents for cover. When you reach the edge of the village, run like hell to the east. Follow the riverbed for five miles, and there's a cavern there. It can only be accessed by deities. It's charmed to prevent human entry. It won't get you to the immortal plane, but it's a safe haven and a quick escape. I'll meet you there when this is over." His words were a rushed whisper, the instructions he threw at me not fully processing in my panicked mind.

As I opened my mouth to refuse, a man wearing a yellow and red scarf turned the corner. He spotted us. Without ever taking his eyes from me, Arrick drew his pistol and blew the guy away. The bullet hit him square in his chest. A constant flow of transparent, ghostly eels swirled along the ground and wound their way up Arrick's legs, but he never took his eyes from me. "You need to go now. Get out of here." He shoved me toward the tents, and I hesitated; then, I shook my head. "Dammit, Bekka. I promised to keep you safe. Don't make me a liar. Now go!"

He shoved me harder this time, forcing me away from him. But he needn't have bothered. The guy with the bullet hole in his chest was oozing blood. My stomach churned at the gore surrounding me, so I clutched the gun to my chest and ran. I glanced back once to see Arrick slip from around the tent and run into the approaching melee.

Men rushed into sight, fighting hand to hand or with their swords and knives. I saw Arrick draw his sword and swing it in a wide arch, slicing a Puhari man through his belly. I turned away, feeling sick at the sight of so much blood and so much pain. I continued to run, squeezing through the tight alley of the tents, checking any crossroads as I came to them. But I had already made up my mind that I wasn't going to do as I was told. Instead, I took a sharp right and headed toward the eastern side of the camp. From what we discussed last night, there was an entire other section of residential tents on that side of town.

Mariah was taking care of her residence on the western side, but who would get the rest of the women and children on the other side of the village out safely? I might not have the constitution to fight in a battle, but I could help in the evacuation effort. The sound of bullets flying roared around me as I ran. I turned one more corner, and suddenly, I was in it.

The heat of the battle.

Men fought all around me. Gunshots rang, and I heard them connect with flesh. I listened to the screams of dying men. I didn't know what to do. I froze.

Two Puhari men locked onto me. They must have seen the fear in my eyes because they smiled, circling me as if I were prey. I held up my gun and hesitated. Before I could make up my mind to pull the trigger, two arrows found their home in each of the men's eyes. Then rough hands grabbed my shoulders and shoved me out of the way as bullets sunk into the trees behind me. They hit with a deafening *thunk* and splinters spewed in all directions.

One more shove from those rough hands and I was at the edge of the village and into the forest, out of sight from the melee. I looked up and saw the man who saved me. His hair was a vivid blonde, almost white, and contrasted starkly with his deep tan. His eyes, though, were crystalline blue and almost inhuman in their intensity. "What the hell do you think you're doing?" He asked, grabbing the gun and ripping it from my hands. He fired off two more shots just over my shoulder, and I heard two more bodies fall behind me. He thrust the gun back into my hands and shook me roughly. "If you're going to carry a gun, use it. Don't hesitate."

Another rustle came from behind him, and he pulled a knife out of a scabbard on his hip and threw it.

"Holy shit!" A male voice exclaimed, dodging to the side as the blade planted into a tree, where his head had been only moments before. "Son of a bitch, Deklan. It's me!" Firelight wavered on the newcomer's face, and as he drew closer, I could make out his features. He was an exact replica of the guy who saved me.

"You should be more careful, Caden. You know better than to sneak up on someone in the middle of a battle," Deklan snarled, striding to the tree and ripping the knife free. He deposited it back into its scabbard and glared at his brother. Or at least I assumed they were brothers— identical twins, from what I could tell.

"Who's she?" Caden asked, ignoring his brother's admonishment and staring at me in confusion.

Dimly, through the fog of my mind, I remembered something Arrick had said about how being his wife would afford me some position here. So, I decided to use it, "I'm Arrick's wife, and I need your help."

They both stared at me, slack-jawed, as the battle raged just outside the tree line. "Arrick's *wife*?"

"Yes, but we don't have time to waste on that now. He tasked Mariah and me with evacuating all the women and children. She is taking care of the west side of town, and I'm supposed to handle the east side." The lie slipped easily from my lips. I couldn't just hide while people were in mortal danger. "Can you help me get there?" I asked. Deklan was a formidable warrior, and judging by how quickly Caden had dodged that knife and the easy way he carried his sword, he was a strong fighter as well. I could use their help protecting the people we needed to evacuate.

"If those are Arrick's orders, then let's move," Caden said. Deklan had a compound bow behind his back, and he drew it, arming it with two arrows. Caden swung the sword he held three times, as though letting me know that he was ready for anything. Then we took off. They moved fast, taking down enemies efficiently and mercilessly as we passed.

But the further east we went, it became clear that there were too many Puhari. The red and yellow scarfed raiders just kept flooding into Itoriah from the north side of camp. For each one we killed, two more seemed to spring up in their place. When we finally reached the eastern residential boroughs, they were smoking. Someone had thrown torches into it. I heard screams of people trapped inside, and my mouth went dry.

"Come on; we need to hurry!" I yelled, running toward the dancing flames that had begun to lick up the tarps that served as an entrance. Caden was close on my heels and passed me up, gesturing for me to follow him. A pair of Deklan's arrows took out the only two Puhari near the tents. We ran along the side of the tarps, Deklan watching our six, as we searched for a good place to cut an entrance.

At the furthest point from the smoke, on the side closest to the woods, Caden stabbed his blade through the canvas and made a doorway. Without thinking, I rushed through it, Deklan staying behind to keep watch as Caden and I went room to room.

In the first room, a mother and her young daughter sat huddled together, trying to ride out the worst of the battle. We pulled them to their feet and showed them the way to our makeshift door. Deklan ushered them out into the forest, and we kept going. Smoke grew thick and heavy as we moved further into the compound. We rescued three more kids, four mothers, and three infants before the smoke began to choke us, so we ran outside, sucked in some clean air, and then rushed back into the tents.

"Is anyone else in here?" I yelled to be heard over the battle outside, terrified that the smoke was getting too thick. Afraid that people would pass out and be unable to answer us.

"Back here!" A female voice shouted. I broke into an all-out sprint and busted through the door from where I'd heard the voice. Flames danced in front of me, and I almost fell backward from the intensity of the heat. I smelled burning hair, probably my own. Then, I looked inside and noticed that a mother, a teenaged boy, and a little girl were bunched against the far wall, as far away from the flames as they could get.

The boy prowled like a trapped wildcat, looking for a weapon or something he could use to force his way out. I thought about throwing them Caden's sword and letting them cut their own door. But the exterior wall was too close to the battle. It would only put them in further danger. I raked my fingers over my scalp and cursed.

Before I could make up my mind on what to do, Caden did it for me. He tossed them a wicked-looking knife and said, "Cut your way through to the next room." He gestured to our right, and I did a mental head slap. *Of course,* I thought, fighting to calm my racing heart. The fire hadn't spread there yet. The boy picked up the knife from the floor and rushed to the wall that Caden indicated. He stabbed the canvas and slid the knife down without hesitation. He held the slit open for his mother and his sister, then came through himself.

They met us at the entrance to the next room over, and we coughed and sputtered as we made our way back to the other refugees. The boy led his mother and sister, his confidence buoying now that they were out of their fire-laden home.

I shouted to be heard above the commotion, "Is there anyone else we missed in here?"

The boy coughed and nodded vehemently, "Far end back to the right. There's a room back there. I think Genie is trapped with her son, Matty. I think they might have passed out from the smoke."

I turned, intending to run back in that direction, but the boy caught my arm and ushered me behind him. To Caden, he said, "Take my mom and sister out with you. I'll show her where they are."

Caden hesitated and then stepped closer to the boy. "Donny, she's Arrick's wife. Take care of her."

Donny did a double-take and surveyed me quickly. Then he turned back to Caden and said, "I'll protect her with my life, Sir."

"Good, now go!" Caden barked.

Donny rushed forward, me on his heels. As we moved deeper into the borough, it became harder to see through all the smoke. The boy pulled his shirt up over his mouth and nose and I did the same with my scarf. My semi-mortal body protested the inhalation of smoke, so I sputtered, eyes watering as we pushed forward. When we neared the end of the apartments, Donny stopped and pointed to his right. I nodded my understanding. This was where Genie and her son would be.

Together, we pushed into the room and were welcomed with a blast of heat. On the floor to just beyond a wall of flames were two bodies, each slumped over on their sides. We both stumbled back a few steps from the heat and turned our heads to look at each other. Through the material of his shirt, I heard Donny shout, "Wait here!"

"What are you going to do?" I asked, eyes wide with concern as he took two steps backward and then rushed forward at a full sprint. He ran through the flames as fast as he could, then skidded to a halt on the other side. He bent down and lifted the boy onto his shoulders and repeated his run through the fire. This time, a couple of places on his shirt caught flame, and I pulled my scarf off and smothered them. When he was no longer on fire, I looped it back around my nose and mouth.

He passed the boy to me and shouted, "One more time." Further into the apartments and down the hallway, the wooden posts crackled and then collapsed, taking a good chunk of the tarps with them.

"Hurry!" I urged, the child now held carefully in my arms. Donny ran through the fire one more time and scooped Genie up from the ground, cradling her slight frame.

On his way back through the fire, he shouted to me, "Run!"

I obeyed his command and dashed toward our exit. I could hear his breathing close behind me and knew he was right on my heels. The closer we got to the cut doorway, the easier it was to see. I heard more crackling and the sound of collapsing tents behind us.

"Faster!" Caden shouted from outside our makeshift doorway. "The borough is coming down!" We stumbled out just as the entire structure collapsed, expelling a wave of hot air out at everyone standing nearby. I winced as it hit my skin and dropped to one knee. The boy's weight became immense as I struggled to gulp air. I laid him gently on the ground and looked him over for signs of life. His chest rose and fell, and his heart was beating, but it was hard to say how long he'd been deprived of sufficient oxygen. I looked at the teenager who'd helped me—the one Caden called Donny.

"That was everyone?" I asked, hoping the answer was yes. If not, there was no way we could go back to save them. The entire structure was engulfed in fire now.

He coughed and sputtered as he nodded his head. "That's everyone who was left in this borough. The rest of them are either fighting or have already fled. We were debating whether to wait it out or evacuate when the fire broke out."

"OK, I'm glad everyone is out," I said, breathing a sigh of relief. "Now, we have to get you all out of here and somewhere safe." The sound of fighting was far too close for comfort, and none of these people looked like warriors. Save the boy. But he was more like a warrior in training. Too young to be a part of the fight, but too competent to stand idly by.

He stepped forward and held out his hands. "We know where to go. Just give me a weapon in case we run into any trouble." Caden, Deklan, and I eyed him, all three of us debating the merits of giving a weapon to a teenage kid.

Deklan relented first, leaning down and removing his gun from his ankle holster. "Don't hesitate to use it,

Donny," Deklan commanded, placing the gun in his hand. "Just like we've practiced in training."

As Donny cocked it, I realized that the kid still had Caden's knife tucked into his boot. "You can keep that too," Caden said, gesturing to it. "I've got more where it came from." Realizing that my own gun was useless in my hands, I looked at him.

I stepped closer and offered him the shotgun. His mother stepped forward instead and said, "I'll take it. I know how to use it." I slipped the shells from around my neck and handed those to her as well. She took the gun and the ammo, nodding in gratitude. They lifted Genie and Matty from the ground with no further hesitation and slipped into the forest, following Donny's lead.

"What did you just do?" Deklan asked. He looked really pissed. "Did you just give away your only weapon?" Before I could answer, a gunshot boomed. The sound reverberated against my skull, and time seemed to slow as Caden jumped in front of his brother and me. He swung his sword, and I heard metal clang along with sparks flying from the blade as he deflected the bullets.

I stared at him stupidly for a beat before he shouted, "Run!" I obeyed. I rushed away from the cover of the forest and back to the village, making a beeline for the thick of the fighting. I refused to lead anyone who pursued us further into the woods. If we did, then they might intercept Donny and the other refugees we just saved. I heard Deklan and Caden's footsteps behind me while I bobbed and weaved through the tents, through scattered belongings and the bodies of the fallen. Bullets whistled by my ears and hit tents, trees, and the ground.

I heard the spring of a compound bow release followed by a man screaming in pain. I knew that Deklan had found his mark. We kept moving, never stopping as we fled deeper into the heart of Itoriah.

Suddenly, a shot sounded, and pain exploded in my shoulder.

White lights were dancing in front of my eyes, and everything once again seemed to slow down until I felt Deklan's hand at my other elbow, urging me to keep moving, even as I stumbled from the blinding agony of it.

That was when I felt it—a hum of power deep inside of my body.

It pulsed like an angry, leashed beast. It shouldn't have been possible. I'd had my powers stripped. But then I remembered something. In my drunken haze, I had seen a blue light before I fell asleep last night. Then, before, when Arrick brushed his hand over mine. Was my power only dormant and not truly gone? Was it trying to break free? I could not think of a more inopportune moment for that to happen than right now.

We turned a corner, and I staggered, nearly falling to my knees. My mortal body was collapsing under the strain of pain and exhaustion. But Caden helped me up and forced me to keep going. The deeper we got into camp, the thicker the smoke became. It seemed that everything was on fire, and my lungs rebelled against the spoiled air, but I knew we couldn't stop. Finally, two gunshots sounded and the men behind us yelled, their bodies thudding to the ground. I turned my head back to check our tail and saw that the last two who'd been chasing us were down. Probably dead.

Smoke billowed around us, making me cough. Then, the wind shifted, blowing the thickest of it away and I saw Arrick standing there. His pistol was trained, and I knew instinctively that he had shot our pursuers. Behind him, the battle was still raging on; there had to be at least twenty of the Puhari left alive. In the melee, I saw Kaleb and Niko still fighting nearby. That made five Itorian warriors remaining, counting the addition of Caden and Deklan. My mind struggled to take in the scene as I fought to contain the power growing inside me. If I let it go here, we would be in deep shit.

I locked eyes with Arrick, shook my head in warning, and fell to my knees. I screamed, the sound ripping through my throat as the power surged, grew, and then burned like fire. I could see the fear in his eyes when he holstered his gun as he sprinted toward me.

"I'm sorry," I rasped, the sound inaudible as tears flowed down my cheeks. Then, the energy inside of me exploded.

The resulting shockwave knocked everyone in a hundred-yard radius flat on their backs, except Arrick. He slid under it, avoiding the brunt of the blow. He was on his feet within seconds and running toward me. Blue power swirled around me. My skin flashed in a vivid glow, and the bullet wound in my shoulder healed instantly. Pressure built within me, and I feared what would happen next if I couldn't get this leashed. I couldn't afford to create another sun on the surface of this planet. It would kill everyone.

Arrick's voice broke through my terror, "Focus it, Bekka. Don't let it control you. Remember, you control it!" He was still running toward me, and I tried to absorb the meaning of his words. As I did, the power built, threatening to consume me and every living creature unlucky enough to be in the vicinity. I burned from the inside out, the energy unwilling to be contained. A second passed, and Arrick was at my side. He braved the blue flames pulsing around me and gripped my arm in his fingers. He winced, and I heard his flesh sizzle, "Concentrate," he said, pulling my attention to him. "You can control it. You're *She Who Was Sent*. It's your destiny, so you can do this."

I did as he asked. I breathed deeply, concentrated harder than I ever had before, and groaned with the effort it took. I burrowed deeper inside of myself, into the very core of my being. And that was where I found the center of my power. I focused it, bent it to my will, and the fire shifted and settled around me like a cloak.

I looked out onto the battlefield and saw the men getting up from the blow I'd issued. Every single face stared at me in mute horror, but I ignored them all. Instead, I looked around and saw that the ground was littered with the bodies and blood of Itorian men, women, and children. I'd tried, but I hadn't gotten everyone out in time. A fire burned in my belly as I let the rage of this realization wash over me.

The Puhari started to turn and flee, but I made up my mind then and there. I knew exactly what I was going to do with this power. These were kin to the men who'd tried to kill Arrick and rape me. They committed countless other atrocities that I had witnessed. They didn't deserve the air they breathed.

What kind of monsters killed children?

I focused my power, sought to understand it and what I saw amazed me. Through my magic, I was able to connect to all living things. I could see everything, down to the atoms and molecules that made up the fabric of life itself. Even as the Puhari ran into the woods, I lifted my head and snapped my fingers. My power rushed out of me and through the forest after them. It encircled every last one of them in blue light and then reduced their bodies down to the building blocks of life. I rearranged them into dust, and they floated away on the wind.

As quickly as my power came, it was extinguished, and the dampener was firmly back in place. My chest heaved from the effort I had expended as the silver mist of the souls I had relieved their mortal bodies slipped along the ground. They rushed toward the only death god within a million miles, invisible to everyone but us. Finding him, they swarmed at his feet, surrounding him, and then they passed through his body. He sucked in a breath and grimaced as they disappeared one by one.

Then without warning, Arrick dropped to his knees; he growled and panted as though in agony, clutching his wrist. My legs went slack, and I dropped to my knees beside him, small jagged rocks biting into my flesh through the barrier of my pants.

I pushed through the pain and exhaustion and asked, "Arrick? What's wrong?" His teeth were clenched and bared as he panted and shook his head from side to side. His face finally relaxed, and he slumped forward as though in prayer. The pain was over.

"We are screwed," he said, through gritted teeth and panting breaths. In explanation, he slid up the sleeve of his jacket. The tattoo was gone, replaced with nothing but bright pink flesh. It looked as though an acid wash had removed it.

My heartbeat skittered as I realized one horrifying fact. I had just given humans proof of divinity. Now, our all access pass, the one Arrick had said was our ticket out of here, was gone. We were stuck here. He was right. Only, we weren't just screwed. We were fucked.

The full impact of what I just did hit me all at once with the force of a freight train—we were marooned here thanks to me, and I had just killed dozens of men.

The world went fuzzy, and my body went limp, but Arrick caught me before I could eat dirt and held me in his arms gently. I looked up at him, all that energy rushing out of my veins just as quickly as it had come. He stared down at me with an expression I couldn't quite read. He rose to stand, my body still in his arms, and then set me down, propping my back against a tree.

I covered my eyes with my hands as panic began to push its way into the forefront of my mind. I'd taken a human life. Well, not just one life, but many. And not only that, but I broke the rules. How were we going to get back to save everyone if we were stuck here?

A bone-deep sorrow broke inside of my chest, and tears slid down my cheeks. "What did I do?" I asked Arrick as I covered my entire face and let the sobs rack my body. He knelt beside me and stroked my hair.

Unexpectedly, I heard the shuffle of boots on soil and pine needles as someone else approached.

A whoosh of air rustled my pants, and I removed my hands from my face, looking past Arrick to see what was happening. Deklan and Caden had come to stand before me, flanked by Niko and Kaleb. They were what was left of the Itorian fighters. The rest had given their lives to defend this place, or they had fled into the woods once they realized the battle was lost.

They all looked at me like I was an alien, a foreign object that they couldn't quite understand. Then, Kaleb broke the silence and said, "What the hell are you?" His eyes were fixed on me, and I looked up as all four men stared at me. It was at that moment that I appreciated just how badly I'd screwed up.

What the hell was I, indeed.

CHAPTER 10

Marooned

"Maybe you should thank her for saving our hides instead of staring at her like she's a monster," Arrick snarled, giving them all a warning glare. All four men were looking at me in a way that made me wonder if there were a dry pair of underwear between them. Their mouths hung open, their eyes were wide, and Niko's hands shook visibly.

Kaleb was the first to recover, "She just disintegrated twenty men with the God damn snap of her fingers. I think we have a right to know what the hell she is!" He argued, pointing an accusing finger in my direction.

"He's right," Niko said, stepping a few steps further away from me for good measure. "We deserve to know. Otherwise, how can we trust that she won't do the same to us if the mood strikes her?"

"You can trust her because she's *my wife*. I'll vouch for her," Arrick said, thumping his fist to his chest and angling his body in front of mine. It was a natural gesture of protection, but as much as I appreciated it, I didn't need it. I could take care of myself, and I certainly didn't need anyone to speak for me.

I was still sitting on the ground, resting against a tree, so I braced an arm against the solid bark behind me and rose to my feet. I stood, spine lengthening to my full height. What I wanted to do was bury myself under the covers of my bed in Valeria and never come out again. My shame over what I'd done ran deep, but hiding from it wasn't an option.

"You know I won't do the same to you because I'm not a monster. I'm a goddess, and I'm your last hope to avoid extinction."

Niko and Kaleb's mouths dropped open in stupefaction. Niko's sword slipped from his fingers and plopped onto the ground, his eyes blank. Kaleb blinked rapidly as though trying to process what I'd just said.

"S-S-She's a… what?" Kaleb stuttered as he stared at me. I couldn't tell if his expression was horror or awe, so instead of examining him further, I turned my attention to Caden and Deklan. In contrast to the other two men, the brothers just stared at me with curious expressions on their handsome faces.

I squinted at them in suspicion, but before I could inquire further, Arrick interrupted, speaking through gritted teeth, "Can I talk to you for a minute, please?" He wrapped his fingers around my upper arm and pulled me away from the awe-struck stares of our companions. None of them followed, and I wasn't sure if it was from courtesy or fear.

When we were out of hearing distance and partially obscured in the forest, he asked, "What the hell do you think you're doing? You can't just tell them that you're a goddess!"

I pulled my arm out of his grasp, "What difference does it make? We're already marooned here indefinitely. Besides, do you really think they would have believed anything else?"

He stared at me, wide-eyed, and shook his head as though to clear it, "That's not the point," he growled, and I could see his frustration growing by the second. Slamming his fist into a tree, he snarled, "I can't fucking believe this. You're here less than one day, and the situation has gone to hell in a handbasket. I've lived here for 15 years and never come close to a slip-up. But now we've handed proof of divinity to four mortals on a silver platter."

I crossed my arms over my chest. I was starting to feel defensive. "You're blaming me for this? How is this my fault?" I asked, stepping into his space bubble and glaring up at him.

When he spoke, his voice was low and dangerous. "If you had gone to the cavern, like I asked, none of this would have happened." I could tell he was angry now. His eyes were slanted, and his body was tightly coiled, ready to burst into action at a moment's notice.

"If I had run away as you asked, then seven people on the east side of town would be dead right now. Burned up in a fire started by the Puhari," I argued. "I stayed to help them escape."

Arrick's nostrils flared as he fought to control his anger. He waited until his breathing calmed before he asked, "That's why you stayed behind?"

"Of course. I couldn't just sit back and do nothing. Mariah was taking care of the west side, but no one was helping the eastern borough."

He shook his head and dragged a hand over his sooty face. When he spoke, his voice was softer than I expected. "You should have listened to me."

"I'm not a coward, Arrick. I'll never run away to protect myself when other people need my help."

He groaned aloud in frustration, the sound echoing in the distance. He clenched his teeth and spoke through them, "Noted. But here's the situation we're in now because you disobeyed a direct order. Kaleb, Caden, Niko, and Deklan all know that more than one god exists. The only way for us to get back to the godly realm is to eliminate them."

My mouth dropped open, and I stared at him for a solid three-count; then I took a deep breath and said, "You can't be serious." He'd told me that the only way back to the immortal realm would be unpleasant, but cold-blooded murder? "We can't do that."

He let out a long breath, too, and looked up to the sky, his eyes full of sorrow and regret, "I'm sorry, Bekka. But you've left me no choice. If it's four men's lives bargained against millions… I have to do it." He paused, and I could see the raw pain lining his face. He didn't want to do this any more than I wanted him to. Despite the misery that enveloped him like a shroud, he reached for the gun in his holster, fingers twining around it.

"No!" I pleaded, rushing to cover his hand with mine, not allowing him to draw the weapon. "There has to be something else we can do. They've done nothing wrong. We can't just kill them."

When I looked up, his skin had gone bone-white with anguish, "You think that I want to do this? I've known those men for years. Caden and Deklan are my friends, and Kaleb and Niko are like family to me."

"Then, don't, please. I'm begging you."

His jaw flexed, and he swallowed audibly, a haunted expression washing over his face. "Remember when I told you that I'd do anything, risk everything to save this place? When I said I'd give my very soul to save everyone here?" He asked, resting his hands on my shoulders. He hunched down and looked into my eyes. "This is that *anything* I was talking about."

I stepped back out of his reach and shook my head, "No, you can't."

"I have to," he growled, the regret evident in every syllable.

"Not if you want my help to fix your sun and heal this planet. If you do, then you won't touch them." My voice was steady while I stared him down, daring him to fight me.

In a flash, Arrick's expression transformed from painful misery to anger. His eyes glittered with it as he stepped closer, his presence menacing. I held my ground.

"You wouldn't," he said, lips firm and jaw squared.

"Try me," I dared him, not backing down an inch.

He growled in frustration, and the veins grew taught in his neck as he struggled to restrain his anger. When he spoke, his voice was eerily calm, "This isn't about four men. This is about an entire planet of people and animals. Even if there was another way, which there isn't, we don't have a lot of time to find it. Gabryel is looking for you, *and* this planet is on a rapid countdown to destruction. Every second we spend in this realm is time that we no longer have to prepare your powers for what needs to be done. And believe me, we are going to need every second we can get." When I didn't waver an inch, he took in a calming breath and gripped my shoulders so that he could look into my eyes once more. There was a combination of desperation and sorrow in them. "I know you don't want to hear this, but they can't exist here after what they witnessed. The portals will only reopen once they can no longer share what they saw with others. There is only one that way we can be sure that they won't. That is the sacrifice that's required for reentry."

My mind reeled as I absorbed what he said. Could he be wrong about another solution not existing? Was I willing to risk it? "Give me two more days," I said before I could second guess myself further. "Please. Only seven hours will have passed in the godly realm by then. We have to at least try to help them, Arrick." I thought about all those images hanging on the walls on our way to this place—all that death and senseless killing. I thought about the men who attacked me. That was the kind of danger these people must face every day here, and I did not want to contribute to that; I needed to find that third option.

Arrick turned his back to me and dragged his fingers through his filthy hair. I could tell that he was considering my offer carefully, weighing the cost versus the benefit. On the one hand, it cost him two extra days on this planet and five fewer hours to stay ahead of my grandpa. On the other, his agreement guaranteed my assistance when we returned to the immortal realm. He could take a gamble, say no, and hope that I would help Moldize anyway. But he couldn't be certain that I would. If he took my offer, then we were making a deal that each of us would consider binding, and he'd have my help no matter what.

When he turned back to me, his face was composed, so I realized that his mind was made up, "If I give us two days to find a loophole, you'll help us fix our sun? I have your word on that?"

"You do." I held out my hand to seal the bargain, so he took it in his and shook. Despite his frustration with me, I could see his shoulders relax with relief. He hadn't wanted to kill them any more than I had; he'd just thought it was the only option. I hoped for everyone's sake that he was wrong.

When he spoke again, his words were filled with warning, "Then we have a deal. But when that time is up, if we haven't found a way back home, we'll revisit this conversation."

Goosebumps prickled on the back of my neck, and I swallowed. I could only hope that we would be successful and never had to talk about this again. Deklan and Caden had saved me from unspeakable pain and torment during the battle, and from what I'd seen of Niko and Kaleb, I liked them. I didn't want to see any of them dead.

When we turned back to what was left of the village, intending to join the others, Niko emerged from behind a nearby tree. He was close… close enough to have overheard our entire conversation. He stared at us and shook his head in what I guessed was a mixture of confusion and shock.

"Shit," Arrick breathed. "Whatever you heard, Niko, I can explain."

Niko raised his hand and shook his head, mouth still open. Realizing this, he snapped it shut and asked, "Explain what? That you are both gods, and you're trapped here now? That the only way you get back to your realm and save our planet is to kill us?" With each word, his voice got louder and louder, and at the end, he was nearly shouting. His voice carried to the other men, who had kept their distance.

All three of them turned their heads to stare in confusion, so Arrick pressed his fingers over his lips, "Please, Niko, be quiet. We can talk about this."

"What's there to talk about?" Niko asked. "It's four lives bargained against millions. Isn't that right, Arrick?"

Arrick shook his head, trying to soothe his friend, "That's not what I meant."

But Niko was having none of it; he'd lost himself to rage and frustration. His face was red and mottled, and his eyes were filled with desperation. He gestured to me, "Just because Miss Merciful over here is not getting the importance of this doesn't mean that I don't. Trust me, brother," Niko said, nodding fanatically. "I get it." Then he reached into his holster and pulled out his 45 long barrel. He pointed it at Arrick for a split second before he trained it to his own temple. "You're talking about my life weighed against my wife and daughter's lives. I'd go to my grave any day of the week to save them. Just say the word, and I'll pull the trigger. I'll make it nice and easy for you. It's the least I can do, after everything you've done for us over the years."

"Niko, don't," Arrick pleaded, stepping forward, hands raised in surrender. "Please, brother. Bekka's right; we have time. We'll find another way."

I pressed my hands to my mouth to stifle the scream that itched its way up my throat. I turned my head and saw Kaleb, Caden, and Deklan sprinting toward us.

Caden and Deklan got to us first and circled behind Niko, just out of his line of sight. Kaleb, on the other hand, approached him head-on, taking his position next to Arrick and raising his hands in a pacifying motion. When he spoke, his voice was soft and full of worry, "Niko, whatever's going on in your head right now, you need to stop. Think about Eryn and Kimmy."

Niko laughed, shaking his head, "That's exactly what I'm doing, Kaleb. You didn't hear what they said. You don't understand. We all have to die. To save everyone else, we all have to die." Though he spoke the truth, he sounded deranged, and it was clear from the expressions of those around me that they thought so too.

I gasped as Niko's finger tensed on the trigger. Arrick gave an imperceptible nod, and before his friend's finger could finish its backward motion, Caden and Deklan were on him. They moved faster than I imagined possible, and I blinked stupidly in reaction.

Caden ripped the gun from Niko's hand, ejecting the clip and clearing the chamber. Arrick shoved him as Deklan held out his leg to trip him and bring him to the ground. Then, Arrick and Deklan held either arm as he kicked and thrashed.

"No!" he yelled. "Why'd you stop me?" He was frantic now. "They're all going to die. You shouldn't have stopped me!" Kaleb hauled back his fist and planted it directly into Niko's face. The resulting crunch made me wince, and Niko's body automatically went slack. He was out cold.

Following Arrick's lead, Deklan let go of Niko's arm and rose to his feet, wiping sweat from his brow. "Care to explain what the hell that was about?"

Kaleb coughed and rose to his feet. "No shit. What the fuck happened to my uncle?"

Arrick and I looked at one another. The cat was out of the bag now. When Niko came around, he was going to tell them everything, and we wouldn't be able to lie to them, even if we wanted to.

Arrick had been right.

Since the moment I stepped foot on this planet, it had been nothing but a non-stop disaster. And now, we were going to have to explain to four mortals who we were, why we were here, and why we were trapped. Exhaustion washed over me, and I hoped that fate knew what the hell it was doing. Because if this was part of my destiny, then she was one cold-blooded bitch.

CHAPTER 11

A Third Option

Before Arrick explained our situation, we took a few moments to venture further into the forest. We wanted to get a safe distance away from the wreckage in Itoriah just in case any enemies came sniffing around. We also restrained Niko using some rope we found in the smoldering rubble that was left of the place before we departed. We then tied him to a tree and brought him around using the very strategic method of snapping near his ear and gently patting his cheeks.

He woke up confused at first. But then he took one look at me and became incensed. He fought against his bindings and shouted at us, commanding that we free him.

Kaleb knelt beside his uncle and looked at him with pleading eyes, "Niko, you need to stop. You're acting crazy, man."

When he only snarled like a rabid animal, Deklan ripped a section of his shirt into a thick strip, stepped to Niko's side, and slipped the fabric into his mouth, creating a makeshift gag. The shouts were instantly muffled, and I felt my shoulders relax in response.

"What the hell happened to him?" Caden asked, his voice filled with worry. "It's like he's lost his senses."

Arrick dragged a hand over his face in frustration. He looked at me and then back to Niko, his eyes filled with regret. I couldn't say for certain what had caused Niko to snap. My best guess was that it was because we'd given him hope of saving this world. Couple that with the knowledge that there was only one thing he could do to aid this cause. Die.

I shivered as I tried to determine how we could answer Caden's question without eliciting a Niko-like response from the other Itorian men. I turned to Arrick, leaned close to him, and whispered in his ear, "I think we are going to have to tell them everything. Niko already heard it. They're going to find out."

Arrick cleared his throat and stared into the forest. He looked resigned when he turned his attention back to his friends. "I guess we don't have another choice." Hesitating, Arrick pressed his fingertips to his eyes as though a sharp pain throbbed there. Taking his hand away, he leveled his gaze on his friends. "Before I tell you this story, you need to understand something about the world we live in. There is not one god. There are millions of gods across over a dozen universes that we know of, and hundreds of galaxies. And we operate differently than the Moldizean religion tells you. We are not all-powerful and omnipotent. Instead, we all have gifts uniquely suited to keeping those universes, galaxies, and planets running smoothly. It's our job to sustain life."

After a long pause, Kaleb let out a snort of awkward laughter. When we just stared at him, he cleared his throat and rolled his eyes meaningfully, "I mean, you're kidding. This is a joke, right? You're fucking with us."

Arrick and I exchanged a look before we turned back to him and shook our heads in unison. He ran a hand down the back of his neck and replied, "No, I'm not kidding. We're not screwing with you, and I'm not making this up. This is the truth." When everyone except Niko continued to stare at him in a combination of disbelief and dismay, he continued, "You have my word as a leader of Itoriah. And if you need more than that, then you have concrete proof. Think about what Bekka did to those Puhari."

The general reaction to this statement was complete and utter stupefaction. Kaleb slumped to a sitting position abruptly, mouth agape; it opened and closed at odd intervals, like a fish sucking air. Caden's eyes were wide, and his brows raised; his mouth was also slightly open. He backed up, hit a tree, and slowly slid down it, his descent slightly more controlled than Kaleb's. Niko's eyes went buggy, and he grumbled against his gag.

Deklan was the only exception. He leaned his shoulder against a nearby tree and pulled his knife out of his ankle holster. He wedged the tip under his fingernail, the picture of casual indifference. He asked, "If there are so many of you, and it's your job to sustain life, then why didn't you save Moldize before 80% of it became uninhabitable?"

Arrick clenched his jaw, the strong line of it flexing in the dawning sunlight, "Deities rely on a *network* of gifts. We didn't have access to the one we needed to save this place. Until now." His eyes settled on me, making my belly clench because it caused all eyes to follow his, fixing on me in a combination of wonder and curiosity.

"What's so special about her?" Deklan asked, eyeing me up and down. "Aside from the fact that she can disintegrate human bodies into dust, that is."

"I'm sorry to interrupt," Kaleb interrupted. He didn't look all that sorry if you asked me. He continued, "But this doesn't explain why Niko lost his shit. There has to be something else." Niko struggled against his bonds, mumbling against his gag and nodding his head furiously.

Arrick slid a hand over the back of his neck and said simply, "You're right. There *is* more." Then he launched into the story. He left no detail to their imagination, divulging everything. He explained the prophecy, that I was *She Who Was Sent*. He discussed how I'd gotten here and my tenuous agreement to visit Moldize to see the people firsthand. He described the relations between my home realm and his own, letting them know just how meaningful it was that I was even here.

He explained the rules that deities had to operate under in the Moldizean mortal realm. Then he explained how what I'd done tonight had broken them. He told them the punishment for breaking those rules, namely our exile. He conveyed that the only way back to the immortal realm was to eliminate all witnesses to my divine act. He made sure that they understood that their lives were all that stood between us and saving Moldize. He finished the story by going through the deal we'd just made. Two days here to find a loophole in exchange for a guarantee of my help once we returned to the immortal realm.

To say that only their lives stood between us and saving Moldize was overstating the facts, in my opinion. There was a lot more between us and the end goal than the lives of these men. There was my own inexperience *plus* my lack of control over my powers. Then there was my grandpa, who would present another obstacle for us to overcome.

But he continued, undaunted by my narrowed eyes and pressed lips. "That's why Niko flipped out and tried to kill himself. He heard me tell Bekka that it was the only way to save everyone else. He heard the deal we made, and he decided to take matters into his own hands."

All three of the men cut their stunned expressions to Niko. Kaleb was the first to react, moving closer to his uncle and removing the gag. Niko coughed, spat, and glared at Arrick before adding his two cents to this challenging conversation, "Making that deal with her was insane. You're wasting precious time we don't have for a pipe dream." Then he looked to the other three men, a plea in his eyes. "You know I'm right. We should face this head-on and do what must be done. We are not cowards. We're warriors."

Kaleb turned to Arrick, his voice level as though carefully considering Niko's words, "Is there any hope that we can find another option? Or is Niko right, and we're just deluding ourselves? Because if that's the case, then I'm with him." He flung a hand to Niko's bound figure for emphasis. "Our family founded this tribe over 20 years ago when The Burning forced us to relocate, and I'm sworn to protect it with my life. I know you, of all people, can understand that." Though I could tell he was trying to control his emotions, I could still see anxiety vibrating off him in waves. He meant every word he said, and I knew that he would act on them, if necessary.

Arrick rubbed a hand over his chin in thought and then looked at me. "If Bekka can access her powers, we might be able to find a way. There are portals all over this realm; she might be able to punch through despite our exile."

Caden looked at me. His eyes were full of wonder as if I was some rare object—an alien. *Which I technically was,* so it made sense. "Can you do it? Can you access them again?" he asked hopefully.

Arrick had told them about the rules, explained how our powers had been stripped. But it left me questioning, wondering if stripped was the wrong word because it seemed like suppressed would be more accurate.

In response to Caden's inquiry, I closed my eyes and delved deep inside my being. I found that center of power once more, coaxed it out. I felt it pull to the surface, and when I opened my eyes, I saw my fingers glow blue. But before I could do anything, it guttered, evaporating into nothing but air. When I tried to find it again—eyes and nose scrunched with the effort—there was nothing there.

I felt empty.

I looked at them all and shook my head. "Something's blocking me. It's like there's a shroud covering them. It will only let me get so far before it smothers them."

Deklan was still cleaning his nails when he asked, "Then how were you able to do it before? You didn't seem to have any access problems when you dusted those men."

In response to his challenge, I closed my eyes tightly and tried a third time. Panting from the effort, I dug deeper, looked harder. Then a blinding pain, unlike anything I ever experienced before, pierced my brain like a white-hot poker through my skull. I screamed, clutching my head in my hands. I slouched down into a crouch, involuntary tears flowing down my cheeks.

Suddenly, Arrick was there next to me, holding my face with each of his hands and looking into my eyes, trying to comfort me. "Bekka, stop. Please, you're hurting yourself. You have to stop."

Dimly, I realized that I was sobbing all-out now, my shoulders shaking with the agonized cries. I tried to calm my body, but I couldn't seem to control my own reaction. The pain was unlike anything I had ever felt before.

"What *the hell* just happened?" Caden asked, and I could tell that there was concern in his voice. I couldn't be sure if it was for my own sake or for the salvation I represented. "Is she OK?"

Sweat slid down my back, but the shaking had subsided now. Arrick still held my face and stroked my hair to comfort me. I shuddered a little in reaction, feeling oddly soothed by the gesture. Then I tilted my head up to his, our eyes locking.

When I spoke, my voice was weak and wobbly, "I'm not sure I'll be able to help. It's like I'm being punished for breaking through the wards."

He nodded in response and released me from his soothing hold. "It's OK, Bekka. We'll find another way. Don't try to access them again. We can't risk you."

"What *other way?*" Deklan asked, his voice calm and logical. "And why was she able to do it before but now she isn't? It seems a little too convenient."

"It's anything but convenient," I retorted, anger restoring my energy, so I pushed out of Arrick's arms to glare at Deklan. I wiped my palms on my filthy pants. Though I was loath to admit it, he made a good point. *Why could I do it then but not now? The answer might be able to help us.* So, I thought back to when my powers had erupted from me like a geyser boiling over. That was when I realized that there had been one very specific difference. "I'd been shot.

It seems like my power can only breach the wards when I'm in serious distress. It's like it overwhelms them, and the counter-magic can't stop me."

Deklan nodded in thought. Casually, he pulled a pistol from his waistband and trained it on me, "I could shoot you again if you think it'll help?" I flinched and shied back, remembering the explosion of agony from the battle. Getting shot hurt—*really bad*—and I wasn't ready to relive the experience. At least, not just yet.

Arrick stretched out his arm and leaned protectively in front of me, "No one is shooting anyone, alright? We still have time to figure this out without causing Bekka grave bodily harm."

"What harm?" Deklan asked, gesturing at my perfectly healed shoulder. "She should still have a bullet hole right there, and look, there's nothing. She's fine."

I pressed Arrick's arm away and spoke directly to Deklan, facing down the barrel of his gun, "Arrick is right. We still have some time to figure this out. But, if we can't, then I'll let you shoot me so we can see if it works. Fair enough?" I thought it would best to keep the fact that I was just as likely to dust *them* as I was to create a portal to myself. My control had been non-existent the first time I'd used my power and tenuous the second time. Who knew what the next time would be like? But Deklan's lips twitched in response to my suggestion, and he nodded his head in acquiescence, slipping the gun back into its holster.

Niko spoke then, "You keep saying we have time. But two days is too long to waste on a lost cause. Why don't you just kill us and be done with it?"

Arrick looked at Niko, and I could see the irritation in his eyes. "Listen carefully," he said, expression darkening. He prowled closer to Niko with a predatory gait. "You can trust that if we didn't have the time to sort this out, I never would have made a deal with her. I'd have killed you myself. Now nod that you understand."

Niko had gone stark white, and everyone else had fallen silent. I got the impression that they'd never seen Arrick in his death god mode before. Or, at least, it had never been directed at them. After a brief hesitation, Niko nodded, the Adam's apple at this throat bobbing as he swallowed.

Arrick smiled, but his teeth held a distinctly feral quality. I shivered in reaction as he said, "Good. Then stop trying to be a goddamn martyr and help us think of another way around Afryel's rules."

Caden sucked in a quick breath, his already white face going ghastly in the dawning sunlight, "Did you just say Afryel?" His expression held a combination of confusion, disbelief, and most importantly of all, recognition.

I cinched my brows together in curiosity, "Yes, Afryel. He's the creation deity who built Moldize. Do you know that name?" I asked, edging toward him.

Caden shook his head as though to clear it and turned his attention to his brother, "This is—" he shook his head again. "This is insane. It can't be."

Turning to Deklan now, I could see the shock etched plainly on his face. He'd paused mid-nail cleaning, the blade hovering over one fingertip. Snapping out of it, he slipped his knife into his scabbard and chuckled in disbelief, "Actually, it makes sense if you think about it."

"But they were crazy. We both always thought they were crazy," Caden said, raking both hands over his scalp.

Arrick cleared his throat, and we all turned our attention away from the brothers, "Care to tell us what you're talking about? How do you know Afryel's name?"

Deklan flashed an arrogant grin and said, "Why don't you sit? Because we have something to tell you all.

Something that might make that nutcase over there relax for a few minutes." He gestured to Niko with his chin. "Meaning, I think we have a way to get you out of here without killing us to do it."

CHAPTER 12

Legacy

After Deklan's declaration and Arrick's promise that we had time left to find another answer, Niko had regained most of his composure. We were able to untie him, and he now sat in a circle, with the rest of us, all eyes trained on the brothers. He still looked a little rough around the edges, if you asked me. But on the positive side, he wasn't aiming a gun at his own head anymore. Probably, we wouldn't know the full extent of the gasket he'd blown until another stressful situation presented itself. I could only hope that he would recover and be back to the fearless leader I'd met the night before.

Caden and Deklan sat close together, conferring with each other in hushed whispers and gesturing wildly. After a few moments passed awkwardly, they seemed to have reached a decision. They then retrained their focus on us.

Caden cleared his throat and rubbed at his chin, "Our family has a… legacy, of sorts. A legend that's been passed down from generation to generation. My brother and I always thought it was a bunch of nonsense. Something one of our ancestors made up to screw with the subsequent generations. But when you said that name… *Afryel.*" He shook his head. "I wonder now if it's true. Maybe you can tell us one way or the other, once and for all."

"More importantly," Deklan interrupted, holding up a finger to emphasize his point. "Maybe this story will get you both the access you need to get back to the godly realm. My brother insists that I tell the story in full, though, just as it was passed down to me from my mother. He believes the context is important, and I'm inclined to agree. So, in the spirit of that, I guess I should start by telling you that our family, on our mother's side, is different. Many of us have possessed what you might consider 'gifts.' Nothing extraordinary, but talents beyond the scope of what most people deemed normal."

Deklan's serious-as-death expression as he spoke and Caden's earnestness created a strange and ominous feeling that crawled up my stomach. Everything he was saying kept me on my toes; and I listened to him in rapt attention as I wondered, *what the hell is going on?*

"For example, many of our relatives have had a special talent for interpreting past lives or an ability to see auras. Some could even see into the future, though that was a long time ago. But our mother, for example, had a gift with plants. She could grow *anything,* and faster than you can imagine. Plants that she'd start from seed would be fully grown and fruiting within a week."

My eyes widened. That *was* unusual. As far as I knew, only gods or goddesses of agriculture in the Mortal & Godly Affairs Pillar of the godly governments could accomplish such a feat.

I leaned forward in interest, and Deklan took a breath before continuing his tale, "According to family legend, this all started with our great grandmother and grandfather, ten times down the line. That great-grandmother was so beautiful it would hurt your eyes to look at her. She had silvery blonde hair and electric blue eyes. Her skin was velvety peaches dipped in warm cream, and she was the envy of every woman she met. She was also the desire of all the men in her village, and many proposed marriage to her once she came of age. At that time, marriages were arranged by families or chosen by the men themselves, unlike the freedom to choose that we have now."

That made me think about my sister and her marriage to Thayne, of the responsibility she bore to ensure that our people had the resources they needed to live full, safe and happy lives. *Focus, Bekka,* my mind screamed when the anguish of the prospect of not seeing her again began to swell in my chest. I forced myself to pay attention once again.

"But her father was a kind man, and he loved his daughter beyond comprehension. They were not a wealthy family, and though her beauty could have made them so, he did not pressure her into choosing someone she didn't love. So, many suitors came, and they left disappointed, as she refused them all. Until one day, an injured man came to their door. He'd been attacked by raiders, who plagued the roads by their village and had lost all his worldly possessions on his journey north. She and her father gave him aid and a place to stay while he recovered. Both were amazed at how quickly his wounds healed. What they thought would take months to knit together and fully heal took only days."

Arrick leaned forward and asked, "Only days?"

Caden had a sardonic smile when he replied to Arrick, "Yes, like your Bekka." I didn't know if I was more impressed by his *'your Bekka'* comment or by the craziness of the tale. No mortal could heal at that speed. But if this mysterious traveler had been a deity, then what or who attacked him to give him those kinds of injuries? It couldn't have been human raiders. Rather than ask the million questions swirling in my mind, I refocused on the story, hoping that maybe it would hold the answers.

"At first, she didn't have any idea what the man looked like since long gashes, dirt, and blood had covered his face entirely. But, as he healed, she could see what was beneath all that injury and grime. According to her, he was the most beautiful man she'd ever laid eyes on. His skin was tawny and bronze, and his hair, once cleaned, had dark waves of chestnut color. His eyes were the most vibrant green she'd ever seen. She said they reminded her of the fresh green of springtime foliage."

Like Arrick's, I thought, while that ominous feeling increased ten-fold.

"When he was fully healed, he repaid her family by helping around their small farm. In the evenings, he'd go riding with her, and they'd watch the sun dip over the horizon. They'd be gone for hours, talking about everything that mattered to them most and about nothing at all. Eventually, they fell in love and began a passionate affair in secret, worried over her father's disapproval. One night, after they'd made love, she began tracing the lines of a tattoo on his wrist. She asked him what it meant, and he said, 'It's my ticket home, my love. One day, I will take you with me, and then we can be a family.' When he rested his hand on her belly, she felt it, the baby growing within her. She hadn't known before then, but she was overjoyed at the prospect of a family with this man who had come to mean so much to her."

I snuck a look at Arrick and then down at the wrist that had held his tattoo, his all-access pass to what lay in the immortal realm. He reached for me and tightened his grip around my hand in acknowledgment that he saw the parallel.

Deklan continued, "Soon after, the man asked for her hand in marriage and, seeing his daughter's happiness, her father agreed. They were married in a small, private ceremony on her family's farm. Afterward, they decided to go back to the man's home. He said that he came from a prominent family and promised that she would be safe and taken care of there. On a brisk fall morning, they departed together, her belly just beginning to swell with her pregnancy. Her father's eyes shimmered with tears as they hugged and promised they'd visit soon. They also swore that they'd send word once they had safely arrived at the man's home."

Caden held up a hand to pause his brother's story. "Now, this is where it gets bizarre. Let's just say, no one ever saw our ten times great granny ever again."

My brows rose, and I shifted my gaze back to Deklan, but before he could continue, Arrick spoke, "If no one ever saw her again, then how is there more to the story? Wouldn't it just end here?"

"All in good time," Caden replied as he gestured for Deklan to continue his tale.

"According to the family legend, our many times great grandmother left this plane of existence and went somewhere... else. It claims that she met men and women of great power, immortals who lived just outside our range of perception and who had dominion over all life."

"So," Caden said, "If we put this story into the context of what you told us, they must have been gods, and they must have gone to your realm, right?"

Arrick pulled his hand from mine and crossed one over his chest while the other stroked his chin in thought. "It's possible."

Deklan continued, his blue eyes growing intense in the early morning light, "Her new husband had promised that she would be safe in his home. But when they got there, his family refused to accept her. They claimed that she was unworthy; her lack of immortality and uselessness as an ally made her a disappointing choice for their favored son. Because he was, as she discovered, *special.* Even amongst the glory of the beings she now called family, he was unique."

He took a small pause and looked at his brother, who nodded in silent agreement to an unspoken question. Seeing the ease of their connection made me miss my own sister. My heart squeezed as I realized that she would already be gone by the time I got back to Valeria. I refused to think about the fact that, with my agreement to help Arrick, homecoming may not even be in the cards for me. Everything we planned to do was risky and dangerous as hell, so I pushed this unwelcome thought far back into depths of my mind and shifted all my attention to the story again.

This time, it was Caden who continued with the tale. "According to the legend, the man's family was cruel and had no love for the people they held dominion over. The world was a hard place, and suffering was in abundance. The man sought to change that, and through an alliance with the mortals, he thought he could get his family to realize there was a better way. So, believing they would eventually come around, given the chance to see what he saw, he and his wife stayed. She tried to do whatever she could to please her new family, but each day she felt more and more defeated as she came to the realization that it wasn't who she was that mattered to them. It was *what* she was at the very core of her being that they could never accept."

That broke my heart. I was lucky that my family hadn't rejected me at the prospect of me never getting my powers… but then again, hadn't they'd always known what I would become? That I would get these terrifyingly immense powers? That I'd be my grandpa's heir? But still, if they hadn't known, I knew they'd never have rejected me. *Right?*

"She fell into a deep depression until, eventually, their son was born. He shared his mother's silvery hair and blue eyes and shimmered with power and light from his father. He was half-mortal and half-immortal, a perfect blend of the two species. They loved him beyond measure, and, hoping that the grandchild would change his family's mind, they presented him to his grandparents, uncles, and aunts."

Deklan snorted at that and said, "Rather than the joy and excitement he thought they'd feel at greeting a new child into the world, they became incensed. According to them, he was an abomination, a half breed, and shouldn't be allowed to exist. They'd never expected the baby to have power or to be more than a mortal, but seeing the possibility of a merged race, that's what made them most fearful. So, like any good psycho, to keep this new race from growing, the man's father, their leader, ordered our great grandmother and her baby executed. But before that could happen, the man encircled them into his arms, and they disappeared. Fighting for the lives of his wife and son, he flew into action. He used his great power to hide them from prying eyes and arranged safe passage back to the mortal world for them via a special portal that he created, known only to him."

"Are you guys seeing the coincidences here? With your portals and powers?" Caden said, raising his eyebrows.

Without waiting for an answer, Deklan continued, "He grew concerned that once they were back with her people, his family would trace the boy's magic and find them. So, he used the unimaginable power he possessed to change the game because, in a last-ditch effort to keep those he loved safe, he bound the world of Moldize so that his family could not use their powers while in his wife's realm. The spell would cloak his son and keep his family safe. With everything arranged, they stole into the night, risking life and limb to make it back through the passage he'd arranged to the other side."

"But, before they could cross through, the man's father intercepted them," added Caden. "According to the legend, he ripped our Grandmother's soul from her body and snapped her essence out of existence in an instant, destroying her completely. She died before her husband even knew what happened. When he turned to face his father and saw that his wife was gone, the anger that exploded inside him was so hot, so nuclear that he flew into a murderous rage. He rampaged through his family, killing anyone who condoned the death of his wife. He left only his beloved sister, her husband, and their daughter. Then, with his wife's life avenged and his heart shattered, he took his son and went back to his mortal father-in-law."

"But how do you know that story? Did the god tell his in-law about everything?" asked Kaleb with a frown upon his face. He had stayed silent for so long, not even moving a muscle, that I'd thought he was in a sort of trance.

"He delivered the boy, a diary our Grandmother had kept since the day she met him, and a letter explaining who he was and what had happened. Then, without another word, he disappeared. No one ever saw him again. But his son grew up strong, happy, and surrounded by the love of his mortal family. He is the start of our family line, and his name was Adryan."

I cleared my throat and raised a tentative hand, "What was the god's name, the one who fell in love with your Grandma?"

"His name was Afryel, and our Grandmother's name was Arabella."

I swallowed hard at the confirmation of my suspicions. This story filled in so many of the missing pieces of Moldizean history that Arrick and I had discussed before we came here. Even as I listened, I hadn't been certain that Afryel wasn't the father who'd ordered the execution. At least until their powers became clearly defined near the end of the tale.

I turned my head to look at Arrick, who also seemed to be struggling to process everything he'd heard. When he recovered, he hissed, "That's impossible."

Deklan held up a hand to argue, "Improbable, but not impossible. We have proof." He reached into his shirt and pulled something from over his heart. It was a small, tattered package wrapped in plastic. He took a moment to remove the wrappings and then presented us with an old, leather-bound book. The pages were bent upwards and yellowed slightly with age. "I carry this with me everywhere. It's not the original, but it's been copied and passed down many times over the centuries. Our ancestors even made a replica of the original seal from Afryel's letter to his son. This version is about a hundred years old."

He then opened the book and turned it toward us. The text read, *'This is the diary of Arabella Brannon.'* Folded and nestled between the first and second pages of the book was a letter, the envelope sealed with a red wax symbol. It was titled, *'To my son, Adryan Brannon.'*

Brannon was the house name of the ruling family in Moldize. All the royal families in the multiverse had a house name. My family's house name was Daevos, though it served a limited purpose. We only used it when recording scholarly histories or during multiversal visits with ruling deities from other realms. It helped us easily distinguish interests during negotiations between realms and record any resulting treaties accurately. But why would a human woman have adopted it as a surname? What the—

Arrick took the letter and examined the seal, "This is the official royal seal of Moldize. There's no way anyone in the mortal realm could know about it unless they had a connection to my family." He looked up at me in amazement, and then he began to read. I peered around his arm as he did.

In the letter, Afryel explained everything to his son about who he was and why he had to leave. Killing celestial beings held a high price, and that price was trans-universal. If he had stayed, he would have had to pay the piper eventually. I imagined that exile was preferable to extinction via the surface of the sun, which was the penalty for murder in the godly realms.

He apologized to his son for not being able to stay with him but promised that he would grow up in a better world than his mother had known. Afryel had left his beloved sister, her husband, and their child behind to ensure that. According to him, she shared his desire to make Moldize a better place, and he hoped that she would continue the spirit of his work.

"I don't understand. My grandmother hated Afryel; she blamed him for all the bad things that happened in Moldize. She told us he was a monster. Now, I'm supposed to believe that they were beloved siblings?" He shook his head as though to clear it and looked at me. "This doesn't make any sense."

"Think about it," I whispered, resting a hand on his forearm to soothe him. "Afryel killed everyone in her family and then left her alone with her husband and child to clean up the mess. Imagine how terrible that must have been for them. It probably traumatized her, and that's why she never spoke of what really happened."

"But, based on what this is telling me, it doesn't even sound like Afryel ruled over this world. Then there's the part about his father and the way he killed Arabella." He paused and shook his head in denial. I could tell that he'd made the same connection I had. "Afryel's father had to be a death god. It's the only explanation for why Afryel didn't command the universe he created. That's the only way he could have exerted power over a creation deity."

Death deities were the only power of an equal match to a creation deity. And since Afryel's father was able to take Arabella's soul, we both knew that it was the only explanation. So, if all that held true, then it made sense that Afryel had been a pawn to further his father's darker intentions. Until the day he snapped and killed them all for it.

"This is the gap in history that you've been looking to fill," I exclaimed, eyes wide with astonishment. I looked down at the diary and letter once more as I made more connections in my mind. The injuries Afryel had had when he'd found Arabella, they'd probably been inflicted by his father. Who else could have hurt a creator like that?

Add to that, the reason our powers had to be stripped to come here made sense now. He had put those wards in place to protect his precious son, a demigod. And it had worked. *Thousands of years later, and here we sat with the descendants of his line.* There was no way that it was a coincidence that I had run into them during the battle. What were the odds that my allegiance with them was an accident? Probably slim to none. Destiny was a powerful force, and I was starting to believe that they were meant to be a part of mine. Just like I was starting to think Arrick was, too.

But there was one piece of this puzzle that seemed out of place. Voicing it aloud, I asked, "Why would Afryel have set up the wards to require the death of any human who witnessed the divine? His son was half-mortal. It doesn't make any sense."

Arrick paused and thought about this for a moment. "The story doesn't say that he built all the wards, only that he bound the planet against the explicit use of our powers here. There could have been other rules in place already. Maybe ones he was forced to put in place by his father. Death gods are Nefarals, and just one of the many types of gods that operate under the Nefaric Pillar of Power in the immortal realm, all of which are notorious for cruelty."

Niko's brows furrowed, "Pillars of Power? Nefarals? What does that even mean?"

"There are six Pillars of Power in the immortal realms. Different powers serve different pillars, and they care for different parts of their realms. The Nefaric Pillar houses the gods with the less savory gifts, like war, famine, and death," Arrick explained absently.

Coming out of another trance-like state this conversation had put him in, Kaleb cleared his throat nervously, "I'm sorry, but did you say death god?" he asked.

We fixed our attention on him. He had his knees drawn upward, his elbows resting on them as he ran fingers through his hair. "There really are such things as death gods?"

"Yes, I'm the god of death in Moldize now," Arrick replied. "I must have inherited the gift from my great grandfather." Just like that, everyone stilled and eyed him cautiously. We didn't mention what Arrick was the god of before. It was not an intentional omission. It just hadn't been relevant to our story at the time. But now, it was.

"Not all Nefarals, or death gods, are bad. Not all of them give into the darker side of their power," I said, reading the room and trying to comfort them. "Arrick's nothing like the father in that story. Without death deities, the souls of the departed are forced to wander the world alone for all eternity. Arrick makes sure that doesn't happen." This seemed to settle the men around me, though they still eyed us cautiously.

Ignoring us all, Arrick asked, "This is true, isn't it?" The words were aimed at no one in particular. Then he rose to his feet and began to pace. I watched carefully as he moved. His body was lithe, and I could see the sinew of his forearms flexing as he considered everything he'd learned. "It has to be. It's the only thing that makes sense. How else could they know the name Afryel? And Brannon—the name of the Moldizean royal family's house? There's the seal too. Like I said, a mortal could never have gotten their hands on that. But what about you two?" He finished, stopping to stare at the brothers. "Your last name isn't Brannon. It's Helkum."

Caden shrugged, "The relation is on our mother's side. We took our father's name. It's not like your last name is Brannon either."

Ares shook his head. "That's because it's not a last name. It's strictly for identifying royal houses in the godly realm. Then, as you know, I took Mariah and Jarrod's last name here."

Caden nodded thoughtfully, and Arrick resumed pacing. His mind seemed to be firing in rapid succession, trying to piece together everything he already knew with what this story had revealed. Unfortunately, there was no way we could know what really happened with one hundred percent certainty, not unless Afryel came back to tell us in person. But most likely, he was no longer in exile. Most likely, he had already ascended, like his sister and her husband.

I stepped into Arrick's path to stop him and rested my hands on the diary, which he still held. I carefully closed it, pulled it from his grasp, and handed it back to Deklan, who stepped forward, taking the book from me and holding it reverently.

"Let's focus on the issue at hand," I suggested, directing everyone's attention away from the story Deklan and Caden had just told us and all its mind-boggling implications. "How does this help us get back to our realm? If Afryel really did arrange for safe passage for his family, then he probably used his tattoo. I hate to be the bearer of bad news, but that won't work. Arrick's was removed when we were marooned."

"No, that's actually not accurate," Caden said, striding toward Deklan and holding out a hand for the book. He passed it to him, and Caden flipped the book to the back and then thumbed through some blank pages. He found what he was looking for and turned the book back around, pointing down at a passage. "Read this. It's Arabella's last passage."

We did as we were told. Niko and Kaleb also squeezed in to get a look. When we finished, Kaleb said, "Holy shit." At that moment, I couldn't agree more.

CHAPTER 13

The Fallen

There, in black and white—well, more faded brown and a tinged yellow—was a description of Afryel's secret portal. According to Arabella, buried deep in the bowels of her journal, it had been forged for a single purpose, and only someone with mortal blood, specifically her family's blood, could open it. She described in rough detail where it was located within the mortal realm.

Her description was nowhere near thorough enough to get us where we needed to go, but after flipping a couple of pages, we found that she had very helpfully provided us with a map. Sure, none of those places existed anymore, and it was entirely in reference to her old family home, and who knew where the hell that was. But there were just enough landmarks noted that Arrick recognized. So, we worked backward from there, thank the ascended.

Now for the kicker. We may have found a passage that we could traipse through pretty as you please, with the help of Caden and Deklan's genetic heritage, of course, but it was in a hazardous part of Moldize. According to my new friends, that entire hemisphere was rife with radiation and had been declared inhabitable years ago.

"The hits just keep coming," I groaned, letting my frustration show. "We have a way back, but now we have to figure out how to get at least us four—" I pointed to Arrick, Deklan, Caden, and myself for emphasis— "1,200 miles north without taking so much time that the sun kills everyone before we get there. Then, even if we make it there in time, we have to find a way for two mortals to stay alive in radioactive conditions. That's just perfect. Maybe Deklan should just shoot me, and we'll see what happens! Maybe I *won't* accidentally deposit us onto the surface of the sun or accidentally maim anyone in the process! Let's just find out! Have at it, blondie!" I yelled to Deklan. Then I kicked a rock… *hard,* stubbing my big toe as a result, and then proceeded to hobble in tight, angry circles. That was why I didn't like getting angry; I always ended up feeling like an idiot afterward.

Arrick stared at me for a moment and then chose to ignore my outburst completely, for which I was grateful. Instead, he asked, "Has anyone in your family ever found or used this portal before?"

Caden shrugged. "The more recent generations thought it was just old family lore. They didn't put much stock in it."

"But people have tried. At least a few of them," Deklan argued, engaged fully in the possibility of helping us. "No one ever seemed to find it, though."

Arrick fell silent as he thought, and a minute later, said, "Maybe they didn't know what they were looking for? Or maybe they never found the right place?" We all paused to think about it, unsure of how to explain the lack of successful journeys.

"It also doesn't describe how to use it," I added. I turned to look at the brothers. "It implies that your blood is needed to access it, but I can't tell if it's just your heritage she means or if it's your actual blood that's required." I frowned as I looked down at the text.

"Either way," Caden ventured, "It's not like Afryel would have required that his grandchildren bleed themselves dry to obtain entry, and a drop of blood won't kill us." I nodded, starting to feel like this might work if we could make it there.

Niko interrupted our discussion, "I don't mean to state the obvious, but what's to say that he left the portal open?" He frowned, looking down at the hand-drawn map. "How do we know that Afryel didn't destroy it or seal it shut once he was done hiding his son here? He disappeared into exile, so why would he keep it open?" Niko looked at us, calm once again, and I saw that slice of cunning laced with brutality. But unlike earlier, it was tempered with compassion once more.

We all stared at him, considering his question. He was right, of course. We had no way of knowing whether the portal would be open and usable or sealed shut. There was no mention of it in Afryel's letter to his son, and Arabella only drew a map before she was killed. It made sense that it would stay open while she was alive and Afryel was in the godly realm. That way, she and her son could use it to visit her husband secretly. But with her dead and Afryel fled into exile, what would be the point in keeping it active?

"Well, fuck me. Why does everything keep going wrong?" I shouted, not asking anyone in particular. I thought about kicking a rock again but then decided against it, remembering my stubbed toe from moments before. And the whole idiot thing.

Arrick laid a hand on my shoulder, "If there's a portal that only requires Caden and Deklan's blood and not the tattoo, then I think we have to at least try to find it. Even if it ends up being a dead end."

"We have less than two days left. We might be able to stretch that to three or four days if it comes down to it. But any longer than that and the odds that we can stay a step ahead of my grandpa are slim to none. We can't afford to make the wrong call right now and go 1,200 miles away. How would we even travel that distance in such a short time?" I asked, starting to realize that we might really be trapped and that this might not be the miracle we needed. Because if my Grandpa got here before I fixed this sun, then there was zero chance of us succeeding.

"What does Bekka's grandpa have to do with this?" Kaleb asked, staring from Arrick to me. "And why do we need to stay a step ahead of him?"

Arrick rubbed a hand over the back of his neck in discomfort, "Bekka's grandfather, Gabryel, is... Well let's just say that he won't be happy that I kidnapped her. He'll take her back to Valeria, her home, before she can do anything to help us." He left out the possibility of imminent destruction from my grandpa's wrath if I wasn't present when he arrived. I thought it was a wise decision. Better not to scare them any more than necessary. One crisis at a time was probably the right way to go.

"That bullet is sounding better and better," Niko murmured, shaking his head.

"No," Arrick and I said in unison, voices tight with anger at the suggestion.

He shrugged his shoulders, "Just saying. We need to keep all of our options on the table."

Arrick shot him a stern, warning glare before he said, "I have a way to get us to the portal quickly. It will leave us plenty of time to come up with another plan if this fails."

"How?" I asked, dumbfounded. The speed travel tunnels used his tattoo as a requirement for entry. What else was there?

We waited for Arrick to explain. When he spoke, it was to me, "Do you remember the instructions I gave you when I told you to flee Itoriah?" I eyed him beneath my lashes as I thought back to the battle. Rather than speak and dredge up that argument again, I simply nodded my response. He looked to the rest of the group and continued. "There's a cave five miles east of here. It's spelled so that only those with immortal blood can enter. There's a speed travel domicile inside. It will take us within ten miles of where we need to go." He tapped the point on the map that Arabella had marked as the portal entrance.

"That's what you meant by a quick escape," I muttered, shaking my head at the memory. "You don't need the tattoo to access the domicile?"

"No. These are part of the upgraded system Afryel put into place. They are only for travel within this realm, and they don't cross through to the immortal realm as the tunnels do, so there was no need to link it to the tattoo."

"Sorry to interrupt, but what about us?" Deklan asked, jerking a thumb between himself and Caden. "You need our blood to open the portal, and as Bekka alluded to before, we won't make it ten miles with radiation levels that high."

Arrick nodded. "The tunnel has supplies. Jackets and glasses for physical protection, and then there's a tonic that our healers make, too. The tonic should block the radiation long enough to get us to the portal."

Caden furrowed his brow. "You're sure it'll work?"

Arrick gnawed on his lip, a flash of concern shadowing his expression, "As sure as I can be. It's made for deities, but it should work for you too since you're demigods. We'll just have to get to the portal quickly once we leave the protection of the domicile. As long as you make it through the portal and into the immortal realm, we should be able to heal you of any ill effects."

Caden ran his tongue across his lips to wet them, and Deklan dragged a hand through his hair. Neither of them seemed too thrilled by this prospect. I couldn't blame them. His response didn't inspire much in the way of confidence. They exchanged a meaningful look, and their resolve seemed to solidify.

Deklan turned to Arrick and me, "OK, we'll do it."

I felt tingles of excitement flow through my body as I realized that this was going to happen. We could make this work.

"You can't leave yet," Niko informed us, his voice calm and reasonable. "We have business to attend to here." My hope deflated like a busted balloon as I gaped at him.

"What are you talking about?" I asked, unable to keep the surprise out of my voice. "What could possibly be more important than saving Moldize?" Wasn't he the one with a gun to his head less than an hour ago begging us to kill him? Now we *had business to attend to?'* Talk about emotional whiplash.

"Like you said, you have time," Niko argued, using our own words against us. "I propose that we use that time to our advantage. And I'll need Arrick for what comes next."

There was a gleam in his eyes that made my stomach knot with anxiety for reasons I could not quite pinpoint. Something about him seemed off.

Before speaking, Arrick laid his hand on my shoulder, and I turned to him. "Niko's right. There's a lot we need to see before we go. We need to get a count of the fallen and give them a proper funeral. Then we need to make sure that all the Itorian refugees made it to the EML." I raised my brows in question. "We have an emergency meeting location, should things ever take a turn for the worst," Arrick explained. "Everyone in the village knows it and how to get there safely. We need to make sure that no one ended up in the Puhari camp before we find the portal and go home."

"But I… took care of the Puhari," I argued, unable to use the word *killed*. It seemed too loaded right now, and I was not ready to face what that meant for me. After an uncomfortable pause where we all reflected on exactly how I had done that, I continued. "Who else would they be in danger from exactly?"

Kaleb spoke up first, "Lorus wasn't at the attack last night, which means that there are still more Puhari out there. We need to make sure our people made it out in one piece." And here I thought I had put an end to that miserable tribe. I ground my teeth at the thought of more of them nearby, the possibility of them intercepting the women and children we had worked so hard to evacuate. Or Mariah and Jarrod, for that matter.

Arrick nodded. Then he said to me, "If we left now, the time differential in the immortal realm will keep us away too long. The situation here is too dangerous to risk it."

"OK." His logic was sound. The amount of time we spent in the godly realm could lead to drastic changes here, and I understood his desire to see his people safe before he left. My only concern was that we were putting all our eggs into this portal's basket. If we used up all our time putting things right here rather than looking for another loophole, what would happen if the portal were a bust? I shuddered to think of the ramifications.

Niko spoke up then, giving orders, "Then we go back to the camp and see to the fallen first. Once we have a count there, we head to the EML." He turned on his heel and walked back toward the destruction that was Itoriah. Kaleb, Caden, and Deklan followed close on his heels. Despite his break from sanity earlier and subsequent about-face, he was still their leader, and apparently, old habits died hard.

As I started to follow behind them, Arrick reached for my hand. He tugged, keeping me back with him. When they were out of earshot, he said, "There is one other matter I'd like to discuss." He wound his fingers through mine and pulled me closer. He slid his hands up and down my arms, and goosebumps rippled up my flesh as he spoke. "It's possible that not everyone made it to the EML. If that's the case, then it could get dangerous while we search for them. We can't risk you getting injured again and—"

"And killing everyone with my monumentally fucked up powers," I finished for him.

He pressed his lips together and nodded, "For lack of a better way to put it, yes."

"So, what do you propose we do about it?" I asked, chewing on my lip and staring at the ground. He made a valid point. If we were in a battle again and someone shot me, what would happen? Would power explode from the core of being, like it did last night? Would I be so lucky as to have any control over it? I couldn't say one way or another.

"Would you consider allowing me to take you to the cavern? You can wait for me there, and no one will know your whereabouts. You'd be safe."

"And so would everyone else," I muttered, feeling miserable and understanding the truth behind his request. He thought I was a liability. I ran a hand down my braid and stepped away from him. Being this close to him made it harder for me to think clearly. His touch made my heart hammer in my ears, and my awareness of his body at a time like this felt inappropriate. When I gathered my wits again, I turned to him. "There has to be another way," I argued. "You can't leave me in the cavern, please. I need to help. If there's a fight, I can run. When the men attacked us the first time, I didn't go all big-bad creation deity on them. Surely, that means that it won't happen every time. Now that I know it's a concern, I can keep it under wraps. Besides, the last time I tried to access my gifts, it damn near gave me an aneurism. I probably wouldn't be able to again, even if I wanted to."

Arrick looked down at me, his eyes full of uncertainty. "It's not just that. It's also the promise I made you."

I gave him a confused look. "I'm drawing a blank here."

"The first day we met, I promised to keep you safe. I've done a piss-poor job of it since the moment we arrived here. First, you were attacked and nearly raped, and then you were shot. I don't want to see you hurt again. Haven't you been through enough for our sake?"

I shook my head at him, but the gesture held no anger, "My safety is my own responsibility. Please, don't send me into exile in that cavern. I want to stay and help your people."

Arrick ran a hand over the back of his neck in thought. He let out a long breath and held up two fingers. "Two conditions. The first is that if we get attacked again, you run as far away as you can. When the fighting ends, I'll find you." He didn't need to explain why. I knew as well as he did that we couldn't afford another divine exposure incident. We already had four people we might have to kill. The last thing I wanted to do was add to the death toll. He rested a palm against my cheek, eyes filled with warmth. "The second is that you learn to defend yourself. You learn to fire a weapon and to use a blade. I don't care if it's a knife or sword, but you learn the basics." He paused for effect, allowing the condition to sink in. Then he asked, "Do you agree to the terms?"

I thought about his words, his directive to run as far away as I could. Then I thought of the millions of ways that plan could go wrong and wondered why he didn't insist that I go to the cavern. Why was he letting me stay? Rather than push my luck by questioning him, I merely nodded my head in response.

"I'm going to need to hear you say it," Arrick insisted, his lips set into a firm line. "Just to be sure we're in agreement."

I resisted the urge to roll my eyes, "I agree," I conceded, voice monotone.

Without warning, he leaned forward and brushed his lips across my cheekbone. The gesture sent an involuntary flood of warmth straight to my lady bits. Then, he whispered in my ear, "You know, I'm starting to think that you Valerians aren't all that bad either."

Embarrassed, I smacked his shoulder, "I was drunk! I didn't know what I was saying."

He winked at me and gave me a half-smile, "We should get down there to help. They'll skin me alive if I shirk my responsibility." We moved briskly, hurrying to get back to the village and to see what needed to be done. The sun was high in the sky and beating heat down on us in unrelenting waves.

When we caught up to Niko and the others, they were already searching through the rubble for the fallen. With the sun now fully in place, what I saw in the light of day horrified me. The once-proud village was now a charred carcass of cinders and ash. Piles of canvas still smoldered, and bodies of both Puhari and Itorians littered the ground. I had to swallow hard and take shallow breaths to keep my gorge from rising. I couldn't believe how much destruction had been wrought in such a short period of time. Had it only been hours ago that we had enjoyed blackberry wine and a game of hand slap with Mariah and Jarrod? My heart squeezed as I realized for the first time that they might not have made it through the battle.

I looked up at Arrick, moisture swimming in my eyes. I blinked hard and pushed against any softer emotions I may have felt. Closer to the surface than I might have expected was anger. I felt pure outrage for what happened here.

Arrick whispered so that only I could hear, "Now that you've seen this in the light of day, do you believe me when I say that those Puhari men were rabid? And that they deserved to be put down?"

I nodded once, and he squeezed my hand for reassurance before venturing deeper into the belly of the village. We spent the next few hours working side-by-side. We moved our fallen men to the edge of camp and prepared them for their last rights away from the ruins. We checked for signs of life, hoping we would find someone still breathing. But there was no one. Sweat ran in rivulets down my back and between my breasts, but I didn't dare complain. Instead, we worked in silence, the grim duty before us too horrible for words.

When we had finished, we counted 48 dead and 20 missing. Arrick and I were relieved that Jarrod and Mariah were not among those 48 people. We hoped that, wherever they were, they were safe.

Niko walked down the line of warriors we had arranged and kissed each of their foreheads. Arrick did the same. Then Kaleb, Deklan, and Caden. I felt tears well into my eyes as I followed suit. I may not have known these people, but they had died an unnecessary death. One caused by evil men. Men who, thanks to me, were mostly dead.

And with the evidence of what the bastards did laid out before me, I felt a little of my guilt and regret ease. Suddenly, Kaleb began to sing, his voice soft and heartbreakingly sad. I tried to understand its language but found that there were no words, only a melody. A lament. When he finished, my companions all thumped their fists to their chest over and over. Until, on the tenth hit, they stopped and raised their fists to the sky. Then Niko grabbed a torch from the ground, moved back to the city, and used one of the still smoldering tent enclosures to light it. He strode to the assembly of fallen warriors and lit the bundle of pitch sticks laid under their folded hands. The fires caught quickly and rose high into the daytime sky. It wasn't much, but it was the least we could do to honor their sacrifice.

I reached out and grasped Arrick's hand, squeezing it tightly as I turned my head to peer up at him. He looked down at me, and I could tell that he was surprised by the lifeline I offered. After a brief hesitation, his hand tightened around mine in acceptance as his eyes filled with sorrow. I stepped closer and noted that he smelled of sweat and blood, and I imagined that I did, too. It hardly mattered.

We held fast as the flames danced before us, each seeking the strength of the other as we watched the fire consume what was left of the departed fighters. I couldn't imagine the pain he must be feeling. He had been with this tribe for fifteen years, lived as one of them. He probably knew every one of the men we laid to rest. I didn't know any of them personally, but my heart still weighed heavy with so much loss of human life.

The village he loved so much was destroyed, the 20 potential survivors scattered, and I understood why he wanted to get it all back. He needed to make sure that everyone was accounted for and safe before we journeyed back to the immortal realm. Because once we were home, one day was equivalent to ten here. A million terrible things could happen in ten days in this place. After all, look at what happened in just one so far.

Everything had gone so incredibly wrong since we'd been here. Life had a funny way of reminding you how little control you really had over it, even as a deity. I needed to remember that even in the face of what seemed like insurmountable odds, I was destined to do this. Arrick, Caden, and Deklan were fated to be here. Though no one mentioned that, I could feel it deep in my bones as part of the prophecy. We were all meant to be here, and we were meant to face this together.

When the funeral was over, we rummaged through the rubble of town and grabbed what supplies remained. Three tents, one backpack, some scattered food, and a few jugs of water. All the clothes and blankets were burned beyond usability, so we would travel with the clothes on our backs and sleep two to a tent for warmth at night.

Niko and Kaleb led us deeper into the woods, presumably in the direction of the EML. The sun hung heavy in the sky now. Nightfall would approach soon, and we needed to use this last shred of daylight to cover precious ground. As we set off, we traveled in silence, following the minute tracks left by Donny and his escapees. It turned out that these led to the EML.

I could only hope that we would find them in one piece and safe. As I contemplated the alternative, anger swelled up inside of me. I felt my power build, slowly like the flow of lava from an underwater volcano. I reached inside my being and tugged. A blue light shone through my fingertips an instant before pain rocketed through my skull. I slumped to a knee, breathing heavily, hand clasped to my forehead.

Arrick was instantly next to me, Kaleb at my other side. "What happened?" Arrick asked, voice filled with concern.

"Nothing," I lied, forcing my body upright once more. "I just tripped." I wasn't sure why I lied. If I had to guess, it was probably because I wasn't ready to tell him just how shut off my powers were now. Even if Deklan shot me, I wasn't sure that it would make a difference. Because I knew deep down, if I fought too hard against that invisible fire poker and tried to use my powers again, it might just kill me.

CHAPTER 14

Complications

Not long after we departed from Itoriah for the last time, we were forced to make camp. Exhaustion and weariness weighed on us, and we each found that we were incapable of pressing forward. Due to the low supply of surface water, we could only wash with a damp cloth, torn from the least dirty part of our clothes. The result left a lot to be desired, but at least I was able to remove the worst of the grime. Once finished, we all settled into our respective tents, each of us too exhausted and emotionally drained to eat.

Arrick and I slipped into our shared tent, with no blankets or coverings for warmth. As the sun set, the temperature dropped, and I began to shiver. I curled into a tight ball and chafed my arms to keep warm before Arrick cleared his throat behind me. He rested a hand on my shoulder and scooted closer. I turned my head to face him and saw the question in his eyes despite the darkness. I nodded, and he closed the gap, pressing the warmth of his body against me. A few minutes later and the shivering had stopped. I sighed with relief and let sleep take me under.

When we woke to the rising sun, I realized I'd turned in the night. My face was now snuggled on his shoulder, one leg sprawled over his lap, and an arm stretched across his chest. I did a mental head slap at my apparent brazenness. I couldn't believe that I'd treated him like my own personal heated blanket. I prayed to the ascended that he wouldn't wake as I extricated my limbs from his and put some distance between us. Though I knew that we'd had to sleep close to share body warmth during the chilly night, I still felt just a little embarrassed now that the sun had risen. But the worst part was that, if I were being honest with myself, I'd kind of enjoyed it.

Rather than dwell on all those uncomfortable feelings, I watched him for a few minutes, his face placid with sleep. Then unable to stop myself, I let out a jaw-cracking yawn.

Stirring in response, Arrick murmured, "Good morning." I found the refrain odd considering our current predicament. Was it really?

"That remains to be seen," I retorted, "We need to find those Itorians and quick. We don't have a lot of time to find another loophole if this portal doesn't work. One more day left in our deal. We need to focus."

Arrick groaned. "That's a lot for six AM," he observed. "How long have you been awake?"

"A while," I answered vaguely.

"I can tell," he grumbled. "You sound perky."

"Well, no one's ever accused me of that before." I rolled onto my side to face him fully. His eyes were hooded with sleep, and his mouth smiled just the tiniest bit. "How much longer until we reach the EML?"

"A few hours, tops. We would have pushed through last night, but the battle took a lot out of everyone."

I nodded, "Makes sense. Do you think we'll run into any trouble?"

Arrick shrugged, "This is Moldize. There's always the potential for trouble."

"You're not exactly filling me with confidence."

He chuckled, the sound low in his throat. Then he rolled over and sat up to survey me, "Would you rather I lie?"

"No, I'm just saying is all," I replied, rising to a sitting position as well. "It would be nice if *something* went our way."

His smile turned distant, "I couldn't agree more. Let's hope it does." With that, he stood up, pulled on his jacket, and left the tent to see about breakfast. Alone now, I realized that my emotions had grown complicated where he was concerned. I had always found him sexy as all hell, and who could blame me? The man defined the word hot. But the trouble was that there was something more to it now.

He had the capacity for such goodness and compassion. He was selfless and sacrificed willingly for the people he loved, mortal or immortal. He did it effortlessly and with no need for acknowledgment. So, I didn't just think he was smokin' hot anymore.

I actually *liked* him.

How had I let myself get so close to him so quickly? I wondered, groaning aloud. What was I thinking? What was

I doing? I resisted the urge to bang my head against the ground to dispel the wildly inappropriate thoughts I had about his body. But the truth was that I wanted him.

With a disgusted clearing of my throat, I pushed those thoughts from my mind and got dressed as well. Unfortunately, they were the same clothes from the battle, and they were filthy beyond repair. But there was little choice in the matter. It was either wear them or go naked. I gave serious consideration to the latter, but then dismissed it out of hand. When I was finished braiding my hair, I went out to join the rest of the group.

We ate breakfast, a mixture of dried meat and grainy bread that might have had a little dirt mixed in for good measure. It was all leftovers from the ruins in Itoriah, so we were running low on supplies, and for some strange reason, no one seemed too worried by this prospect. I wondered why.

When we were finished, I packed the food away, calculating that we had enough left for one small meal each. I had no idea what we were going to do once it was gone. Animals were scarce, and we had no means to grow food of our own. Even if we could, it would take weeks before it bore anything resembling edible returns.

Once everything was packed and broken down, we started walking. Niko instructed everyone to break into "formation." The men split into a four-point positioning, where we were spaced just far enough not to see each other but close enough to be within shouting distance should any problems arise. Niko and Kaleb took the head of the group, Deklan and Caden on either side, and Arrick and I brought up the rear.

Ten minutes passed, giving me time to think through everything that happened on the last day. There was one question that bothered me. Turning to Arrick, I asked,

"Why do you think I was able to access my powers? From what you told me, none of the other deities can."

Arrick paused, thinking, then he replied, "I've been asking myself the same question. The truth is, I don't know."

"I'm willing to accept theories if you have them."

He pressed his lips together and shrugged helplessly, "You want me to guess?"

I gave him a small grin, "That would be nice, yes."

He laughed a little and shook his head in bemusement. "OK then, my best guess is that it's because you're a creation deity. The wards were created by Afryel, who shares your gift. Granted, your magic is not precisely the same, but they are kin to each other. Maybe that makes the wards less effective against you."

"That's a pretty good guess," I replied, impressed. "You must have given it a lot of thought."

Ignoring me, he continued, "What's strange is that now the wards seem to recognize their mistake and have adjusted to fix it."

I shrugged my shoulders, "I don't think so."

"What do you mean?" He asked.

"I think it's more like because I'm *trying* to access my powers, they are pushing back. Before, I didn't try to access anything. It just happened. But now that it's a conscious effort, the reaction from the wards is different."

He stopped walking and looked at me, considering, "That's possible. But I've tried to access my power here too, and it's completely cut off. I don't get punished with pain. There's just nothing there."

"Maybe you're right, and the wards are less effective on me. The pain could just be another layer of protection that no one knew about until now. Maybe it's just that punishment was never necessary before."

Resuming our pace again, he nodded in thought. "That's possible. But again, these are just theories. There's no way for us to really know." He was right, of course. The deity who'd made the wards was long gone, and we didn't exactly have access to their records.

After a few moments of silence passed, Arrick slipped his pistol out of the holster, still strapped around his shoulders. "Here," he said, handing it to me without breaking his stride. "It's time we got started on that second condition." Tentatively, I took it, surprised by its heaviness, and pointed the barrel down. "That's a good start," he observed, gesturing toward the barrel. "Never point a gun at something you don't intend to shoot."

I thought about his words and mulled them over. "This may sound ridiculous after what happened in Itoriah, but I'm not sure I could shoot anyone."

He looked at me from the corner of his eye and shook his head. "Maybe not to save yourself. But you'd be surprised what you're willing to do to save someone else."

I considered his words, tried to imagine myself in that position. Once I did, I found that I understood exactly what he meant. "I guess maybe *then* I could."

He nodded in approval and then reached for the weapon. His fingers encircled my own, and he slowed to a halt. He lifted the gun, showed me how to eject the clip and load the bullets. Then he slid the clip back into place slowly and chambered a round. "Now you," he instructed. He watched as I fumbled through the routine and offered me pointers to keep from pinching my fingers. I could not wait to get back to the godly realm and have my real body back, where small things like metal sliding against metal couldn't penetrate my immortal skin.

When I finished, we walked for a little while, not wanting to fall too far behind our team. After we made up some more ground, we stopped, and he showed me how to sight. I closed one eye and stared through the sights, aiming at a nearby tree. "It would be ideal for you to fire a few rounds, but we can't risk the sound attracting what's left of Lorus's forces. Also, we're running low on ammo," Arrick said. "So always make sure you sight before you fire. You can't just point and shoot and expect these bullets to hit home like you could with the shotgun. That kind of control takes time and experience."

"Got it. Take the time to aim and don't point and shoot." I clicked the safety into place and slid the gun back into his shoulder holster, glad to be rid of it.

"Have you tried to access your power since the last time?" Arrick asked, changing the subject as we picked up our pace again.

I grimaced at the memory of the last two times I had tried. "Yes. The most I've been able to get is a flash of blue under my skin before it's extinguished. But the pain is excruciating. Like I said before, it feels like the wards are punishing me for trying to break through them."

He eyed me, concern plain in his expression. "Then you should stop trying. I don't want to see you hurt."

I nodded thoughtfully, wondering if he meant for the sake of the cause or for personal reasons. I found myself hoping it was the latter. "But we'll need a backup plan if the portal is sealed. It seems like I'm the only viable option."

"Not if we risk your safety to do so. We need you in one piece when we get back to the immortal realm. And if the wards really are punishing you, then we can't know how far they'll go to keep your power at bay. We'll find another way."

I looked at him. The determination on his face was unimpeachable. He believed that we would prevail over all odds. More than that, he refused to allow for any other outcome. I wished I shared this certainty. Despite knowing that we had destiny on our side, I was still not convinced that it was enough. I thought about the prophecy aversion missions we ran in Valeria. Prophecies were hard to derail since destiny always pushed the people involved toward their fate. But they could be disrupted if enough happened. That was what worried me. How far off the beaten path were we, exactly? How much had already happened to diverge us?

"I don't understand. How can you be so sure we're going to succeed?" I asked, my voice barely above a whisper.

He paused his forward progress. He reached out a hand and tugged mine to stop me. I turned to face him, and he said, "You're not losing faith on me now, are you Bekka?"

"Not exactly. I'm just afraid that a million other things will come between us and what needs to be done. I mean, look at what's happened so far."

"Hey," he said, tucking a finger under my chin and looking into my eyes. "If you ask me, too much has aligned for us not to be on the right path. Think about Deklan and Caden. That had to be fate intervening. If that doesn't convince you, then you can count on one thing at least."

"What's that?" I asked, my eyes searching his face.

He whispered, "That we're in this together. I'll be with you until the very end, no matter what." He paused and looked up at the massive orb in the sky before he fixed his attention back on me. "I need to see this through just as much as you do."

My shoulders relaxed as I soaked in the meaning of his words. He would be there with me through it all. At that moment, it didn't matter *why*. All that mattered was that I would have someone with me to share the burden and that

I wouldn't be alone. Relief washed over me, and on an impulse I didn't question, I moved closer to him and rested my hands against the firm muscles of his chest. I twisted my hands into his shirt, my fingers burrowing into the fabric. He brushed his hand across my cheek, and I leaned into the touch, licking my lips. His gaze locked onto my mouth as though he envied my own tongue's journey across it. My heart stuttered in my chest as he leaned down and kissed me.

His lips were soft and full as they moved over mine. One hand found its home on my cheek, and the other looped to my lower back, pulling me in tighter against him. I felt his tongue part my lips, and I opened to him, allowed myself to taste him, groaned at the pleasure of it. The heat of his body and the feel of him against me caused something to burn deep in my belly as I buried my hands into his hair.

Before I even realized that we were moving, my back was pressed against the rough bark of a tree. He slid his fingertips down the sides of my waist, and I shivered in response. I turned my head and deepened the kiss, pressing my body closer to his, enjoying the warmth that emanated from him.

All the alarm bells that should have been ringing in my mind stayed silent, and all that existed was his body against mine, his lips moving over mine. We had been through so much together already, and it was like all of that built-up emotion was pouring out of us in a single act of passion. I could fall into this moment forever and never let go.

Dimly, I became aware of noises that seemed out of place—shouts, grunts, and scuffles nearby that sounded like a fight. Abruptly, Arrick pulled his mouth from mine; my body was still pressed against a tree. He stepped away from me, leaving me cool in his absence. He trained his head, listening for what had interrupted us.

The shouts grew louder, and I heard Caden's voice yell, "Get him! Don't let him get away!"

Arrick gave me a pained look, frustration mixed with disappointment, and we both took off running toward the sound of fighting. A few seconds passed, and we had caught up with Caden. Niko, Kaleb, and Deklan were already there. Probably, they were not as distracted as Arrick and I were when the fight started. Deklan and Kaleb joined in the fray, but Niko stood back. And unless I was mistaken, he looked amused.

When I surveyed the brawl—if one could call it that— I could see why. A young guy, no more than sixteen and wearing the Puhari colors, shouted unintelligibly and lashed out at the brothers, who were in the process of trying to contain him. He raked his nails across Caden's face and gained a precious second of freedom before Deklan grabbed him from behind and picked him up. Fighting like a wildcat, the guy reached back and pulled Deklan's long hair, ripping out a fistful of white-blond locks for his effort.

Deklan roared with frustration and then lifted the guy over his head and chucked him. His slender body soared through the air, covering a substantial distance, before he slammed into a tree, thus ceasing his forward progress. His legs smacked against the bark, and he executed a rather impressive 360 before he landed on the ground, gasping for air. Apparently, the impact had knocked the wind out of him. *Served him right.* Hair was sacred.

Kaleb stepped toward the Puhari now, drawing his pistol. Seeing his approach, the kid scrambled backward, crab-walk style, and held up a pleading hand.

Still gasping, he said, "Wait! Please! I'm not here to hurt you."

Arrick and Kaleb exchanged a look that said *No Shit*, and Niko snorted in disbelief.

"I'm serious. I've been trying to find someone to help me, and you're the first Itorian fighters I've seen."

Kaleb paused, lowering the muzzle of the gun, and stared at the guy, surprise lining his face.

"Then why did you attack me?" Caden asked.

The kid rose to his feet and brushed off his jeans, looking annoyed. "I didn't, man. You attacked me. I was defending myself." Looking down at the lock of blond hair still clutched in his fingers, he made a disgusted face and dropped it on the ground. Deklan's lip curled in response, and Arrick slapped a hand over his chest to hold him back. It was a smart move too. I think Deklan would have torn him limb from limb if given half the chance.

"Who the hell are you?" Arrick asked. "And what makes you think we'd ever help a piece of shit Puhari?"

Niko spat on the ground, seconding Arrick's sentiment.

The guy swallowed hard, his Adam's apple bobbing, "My name is Brandt." He squared his shoulders and looked Arrick right in his eye when he said, "And we have mutual interests. So, if you help me, it also helps you."

"I know what mutual interest means," Arrick snapped, glaring at him. "What could we possibly have in common?"

"You're looking for your missing people, right? From the battle?" Brandt asked, an eagerness infusing him as he spoke. "I know where they are. I can help you."

"Nice try, kid," Niko growled, stepping forward menacingly. "We know exactly where they are."

Brandt shook his head. "Not unless you know where the Puhari camp is, you don't."

A silence fell over the group, all of us staring at him now. "Bullshit," Niko challenged, dangerousness coming over him as he stepped closer to Brandt. A look passed between the other Itorian fighters, and I got the impression that they did not think this was bullshit.

Brandt shrugged and said, "I don't know if they're all there. But Lorus set up a perimeter around Itoriah before the attack. He rounded up all the people who tried to flee. There were about twenty of them, give or take a few. Mostly women and children, but a few men too. They're keeping them at the camp, but I don't know how much longer that will last."

Everyone paused, trying to determine if this could be true. If it was, then that changed the situation significantly.

"Why are you telling us all this?" Arrick asked, his expression betraying nothing.

"Because," Brandt replied, drawing himself up to his full height, "I'm going to help you rescue them."

CHAPTER 15

Unexpected Consequences

"You want to betray Lorus?" Kaleb asked, the first to recover out of all of us.

Brandt shifted uncomfortably from foot to foot and nodded his affirmation.

"Why?" Arrick asked, staring at him like he was one knife short of a set. "You know what the penalty for helping us would be? He'll kill you and everyone you love."

Brandt paled and leaned heavily against a tree for support. Quietly, he whispered, "He has Emily."

"Who?" Caden asked.

"Emily Lyle."

"Emily Lyle from Itoriah?" Caden asked, narrowing his eyes in suspicion. "How do you know her?"

Before he could answer, Niko scoffed and shook his head, "Why are we even listening to him? It doesn't matter what this guy has to say or what he wants from us. He's *Puhari*. We can't trust a word he says. This is probably a trap."

"I'm not lying!" Brandt shouted, appealing to us with wide eyes. His auburn hair and smattering of freckles added to the general sense of innocence that emanated from him. I wondered how he could be part of the Puhari tribe and found that I couldn't picture it. "I hate Lorus more than anyone. That bastard tried to kill me, and he's the reason my father is dead!" He spat on the ground for emphasis. Then he snarled, "He won't be the reason Emily dies. I won't let him take her from me too."

His declaration was met with silence from all of us. None of us were exactly sure what to say or do. Niko stepped forward first. He drew his knife from the scabbard on his hip and pointed it at Brandt. "You know what I think?" Niko asked, stalking closer. "I think you're lying. And I think you want to lure the last of the Itorian fighters into the Puhari camp so that Lorus can complete his victory."

Arrick stepped forward and rested a hand on Niko's knife arm, pushing it down. "What if he's telling the truth?"

"A Puhari raider?" Niko scoffed, his opinion on this possibility clear.

Deklan cut in then, "He took a big risk approaching us alone. He's lucky we didn't shoot him on sight. Why would he do that if he were lying?"

Brandt appealed to us one more time. "I'm not lying. I swear! I was raised in the Puhari clan, but I was never one of *them.*" He sneered at the word as though it disgusted him.

"Before this happened, Emily and I had a plan for me to leave the Puhari and join her people. Your people. But when Lorus found those three bodies on your land and the order came down to attack Itoriah, I knew it was bad. He was in a rage like I had never seen him before. He didn't just want to steal supplies or resources this time; he wanted to destroy you. So, I snuck out to warn her, but I got caught up in the battle and couldn't find her. At least, not until it was over. She was captured, along with the rest of the people lucky enough to get away. All the survivors were forced into the prison at the Puhari camp. I tried to rescue them. I had a plan to sneak them away, but Lorus caught me. He shot at me and sent people after me. Only, his most loyal lackeys hadn't returned from the Itoriah yet, and that gave me an edge. I might not be much of a fighter, but I'm a good tracker and an even better scout. I know how to stay hidden. So, I got away and traced my steps back to Itoriah. I hoped, by some miracle, that I would find other survivors. Anyone who might help me save Emily. And that's when I ran into you."

My heartbeat had stuttered and damn near stopped at the beginning of his story, "What do you mean, three bodies?" I asked, looking to Arrick from the corner of my eye, my belly filling with acid.

"He found three of his men, dead on Itorian land. A scout watched from a distance as they were killed. He said that an Itorian man and woman did it. Then they tried to cover it up. The problem was that one of the guys they killed was Lorus's brother. A real sick bastard if you ask me. The world is better off without him. But it sent Lorus over the edge."

I practiced deep breathing to avoid the panic attack that threatened to overtake me. It was our fault that Itoriah had been destroyed. I pressed a fist to my mouth to keep from screaming as Arrick rested his hand on my shoulder.

"They attacked us," Arrick explained, trying to reason with me. "On our side of the border. They tried to rape and kidnap my wife. We defended ourselves."

"Oh, shit," he said, looking from me to Arrick. "That was you guys?" Guilt roiled inside of me as I fought against the knowledge that we were to blame for all the pain and suffering that had happened since that moment. No, not us. Me. Arrick only killed them to defend me. If I never came here, then 48 decent people would still be alive, and everyone present would be better off right now.

As my mind spiraled, Arrick leveled a steely glare on Brandt. He spoke, but the words didn't register. I pressed my hands over my ears and turned away from Brandt, from all the others. Panic rose inside of me as I realized that I was to blame, "I'm sorry, I just—I need a minute." Moving quickly, I broke away from the group and rushed deeper into the forest. I heard Arrick call after me, but I did not stop. I wanted to scream. I wanted to rage against the unfairness of this prophecy. I wanted to beg my family to tell me why they had not prepared me for all this.

Running out of energy altogether, I skidded to a halt. I dug my fingers into my scalp and choked on a sob, my world spinning out of control. How many lives had been lost because of my ineptitude? I had killed dozens with my own hands and been unintentionally responsible for even more deaths. How many more people's lives would I destroy before I finally spared these people from my disastrous presence? Sinking into a crouch, I swallowed a scream as despair overtook the anger. How would I ever make this right? Alone in a small clearing, I stared up into the sky. The red giant beat its oppressive rays down on me, and I wished that all this responsibility didn't rest squarely on my shoulders.

As ridiculous and counterproductive as it was, I wanted my grandfather. He was the only person who might have some basic inkling of what I was going through. But even if I were in the position to contact him, doing so would put everything Arrick loved at risk. So, I knew I would never act on this desire. It was just that I had never felt so alone in my entire existence, and my grandpa was the one person I could always count on to make things better. I wished that we were not on opposite sides of this and that we could somehow work together to help these people. But I knew, deep down, that he would never allow it. His hatred for Moldize ran too deep.

A twig snapped nearby and, slowly, I turned my head to see who was there. It was Arrick, his eyes full of empathy. I sniffed loudly and said, "It's all my fault. I should never have come here."

I heard more footsteps and saw Kaleb there too. To my surprise, he spoke instead of Arrick, "You're wrong," he said, his voice softer than I had ever heard it. "This wasn't your fault, Bekka. Lorus has been sending people onto our land looking for a fight for weeks. He wanted Itoriah gone, and all he needed was a reason. It just happened that you and Arrick were unlucky enough to give it to him. But trust me, if it weren't you, it would have been someone else."

"He's right," Niko agreed, stepping into the clearing to join us. "Lorus is a madman. This was just an excuse to do what he's always wanted to do."

I considered Kaleb's denial and then Niko's confirmation. Somehow, their opinion held more weight than Arrick's would have. The latter remained silent, letting them comfort me, and I realized that he understood this.

Within a few moments, Brandt, Deklan, and Caden had joined us. And when they looked at me, I didn't see blame there. I saw sympathy and understanding.

After a long pause, Arrick offered his hand to help me up. I hesitated, but his voice was a gentle caress over my jagged edges, "They're right. You can't blame yourself for the terrible things other people do. Lorus is the only person responsible for what happened to Itoriah. You can ask any man here, and he'll tell you the same."

I looked to Deklan, who, for some reason, I trusted the most. I knew he would not lie to spare my feelings. He would give it to me straight. He shrugged his shoulders, "What were you supposed to do? Let them rape and kidnap you? Kill Arrick?"

I sniffed a little and thought about it. "No, I guess not."

Deklan answered, "Exactly." The fist that clenched around my heart loosened, and I found that I could breathe a little easier. Despite all the reassurance they gave me, I still could not let go of some of the responsibility. There was one way that all of this could have been avoided. If I had accepted my destiny right away and stayed in the immortal realm, then Itoriah would still be here. But I thought a little harder about what they said and realized that maybe it was always going to happen. The only difference that someone else would have been the catalyst for it instead of Arrick and me.

A calm settled over me, and I accepted Arrick's offer. He helped me to my feet, and I brushed the dirt off my pants. My emotions were under control once more, the initial shock having worn off.

Brandt spoke up again, his voice firm, "Look, I hate to interrupt, but we don't have a lot of time here. I don't think Lorus will hold them for long before he decides to do something terrible. If we're going to help each other, then we need to come up with a plan. Like now."

Everyone turned back to Brandt, and he blanched at gaining their full attention. These were five of the toughest men I had ever met in my life. I could hardly blame him for fearing them. He would be an idiot not to.

"What do you think?" Arrick asked, looking from Niko to Kaleb and then from Deklan to Caden. "Do we trust him?"

Niko rolled his eyes. "No, we don't trust him. There's no proof that anything he says is true."

"I'll draw you a map. You can scout the camp yourself if you want. If I'm lying, you can kill me," Brandt offered, aiming a finger gun at his own temple to demonstrate.

Arrick's jaw flexed as he considered. Then he bent down, grabbing a stick from the ground. Jerking his head at the sandy dirt below, he said, "Go ahead. Draw."

Brandt examined the twig in his hands and opened his mouth to say something. But then he seemed to think better of it and did as he was told. He drew the layout of the Puhari encampment in intricate detail. It was long and narrow, with a small trading area in the center of the camp and residential areas on either end. The prison was located on the closest side of the camp to our current location. Directly across from the prison was the Puhari's weapon's cache. Brandt drew it as a shabby lean-to of moderate size.

"OK, explain how the prison works," Kaleb commanded, ever the general, and crossed his arms over his chest as he surveyed the drawing.

Brandt tapped his fingers on what he drew as a large, circular structure. "This is where they're keeping Emily and the other Itorians. Four men guard it at all times." He drew four X's around the circle and explained the details further. "There is one positioned along each ten-foot section of the corral, give or take a few feet. The area is fully fenced, with only one entry point, and that's secured with a padlock."

Kaleb asked, "Do the guards change shifts, take breaks? They would have to, right? Four men can't be responsible for guarding the prisoners 24/7."

Brandt nodded and elaborated, "Normally, when we have prisoners, the guards work on rotating shifts. Every four hours, there is a complete changeover. It's always predictable, like clockwork."

Arrick nodded, and Niko stroked his chin, "What did you do wrong last time? How'd you get caught?" Niko asked.

A blush crept up Brandt's neck, and he cleared his throat. When he spoke, his tone was defensive, "It's not a one-man job. The guards got organized faster than I expected, and I couldn't pick the lock in time." He frowned as he stared at the camp layout. "They saw me, and Lorus went insane. He grabbed a gun from one of the guards, and that's when he started shooting at me."

Dismissing Brandt's explanation, Deklan pointed at the weapon's cache, "If this is going to work, we'll need a distraction. Something that draws the guards away and keeps them busy while we help everyone escape. This seems like the perfect place to start."

"What did you have in mind?" Arrick asked, one arm crossed over his chest, and the other propping up his chin.

"We torch it," Deklan replied evenly.

Brandt's eyes lit up. "Oh, yeah, that would be perfect. It might even pull men from the guard to help put the fire out. The weapons cache is disguised to look like a hut and is not guarded heavily. That way, if there are any spies brave enough to get close, no one would suspect what's in there."

Kaleb added, "If we time our distraction with the shift change for the guards, then it's likely no one will be watching the prisoners in the confusion."

"One problem," Caden said, cupping his chin in thought. "The gate would still be locked. We'll need a key to access it."

Brandt shook his head vigorously. "No way. I've got that covered." He reached into his jacket pocket and produced a lock pick set, meticulously organized in a soft, leather holder.

Caden looked skeptical. "Didn't you say it took you too long last time?"

"Yeah, but that wasn't my fault. I only need a minute. I had about half that last time. So long as the distraction works, I should have plenty of time. Besides, it would be too risky to try and take a key off one of the guards." Brandt closed the set and slipped it back into his jacket.

Niko, who had remained silent and broody through this conversation, spoke up, his disbelieving gaze fixed on Brandt, "How the hell did *you* come out of the Puhari camp? You don't make any sense. You're not anything like the rest of the hoard Lorus commands."

Brandt flushed and stared at his feet. "It's different than you think there. Not everyone worships Lorus, you know."

Niko rose a brow and crossed his arms, "Then enlighten us."

Brandt swallowed audibly, clearing his throat, "My father was captured during a Puhari raid when I was an infant. That was also the night my mother died. They rounded up all the surviving men at the end of it, forced them to their knees, and gave them a choice with guns to their heads. Either join up or die. My father had me, a baby who needed his protection. So, the way he saw it, there was no other choice. He joined."

Brandt paused and stared into the distance, as though working through strong emotion. Refocusing on us, he continued his story, "So, even though I grew up in the Puhari camp, we were never really one of them. We were just trying to survive. My dad taught me about our old tribe, and he made me swear to play the part of a Puhari in public. But in private, that was never who we were. We were Hesperians."

Kaleb raised an eyebrow. "If your dad was so against becoming one of them, why didn't he run? Try to escape?"

Brandt shook his head and laughed as though this were a ridiculous question, "He wanted to, trust me. We both did. About five years ago, when I was old enough to decide for myself, we had a plan to run. We mapped the whole route out. Then three days before we planned to make our attempt, another group beat us to it." He trailed off, a distant look in his eyes.

"What happened?" I asked, unsure if I wanted to know the answer.

"Let's just say we never talked about our plan again after that. Then my Dad died a few years later, killed during a raid. Though Lorus tried to convince me otherwise, I know it was friendly fire. Since then, I've just tried to fade into the background. Go unnoticed. At least, until Emily. But then… well, you know what happened."

We let that linger for a moment, all staring at Brandt in surprise. From what Arrick had told me, the Puhari were loyal to the point of insanity. But what if Brandt's story was true? It would mean that there were others, of like mind to him and his father, who were trapped. Too scared to get out of the camp and in fear for their lives. If we were successful, maybe it would encourage others to defy Lorus as well.

Breaking the silence, Brandt asked, "Now that you know where the camp is, are you going to scout it?"

"Yep," Arrick answered easily. "And you're coming with us."

Brandt's eye grew round as saucers. "But how do you know I won't give away your position? Or turn you over to Lorus?"

Deklan glared at him, "Are you planning to turn us over to Lorus?"

"No, I just mean…well, does this mean you believe me?" he asked hopefully.

"No," Arrick replied. "This means that if you double-cross us, we can kill you faster."

Brandt gulped, apparently rendered speechless. I almost felt bad for him. Because from what I could tell, Brandt was no liar. He was a young man in love, desperate to save Emily. He sought us out, risked death to ask for our help, and provided us with information that we desperately needed. If he hadn't interrupted our journey, we would be at the emergency meeting location right now with no sign of any Itorians and with no way of locating them.

Looking at the sky, which now showed signs of sunset, Kaleb gave his orders, "We'll wait until dark. Then you'll come with Caden and me to verify what you've told us. If it all checks out, we'll regroup here to figure out our next steps."

Nervous energy pulsed from Brandt, "OK, but we need to hurry. Lorus is nuts. The longer we wait, the more likely he is to do something crazy."

I thought of Donny and all the other people that Deklan, Caden, and I had saved. I thought of Niko's wife and daughter, and of Mariah and Jarrod, none of whom were among the dead. My belly clenched. According to Brandt, they were all trapped in that prison right now. I could not imagine that the conditions were good there. I remembered how those three raiders had treated me and felt sick when I thought about what more like them would do to the Itorian women.

"We'll work out the details of the plan while you guys are gone. If everything checks out, we'll see it through before sun-up," Arrick assured, putting Brandt at ease. "You have our word."

Brandt let out a relieved sigh and nodded appreciatively. "It'll check out. So, be ready when we get back."

"Did you just give us an order?" Niko asked, the dangerous edge still there. Out of all of us, he was the one who seemed most skeptical, most unwilling to trust the Puhari defector. I wasn't sure if this was a calculated decision on his part or if he was simply unable to separate one Puhari from the others.

"Uh, no," Brandt replied, hesitating at Niko's challenge. "Just a suggestion."

"Good, that's what I thought."

CHAPTER 16

Damned Heroes

The sun disappeared under the horizon as we watched Caden, Kaleb and Brandt disappear into the woods, heading to the Puhari camp. It was a few miles away, deeper into the mountains and well into the Puhari side of the treaty line. We estimated about two hours total for them to get there and back and perform the necessary recon to verify Brandt's information.

From what Arrick told me, the Puhari encampment's location had been a mystery to the Itorians for a long time. Though, they had not exactly tried to find it. Generally, the Itorians wanted to stay as far away from the Puhari as possible, recognizing the danger of tangling with someone as vicious as Lorus.

Niko started a small fire for light and warmth while we waited. I was in the process of gathering firewood with Deklan and Arrick to help keep us stocked until the others returned. Despite Arrick's warning earlier, I did a quick check, reaching inward for my power. Pain bloomed bright right above my left eye. I sucked in a breath and dropped the wood I held.

"What's wrong?" Arrick asked, stepping to my side and gripping my shoulder in concern.

I gulped in steady breaths, "I tried to access my powers." Deklan stepped closer and eyed me with trepidation.

"I thought we agreed that it was too risky to access your gifts here," Arrick reminded me, looking down at me in disapproval. "We don't know how far the wards will go to prevent you from using them."

"I know, I know," I grumbled, shrugging away from him in frustration. "But we have less than one day left to find another loophole. And we've made *zero* progress. I know we have to help the Itorian captives, but when are we going to the domicile?" We had not discussed this since the initial revelation from Deklan and Caden, and I was getting anxious. When no one answered, I continued. "It better be soon, or we're going to paint ourselves into a corner. We will have one option, aside from the portal, and I don't think any of us like that option."

Deklan stepped forward, squaring his shoulders, "The portal will work."

"You don't know that," I argued. "We're wasting precious time gathering firewood that we could be using to come up with another plan. Another way to get out of here."

"There is another way," Deklan retorted, jaw flexing. "You just don't like it."

My mouth dropped open in surprise as I caught his meaning. I didn't like it. Not one bit. "We're not killing you," I snarled. "End of discussion."

Deklan looked at Arrick and shook his head as though amused, "It's funny that she thinks she has a say in this." Then he turned back to me. "You may be an all-powerful creation deity, but you don't know much about human nature."

"What is that supposed to mean?" Nerves prickled at the back of my neck. His smug yet determined expression had me on edge.

"The rest of us made a pact the night Arrick told us what it would really take to get home. So, if the portal doesn't work, then you won't need to worry about Plan B. We'll take care of it for you."

Horror washed through me, "You can't—"

Deklan raised his hand to stop me, "We can. And we will. But if we aren't successful in our rescue mission, then there won't be much left worth saving for us. So, if you are asking me to choose between spending these last few hours finding a loophole to save our own asses or planning the rescue mission, then you can guess what my answer is."

I let out a long, labored sigh and turned to Arrick, "Will you please talk some sense into them? We can find another way."

Arrick leveled a stern look on Deklan, and to his credit, Deklan didn't shrink away one bit from the Moldizean god of death. "You won't change our mind," Deklan declared. "It's decided."

Arrick turned to me, and I knew that he had no intention of arguing with them, "You can't be serious," I admonished, voice full of disbelief. "You can't possibly agree with this plan."

"Agree with it?" he asked, surprised that I would even suggest such a thing. "Of course I don't agree with it. But if we don't get back home quickly, *everyone dies*. The bottom line is that Afryel's family portal is the only possible loophole, trust me. I know the rules inside out. So, if it doesn't work, we either try your power, which we both agree is far too dangerous to risk, or we let the mortals choose. It's not our decision to make."

I glared at them both, struggling to find the words that might sway them to my side. I came up empty. Growling in frustration, I muttered under my breath, "Trying to be damned heroes, the lot of you. Bunch of freaking assholes, if you ask me." I bent to pick up the wood I had dropped and stomped away from them. Neither of them followed me, and I was glad of it. I couldn't believe they were so willing to throw away their lives without even trying to find another path. Sure, we had found *one*. But if there was one, then certainly there had to be others.

When I cleared a bend in the forest and saw Niko, I gave him the evil eye, "Don't even think about talking to me. Deklan told me about your pact, and I think you're a bunch of assholes." I dropped the wood at his feet and spun on my heel, stomping to the other side of the fire. I sat down hard on the ground and stared into the flame, my anger simmering just beneath the surface.

Deklan and Arrick reappeared, each carrying firewood as well. Niko had positioned the blaze close to Brandt's drawing so that it would stay well-lit while the scouting team was gone. Arrick had promised that we would make our move before sun-up, and we still needed to flesh out the details of our plan.

Giving me time to cool off, they all hovered around the dirt rendering of the camp. I edged closer. I didn't want to get too close to them, but I still wanted to hear their conversation. I was mad, but I would still be a part of this rescue attempt and needed to know the plan. I wanted to weigh in should the idiots try to do anything else *"heroic."*

They talked for a solid hour, strategizing their approach and working through how they could light the weapons cache on fire. The primary concern there was the incendiary device. The more sophisticated weapons in Itoriah had burned up in the fire.

I stared at the glass bottle of blackberry liquor that Niko had recovered from Itoriah, and a plan formed in my mind. I cleared my throat, grabbed the bottle, and rose to my feet. All eyes settled on me as I announced, "I have an idea." I explained my plan to their approving nods. The bottle was about halfway full of potent liquor, not wine. I learned that the hard way last night. My throat burned with the memory, as I explained. "We could use strips from my oversized shirt to stuff inside of this bottle as a fuse. Then with Niko's flint fire starter, we would be in business. You could just throw it into an opening. Once the bottle breaks, the fire should start."

"It's a solid plan," Deklan confirmed. "We could assemble it once we arrive in the Puhari camp."

Niko and Arrick agreed. Arrick tapped his finger on the map. "Before we can go any further, we need to wait for Kaleb and Caden to get back. This all relies on what Brandt told us. But we don't know the surrounding forest. Where's the best cover? What's the best escape route? Those are all questions they'll have to answer."

"Good point," Deklan agreed. Not looking at him, I stared at the map, trying to think of anything we might be missing. Then from the corner of my eye, I saw a gleam and flicker of something large flying through the air. I jumped back just in time for a knife to imbed itself in the ground at my feet. I stared down at the leather handle poking up from the dirt, mouth agape. The blade was at least eight inches long, and it missed my foot by a mere inch. I was speechless.

"Good reflexes," Deklan observed, moving closer. I gave him a death stare. "What?" he asked, throwing his arms up in a display of innocence.

"You almost stabbed me! Not cool."

His lips twitched, and he shrugged, "Oh please, I lobbed that so slow a one-legged crone could have dodged it."

I squared my shoulders and glared at him, bending down to pick up the knife so that I could gesture with it for emphasis. "If that's true, then why do you think my reflexes are good, hmm?"

"I was just trying to boost your confidence. You've got a lot to learn in a short time. Caden, Brandt, and Kaleb will be back soon."

"What are you talking about?" I glared at him. Then, not giving him a chance to answer, I turned to Arrick. "What is he talking about?"

Deklan answered anyway. "Arrick informed me that you promised to learn to handle yourself. Besides, I refuse to go into this mission with someone who doesn't at least understand basic self-defense. We can't be worried about saving you every time something goes wrong. We have about an hour left, and we're going to take advantage of it."

"An hour?" I asked, biting my cheek in concern. "What do you think I'm going to learn in an hour? And what about Brandt? He's an even bigger sissy than I am."

"Sure, but I'm not worried about saving him if something goes wrong," Deklan replied.

"That's cold."

"Yeah, I am," Deklan confirmed, a feral grin spreading over his lips.

"You know, you're even scarier when you smile," I observed.

Arrick snorted with laughter, and Niko cracked a grin. At least our exchange was helping them loosen up a little and take their minds off what was to come.

Deklan circled me and began making observations, as though I were a specimen that required study. "You're athletic enough and have good coordination. Reflexes are strong. Strength remains a question, though."

I hauled back my fist and punched him square on the shoulder.

His jaw flexed, and I could tell that his pride prevented him from rubbing the point of impact. I was as strong as any man in this realm, so there was no way that that didn't hurt. Calmly he said, "Strength is good too."

I gave him an evil grin.

"The point is, I think you can learn a lot in a short time. You do have certain advantages, after all." I could tell that he was referring to my godly prowess. After a millisecond of thought, I gave in. Why not? What could it hurt?

For the following hour and fifteen minutes, Deklan taught me basic hand-to-hand combat and how to wield a knife. Arrick had already covered the gun lesson. Though I still was not 100% comfortable using one, I thought I could manage it if I had to.

As we went through the lesson, Niko and Arrick jumped in with their own helpful tips. By the time Caden, Kaleb and Brandt returned, I had to admit that I felt surprisingly at ease with a blade, and I knew what to aim for in hand to hand combat. Aside from just the crotch, that is, which I already knew about. I was not a professional by any stretch of the imagination, but I liked to think I knew enough to be dangerous. The question remained, was I a danger to others or only to myself?

We ate a small snack, sharing what was left of our food with Brandt, "We can leave our packs here, except for the one with the liquor," Arrick said. "There's not much left in them anyway. We'll replenish once we reach the EML. There are plenty of supplies there, and it's a good five miles from the Puhari camp straight through rugged terrain. We should be safe once we get there."

Everyone agreed to this, and I realized that this was why no one seemed concerned about our dwindling food stores. They knew all along that we had more where we were headed. After that, Kaleb and Caden described the surrounding forest and the best locations for cover. They had found a large boulder on slightly higher ground than the camp. They drew its location on the dirt map, and I had to agree. It would make for a perfect rendezvous location.

The mission would be split into two teams. The first would be led by Niko and consisted of Deklan and Kaleb; they would sneak around the perimeter and set fire to the weapons cache. Meanwhile, Arrick, Brandt, and Caden would get into position near the prison. Brandt would pick the lock once the guards vacated their posts, and Arrick and Caden would lead the captives back to the rendezvous point.

"What about me?" I asked, frowning a little as they finalized the details.

"You'll be waiting at the rendezvous point and staying out of sight," Arrick spoke in a way that brooked no argument.

Unfortunately for him, I was the queen of brooking, "So, I'm just supposed to sit around and wait while you all put your lives in danger? No way. Use me. I can help."

Everyone shook their heads in unison, except Brandt. But to be fair, he had no idea why they disagreed with my request. He wasn't there when I dusted two dozen Puhari soldiers.

"Bekka, you know why you can't." Arrick's voice was a soft caress. "Remember our deal?"

I bit my lip and nodded. I had promised to listen to orders, and I had promised to stay away from any possibility of battle or injury. We could not afford for me to go "kaboom" in front of all the Itorian captives. That would make a bad situation even worse. Fighting the feeling of uselessness, which I hated more than anything, I reminded myself that this was for the greater good. I could sit on the sidelines and watch if it meant that everyone else would be safer for it.

Now that the plans were made and we all knew what part we had to play, Arrick looked up into the moon-bright sky. "It's now or never. We need to go if we want to make it to the EML before sunrise. Is everyone ready?"

We answered in the affirmative, and I swallowed my nervousness as he led the way. We walked for what felt like hours, though it could not have been more than an hour based on the distance. We spent most of that time moving uphill along rocky dirt, dodging trees and thick undergrowth. We stopped when we reached a large boulder, set into a slight hillside. I peered from around the massive structure and bit back a gasp when I saw it—the Puhari camp, in plain sight below.

It was a rough mixture of makeshift tents and permanent structures. Bonfires were spread throughout the camp, lighting it so that we could see all the goings-on within. Men drank out of large caskets of what I guessed was liquor. Shouts of celebration echoed around us periodically, and I wondered if they still reveled in their victory over Itoriah. The thought of it made my belly burn with hatred.

Speaking quietly, Kaleb explained the general layout of the camp, gesturing as he talked. Brandt interrupted as needed, pointing out the prison and the weapons cache. Just as he had drawn, the prison was a circular structure, like a gated corral. The padlock was located on the north side of the gate, close to the tree line. I squinted to try and make out any faces I might recognize. But it was no use. The interior of the corral was dark, unlike the rest of the camp. The other areas had large torches burning and giant fire pits as well. But inside the prison, all we could see were dark silhouettes from this angle.

The weapons cache was located on the far side of camp from the prison, the two destinations equidistant from our current perch. The building was unassuming, a shabby lean-to, just as Brandt had described. It had small cutouts for windows, which remained uncovered, and no one seemed to be guarding it. That would make it nice and easy to lob the firebomb inside. I counted that as a point in our favor.

Brandt pointed over my right shoulder, "That's the escape route. It lines up with what Caden told me about the EML. The passage is full of heavy pine trees. The dried needles make a dense blanket on the ground. We won't leave any footprints, and it will dampen any sound we make leaving the camp. That should make us impossible to track. It's how I got away last time."

Niko hitched his pack high on his back and tightened it. It carried the only glass bottle of liquor in our possession, and we all considered it precious cargo. "When will the shift change happen?"

Brandt looked up at the triple, crescent moons in the sky, "They switch at midnight. So, I think we have about ten minutes to get the fire roaring. It needs to be fully engulfed as they're trying to make the changeover."

"Then we move," Niko ordered, gesturing to Kaleb and Deklan. They slipped silently into the dark and headed downhill toward the far edge of camp and the weapons cache.

Arrick hesitated, looking at me. He slipped his holster off his back and handed it to me, stuffing one of the two guns it held into the back of his waistband. He left the other one for me. "Just in case you need it."

I slipped my arms through it and adjusted it as comfortably as I could manage. Deklan had loaned me his large hunting knife as well. So, in my opinion, I was armed to the teeth.

"You should hurry," I whispered. "We don't have much time to waste."

He leaned down and kissed me hard on the mouth. It was fast, his scent filling my nostrils one second and then vanishing the next. When I opened my eyes, he was gone, along with Caden and Brandt. Despite my inability to see them, I knew that they would move along the hillside, cutting down toward camp once they were level with the prison gate.

Now that our plan was in motion, my heartbeat hammered in my ears, and my palms sweated. This was it, our one shot at rescuing these people. We could only hope that our distraction worked and that everything went as planned. Because if we didn't, then there was no way we would get out of here unscathed.

Following Arrick's request, I crouched behind the rock and peered into the camp. From this spot, I had a good view of both teams as they drew closer to their targets. I clenched my fist around the pistol and took note of the weight of the scabbard on my hip. I was not an expert with either, but I had moderate faith in my ability to do *something* with them. Hopefully, that something would not entail me chucking my gun at a Puhari's head in panic. Deklan's judgment, should such an event occur, would scar me for life.

As I took in the general atmosphere in the Puhari village, I noticed that the celebration was in full swing now. Many of the men were falling-down drunk already, and I counted that as a point in our favor—all the easier for us to slip into their midst unnoticed if they were impaired.

Less than five minutes after they left, Caden, Brandt, and Arrick arrived at the tree line outside the prisoner's corral. They hunkered down, careful to stay hidden from the Puhari guards. There were four of them, just as Brandt had described. They were each patrolling their designated areas, eyes tracing along the trees and then back through the camp. I tracked my gaze along the east side of town toward the weapons cache. Kaleb, Niko, and Deklan kept low to the tree line and were careful to stay out of view from the camp as well. My breath caught as a large group of men walked close to their hiding place.

The cluster of Puhari laughed, punching each other's shoulders in what I thought was a friendly way. But without warning, or at least not one I could ascertain from my perch, they began to shove each other. The small scuffle turned into a fight in seconds flat. Before I even realized the mood had shifted, fists flew, connecting with flesh, and shouts of rage echoed from the hills.

Concerned, I focused on Niko's team, but the Puhari were too absorbed in their own internal fight to notice the Itorians in their midst. Squinting, I saw that Kaleb and Niko had pulled the homemade firebomb out of their pack. They assembled it quickly and efficiently. Deklan kept a close eye on the gathering crowd, a perfect and serendipitous distraction. Once the firebomb was assembled, Kaleb scraped his knife over a piece of flint and caught the cloth that protruded from the top of the liquor-filled bottle on fire. It burned easily, and he passed it to Deklan, who snuck closer to the cache, moving quietly and smoothly. When he was close enough to touch it, he hauled his arm back and chucked it through the open window. To my dismay, I could not hear or see anything through the ruckus going on below.

A few beats passed before I saw tendrils of flame lick through the openings in the shabby lean-to. Smoke issued through the holes that served as windows, and soon, the fire was burning strongly enough that I highly doubted the Puhari would be able to put it out. There was a limited amount of water available in Moldize. They would either have to sacrifice their drinking reserves, smother them, or abandon their camp. And they would have to do all these things quickly or risk getting engulfed in flames themselves.

Deklan, Kaleb, and Niko retreated deeper into the forests, now entirely out of sight. That was when bedlam ensued. Gunshots zinged out of the lean-to and planted themselves into trees and the ground. A couple of them fired into the crowd of brawlers, which caused men to scatter like cockroaches. I heard screams, saw bodies hit the ground, and knew that some of them had been hit.

I cut my eyes back to Arrick, Brandt, and Caden and saw that they were already at the entrance of the corral. The guards had vacated their posts and rushed to the flame-filled cache. Bullets still exploded from the lean-to, piercing through the night, and I worried over Brandt and Caden. There were many people and small structures between them and the weapons, reducing their risk of getting shot. But it could still happen.

Brandt worked quickly on picking the locked gate. I chewed my lips, mentally urging him to hurry. After what felt like an eternity, the lock gave way, and the door swung open. None of the Puhari saw them. Entering the corral, Caden and Arrick crouched low, got everyone's attention, and gestured for the Itorian prisoners to follow them.

As the Itorians wasted no time exiting the corral, the Puhari were working unsuccessfully at putting out the fire that threatened to consume the entire camp. It had leaped from the cache to two of the surrounding huts. The men were gesticulating and yelling wildly as all their weapons went up in a fireball of epic proportions. Before the situation could descend into complete chaos, a man stepped out from the crowd, shouting orders. Everyone gave him a wide berth and jumped to do his bidding.

From their deferential behavior, I gathered that this had to be Lorus. I could not clearly make out his features, the firelight casting the shadows of his face into sharp relief. But he had a presence about him that was different from the other Puhari raiders. He emanated power, wore it like it was his birthright. Hatred seethed through my belly as I glared at him.

At his terse command, dozens of men gathered the water they had secured for drinking and dumped it into the lean-to. Meanwhile, others began to fill buckets with the sandy dirt at their feet and dumped that into the other surrounding structures that had caught fire. They worked quickly and managed to keep the blaze from spreading, though they made little progress in putting it out. I turned back to the corral and watched with intense satisfaction as the last of the Itorian captives disappeared into the forest. Soon, they would meet us here, at our agreed-upon rally point. Then we would leave this popsicle stand behind for good.

A branch cracked behind me, and I trained my pistol at the sound, "Whoa, don't shoot," Kaleb whispered. "It's just us."

Deklan and Kaleb appeared from behind a tree, and I breathed out a sigh of relief.

"Oh, thank the ascended," I exclaimed, pressing a hand to my chest. They had made it back here quicker than I had expected. "Wait a minute? Where's Niko?" I peered behind them, but there was nothing except empty space—no sign of Itoriah's leader.

"Shit, he was right behind us a minute ago," Kaleb said with a hiss, peering into the dark.

Deklan growled and punched the trunk of a tree. Bark splintered, and I jumped back in surprise. "The crazy son of a bitch went back for Lorus."

Adrenaline dumped into my system so fast it made me see stars. "What do you mean, he went back for Lorus?"

Kaleb shook his head as he pressed his lips together. He was just as angry as Deklan, though he took great pains to keep it under wraps. He was not the type to lose his cool under pressure, and I could tell that he didn't want to start now. "We saw Lorus on our way out. Niko must have gone back for him. He wouldn't have been able to resist a shot for revenge."

Kaleb's eyes were harder than I had ever seen them before as he stared into the chaos of the Puhari camp. "He's going to kill him."

"Or get himself and the rest of us killed," I whispered, unable to say it any louder. I could not believe that he would take a risk like this, knowing his wife and daughter were likely here too.

Kaleb shook his head and peered down into the fire laden camp. "He wouldn't see it that way. To him, he's eliminating a threat once and for all. Trust me; I know my uncle."

I followed Kaleb's gaze and stared down into the furiously working Puhari, and tried to pick out Lorus in the crowd. But he had disappeared amid their frantic efforts to put out the fire. I looked harder, but the flames danced high now and blocked a good portion of the camp from our view. A few seconds later and Arrick, Caden, and Brandt, along with the hostages, found us. I did a quick tally, counted twenty-six of us in total, and breathed a sigh of relief. It was a large crowd for this small hiding place. We would need to be underway soon or risk getting caught.

Brandt stepped forward, holding the hand of a blond woman, her face sooty and her hair grimed with mud. It had to be Emily, which meant that he was telling us the truth all along. Not that I doubted him, but it was nice to have confirmation. His face was flushed with the excitement of our success.

Picking Arrick out of the crowd, I rushed to him. Wrapping my arms around his neck in relief that he had made it out with no surprises.

Before I could explain why we couldn't leave yet, Kaleb jumped in for me, "Niko's gone. He's going after Lorus."

Arrick cursed under his breath and ran his hands through his hair, a good indicator of the anxiety he felt at this revelation. "There's too many of us to hide here. If we don't leave now, someone will see us, and we'll lose our advantage."

A woman stepped forward, carrying an infant in her arms, "Please, you can't just leave him there. You have to help him." Niko's wife, judging by the extreme worry lining her face.

Pain washed over Arrick's expression as he looked at the camp, then at her, "Don't worry. We won't leave him."

A voice I recognized as Mariah's flowed from the darkness, "We're going to have to split up." She stepped forward, Jarrod at her side, and I moved quickly toward them. I reached for each of their hands and squeezed tightly, overjoyed to see that they were safe.

Caden jumped in then, "Deklan, Bekka, and I can lead them in the right direction with Brandt. Kaleb, you and Arrick should go get Niko. You can catch up with us once you've talked some sense into him. He's more likely to listen to you than anyone else."

I shook my head. "No. Kaleb goes with you all. Arrick and I can handle this."

Kaleb shook his head harder, "No way. You can barely handle a gun, and you've had, what? An hour of hand-to-hand training?"

I strode toward him, "Yeah, but Arrick and I can't die. You can. Now get moving. We don't have time to waste."

Arrick was the only one near enough to hear my comment. His brows drew together, and I could picture the wheels of his mind spinning, recalling our deal. The one where I was supposed to run at the first sign of danger. But he didn't argue. Instead, he agreed, "She's right, Kaleb. We'll get him back, and then we'll be on our way to you. Five minutes."

I remained silent, not daring to question his decision. I knew that the only reason he agreed to my plan was that the Itorian captives would be long gone, should I go full creation deity again. So, they would be free of any ramifications that came along with witnessing a divine act. The Puhari mortals, though? They wouldn't be so lucky, and somehow, I couldn't bring myself to care. Even if all of them weren't Lorus loyalists, they still committed heinous crimes at his behest. They were not innocent, and I refused to endanger even one Itorian life for their sake.

Wasting no time on debate, Brandt and Deklan ushered the group away from the Puhari camp. They hurried them down the path with Brandt and Emily at the head of it. Quicker than I would have thought possible, they were moving to the escape route. Mariah and Jarrod waited until the end of the line. Mariah hesitated and then whispered to Arrick, "Be safe. Don't do anything stupid."

"Never." Arrick reached for her hand. She squeezed, and Jarrod nodded soberly at his foster son. "I'll catch up soon. But you both need to hurry."

Obeying his command, they turned and followed the rest of the Itorians into the woods. Before they had all disappeared from our line of sight, Arrick and I were moving. We rushed into the chaos of the Puhari camp.

We moved fast, careful to keep our footfalls silent as we executed a controlled slide down the hillside. We kept close to the trees and retraced the path that the firebomb crew had used before. When we were close enough to the village that we could feel the heat from the cache fire, we heard something—a scuffle, a muffled moan, and then a painful gargle.

Arrick took off in the direction of the sound, and I followed close on his heels. Arrick had his palm trained over the knife at his side, ready to draw should the need arise. My gun was clasped in my hand, hanging at my side, and my finger was on the trigger. I was not entirely sure if I could use it, no matter what we found. But I could not take the chance that I would need it and not have it ready.

Suddenly, Arrick skidded to a stop, and I had to dodge sideways to avoid hitting his back. I pulled up beside him and stared in mute horror. What I saw in the dancing light of the blaze sickened me. Niko stood, panting over the body of the man I identified as Lorus. Lorus's throat was cut, and fresh blood streamed down his body in a glossy sheet. The jagged knife in Niko's hand was slick with the dark liquid as well.

In a reaction I did not have time to contemplate, I leaned over and vomited on the forest floor. Because Lorus's neck was not just slit, his head was nearly severed from his body. When I fully emptied the contents of my stomach, I looked up into Niko's eyes.

There it was—that feral gleam.

Only, it wasn't tempered with any of the compassion or sanity I had witnessed before. Now it was naked, exposed. Terrifying. He was wild with the kill, and a large gash sliced down the side of his face. Apparently, Lorus hadn't taken the attack lying down.

Niko let out one shuddering breath, chucked the body to the ground, and then strode forward without looking at us. But before we could escape the grizzly scene and get away clean, a voice called out nearby, "Lorus? Is that you? We need—"

A man broke through the trees and stood before us, even more stunned by our presence than we were by his. We stared at each other for a few moments. Then he looked down and saw it. Lorus's body. His head snapped up at the same time he drew his sidearm. He let out a blood-curdling scream that seemed to shake the forest around us. Then he aimed his gun right at Niko, sighting his victim. My throat squeezed shut in an effort not to scream.

A shot rang out, and I clapped my hands over my ears, eyes fixed on Niko. I searched him frantically but saw no sign of injury. Had the Puhari missed? Then I turned to Arrick, who held his own raised pistol, the smoking muzzle of it pointed right at his enemy. The Puhari slumped to the ground, eyes blank, and a bullet hole sunk into the center of his forehead. His soul slithered out of his body and absorbed into Arrick's skin, along with Lorus's. Arrick shuddered in reaction at the poison that must have entered his body along with the soul of the Puhari leader. I did not envy him.

Footsteps were close at hand now. Called to us by the warning scream the Puhari had issued just before his death.

Recovering his senses, Arrick shouted, "Run!"

Without hesitation, all three of us sprinted into the night back the way we came. The crunching of footfalls and the sound of voices drew closer, and I knew they would be upon Lorus's body soon. From there, who knew what would happen? My best guess was that they would hunt us down until they caught and killed us.

Desperate to keep some advantage, we darted through trees, running as though our lives depended on it. I glanced over my shoulder, silently thanked the ascended that no one had picked up our trail yet. Though I knew that it was only a matter of time since we ran through bare dirt, making an easy trail for them.

We flew up the hill and toward the escape route, gaining a precious minute head start in the process. A few more seconds at our breakneck pace, and we saw signs of people. Deklan and Caden brought up the rear of the group, and they turned at the sound of our feet. Everyone close enough to hear our approach paused, eyes wide with worry as we skidded to a stop in front of them.

"What happened? We heard a gunshot," Caden asked. Another face I recognized pushed his way through the crowd to stand before us. It was Donny. The boy I had saved that night from the burning borough. He took one looked at Niko's blood-soaked body and gagged.

Kaleb surged forward then and took one look at his uncle, disgust plain on his face, "Fuck Niko. What the hell did you do to him?"

Niko growled low, "Nothing he didn't deserve."

Puhari shouts rang up the hill. They were close at hand. Too close.

I spoke frantically, "We were spotted. There's no time. They'll be here soon." My lungs burned, and I breathed hard, trying to recover as my body shook with adrenaline.

Ever the general, Arrick gave decisive orders, "Donny, Niko, you two hold up the rear and make sure everyone moves quickly. Kaleb, you lead with Brandt. Force everyone to run if you have to. Caden, Deklan, Bekka, and I will be the decoy and lead them away from your trail. Now go!"

Kaleb opened his mouth to protest, but Arrick stopped him with a snarl, "There's no time! Go!"

It was clear that neither Kaleb, Donny, nor Niko liked this plan. But the reality was that if we all went in the same direction, then Puhari would catch us. And we would be screwed. So instead of wasting precious time arguing, they turned and took up their positions, rushing everyone deeper into the forest.

The sun had started to peak over the mountainside, dawn rapidly approaching. "We need to wait," Arrick commanded, and I saw that his body was coiled, ready to spring forward at any moment. "They need to see us. We don't want them to pick up the wrong trail." Shouts and footsteps were close at hand now. I saw running men appear between the thickets of the trees. They sighted us, screaming to their comrades, and made a beeline in our direction.

"Now!" Arrick shouted. He turned and moved at a dead sprint in the opposite direction of those we had rescued. We had a solid lead but were still within shooting range. As we ran for our lives, Caden and Deklan kept pace easily. I strained to stay close to them, this mortal body an ever-present challenge. We flew through the trees, not worrying about how much of a trail we left in our wake. It hardly mattered since we were the distraction. We were the bait.

"Where are we going?" Deklan yelled. His voice was steadier than it should have been, given our breakneck speed. But he was trained for this, as was everyone else, except me.

"To the cavern and the domicile," Arrick replied through his rhythmic breathing. "It's close. A little under two miles away. We should be able to make it there before they catch us." A bullet sang through the air and whistled past my ear. I ducked involuntarily and darted to the right.

"Shit," Caden yelled, glancing over his shoulder to look behind us. "We have five on our tail." Shouts erupted from our pursuers, and all the hairs on my neck stood on end.

Arrick kicked up the speed, and we all pushed to follow him. "Scatter," he ordered. Deklan and Caden split from the small group we formed and darted into the woods. I followed suit and watched carefully and copied them as they all wove through the trees, making themselves into difficult targets. More shots rang from the Puhari as they yelled vicious curses at our backs.

Caden and Deklan moved like wildcats, their bodies lithe and sleek with muscle. Watching them like this, I could see that godly heritage and what made them different. As for me, my semi-mortal body was weaker than I was used to, and I struggled to sustain the speed we held. But I didn't dare stop or slow as we sprinted through the forest. I would push my body to its breaking point before I let myself get captured. We had to make it to that cavern.

Another round of shots rang out, hitting no one yet again. We wove through the forest, making it impossible to sight us. I took comfort in knowing that the Puhari were likely wasting the last of their bullets on trying to hit moving targets. I risked a glance behind me. They were still visible, running through the trees. I wondered how the hell they were keeping up—pure rage and adrenaline, most likely. Niko had killed their leader, and now they were out for blood.

We kept going, never stopping, moving like the wind. Little black spots began to bloom in my vision. Another minute passed, and Arrick shouted, "I see it. Keep moving." I looked ahead, sighted the entrance of a cavern in the dawning light. It was so close. Bullets exploded from the guns once again, one of them planting into a tree inches from my head. I felt dizzy, and my legs wobbled beneath me as I pushed forward.

The cave's mouth yawned open before us, large and ominous. It was so close. It was only a few steps more, and we would be safe. Arrick said that the cave was spelled, that only those with godly blood could enter. My legs were weak with exhaustion, and my body ached with the urge to stop. My focus was locked on my destination, and I would make it there, even if it killed me. My gaze was so fixed on the cave that I didn't see the ground beneath me. My foot caught a rock, and I stumbled, losing my balance. Because I was too tired to stop it, I sprawled face-first on the ground, inches from the cavern's entrance.

Arrick, Caden, and Deklan had passed through its mouth and into safety seconds before, and I could no longer see them. It was as though they'd disappeared entirely.

Like smoke in the wind.

I tried to scramble forward to join them, but a Puhari fighter was on me in seconds. He leaped for me, wrapping his fingers tightly around my ankle; I roared, the sound involuntary and filled with frustration and rage. He dragged at my leg, pulling me further from the entrance. My nails dug into the rocky ground, fingertips burning with the effort to anchor myself. Recognizing the futility in the gesture, I let go and came away with a fistful of dirt for my effort.

Acting on pure instinct, threw the sandy dirt right into my assailant's face. His mouth and eyes were wide with the glee of my capture, and he coughed and sputtered in reaction, reeling backward and letting me go. I struggled to my feet, and Arrick broke from the cavern, now a dozen yards away from me.

The Puhari had dragged me further than I'd realized.

Arrick ran full speed in my direction. A hand slapped my back and dug its fingers into my shirt, whipping me around and bringing me face-to-face with another Puhari. I barely had time to react before his fist connected with my face. I staggered backward, away from my attacker. Stars erupted in my vision as strong, solid arms wrapped around my body. Arrick. I shook my head, and then everything turned red. That son of a bitch had hit me in the face.

In a blind rage, I yanked away from Arrick's grasp and lunged at the Puhari. Simultaneously, I slipped Deklan's hunting knife from the scabbard at my waist. I dropped to my knees and sunk the blade into his foot, ripping it out in one quick move. Blood spurted from the wound, and he screamed, right before I planted my fist as hard as I could into his crotch. It was lights out as he keeled over, unable to decide what body part to comfort. I rose and turned; Arrick was watching me with appreciation as more shouts came through the woods. That was when I remembered that there were still three more coming. I grabbed for Arrick's outstretched hand, and we ran like hell for the mouth of the cave.

We crossed the barrier together, in full sight of the other three, slower Puhari. As soon as we entered, we turned and looked at our pursuers. All three of them skidded to a halt and looked around, faces comically blank as though wondering what they were doing there. Unable to process this turn of events in my current condition, I collapsed to my knees and dragged in gulps of precious air. My injured eye throbbed in time with my heartbeats, and I gently probed the painful flesh.

Caden and Deklan stared at the Puhari outside, all of them obviously confused. Caden spoke first, "What the hell just happened? It's like they don't even know we're here. Or what they're doing here either."

Arrick knelt beside me, rubbing my back to soothe me, "They don't. The cave is spelled to prevent mortal entry. They would have forgotten about us completely once we entered the cavern."

Deklan pursed his lips and muttered, "Well, that's a useful trick."

Caden knit his brows together as though deep in thought. Then he asked, "How did you know *we'd* be able to enter?"

Arrick shrugged, still trying to soothe me as he said, "I wasn't sure you could. I just hoped your heritage would be enough." No choice about it anymore, I gave completely into the exhaustion and rolled onto my back, staring up at the ceiling. Massive stalactites drooped down in eerie columns, and I stared at them as I got myself back under control. The combined effects of the adrenaline dump, the run, and the attack had wrought havoc on my mortal-ish system.

Arrick peered down at me, "Are you OK?"

I looked at him and narrowed my eyes, "I'm OK. But I need you to be honest about something."

"Always."

"How bad does my face look?"

When all three of the men grimaced, I knew it couldn't be pretty.

CHAPTER 17

Risk Versus Reward

A few minutes later, Arrick helped me to my feet. I wavered for a moment, using his arm to stabilize my balance. Once I steadied myself, I dusted off my pants and touched a tentative fingertip to my eye. It was already swelling, my vision impaired by my narrowing eyelid. I couldn't help it. I was pissed.

I looked at Arrick. "I can't believe that asshole punched me in the face. Look at me! I'm disfigured."

His lips twitched. "I'm pretty sure you sent his testicles halfway up his torso. So, I'd say you came out on top."

Caden grinned and flung a friendly arm over my shoulder, "Yeah, that guy will be sitting on a pillow for weeks."

"You think?" I said, hopefully.

"No way around it," Deklan said.

I gave them all a tentative smile of appreciation. That did make me feel better. Then I remembered the first time three Puhari attacked me. I had been helpless, desperate to fight them off, but I'd had no idea how to do it. Today though, I disabled two of them long enough to escape. I didn't need to rely on anyone or on my powers to save me. Come to think of it, I felt damn good about that.

Arrick's eyes shone with appreciation. "Honestly, you did well, killer."

Our eyes met, and my body warmed under his admiring gaze. "I'm a fast learner."

"That's exactly what I'm hoping for. We won't have much time left to hone your gifts once we make it back to our realm." We had already used up almost seven hours of immortal time here in the mortal realm. That left us with about half a day to practice, a few hours to sleep so that I could build up my strength, and then a few hours to come up with a plan and execute it. That was if everything held steady from when we left. The situation with the sun was, as Erykha and Damion had explained, unstable. Then there was grandpa Gabryel and the window of time it would take him to find us. That also held a wide margin of error.

I chewed on my lip in worry. "We should hurry."

Deklan interrupted, his attention fixed on Arrick. "She's right. What's next, then? You said something about a dom—?"

"A domicile. It's a method of speed travel used by the gods to get around the mortal realm," Arrick explained. "If you're all ready to move, it's back this way. The sooner we get home, the better."

"I'm assuming you mean me since you guys all are fine. So yeah, I'm ready," I snarked, still a little irritable. I couldn't help it. I'd been punched in the face. It hurt.

Arrick led us deeper into the belly of the cave. It was dark and damp and somehow otherworldly. We all seemed to sense this and walked in silence until a faint glow appeared just around a bend ahead. It shone blue and an iridescent white, a beautiful blending of magics.

The blue reminded me of the way my body blazed when my gift made itself known. I knew instinctively that this was Afryel's power. I could feel it radiating down the tunnel and stroking against my skin. It sang to me, recognizing a twin to its own nature. I breathed it in and reveled in its similarity, wished that I could call my own forth, tempted by something so similar. Only, I knew this was a ruse. If I tried to break through again, as I had before, it would punish me. And I couldn't imagine to what extent. But based on the agony I'd been dealt the last time I'd tried, I didn't want to find out.

When we got to the end of the bend, the domicile sat before us. It was massive, black with that magical glow surrounding it, and it was as sleek as a panther. Nothing like the practical domiciles we had back in Valeria, this thing looked mean, sexy, and fast. Surrounding it was a control room of sorts. A holo box was placed in the middle of the open space behind the vehicle, and large lock-boxed shelving units lined the makeshift room. Everything was made from the same black material, and Arrick strode to the holo box and placed his hand on the ebony surface.

In response, everything surged to life. The domicile vibrated with barely contained energy, and all the lockboxes unlatched. Then a hologram appeared in the center of the room, showing a map of possible travel locations. Caden and Deklan both stared wide-eyed at the transformation.

"This is incredible," Caden breathed, moving toward the domicile. He rested a hand on its smooth exterior and grinned at me when the vehicle hummed in reaction.

Deklan took one glance at the domicile hovering above the ground and crossed his arms over his broad, leather-clad chest. "Since we're about to walk into a microwave, I'd like to see that tonic you told us about."

Arrick moved along the wall to one of the lockboxes. He opened it and pulled out four bottles. They glowed gold, and we had to squint to see them through their vivid light. They each were topped with a cork and ran about the length of my hand. Arrick explained before we could ask, "Our goddess of healing makes this for when we go in to survey the damage caused by The Burning. We keep tabs on the extent of the destruction, even though we haven't been able to do much to combat it in the past few years. But the point is that the tonic has magical properties to keep the radiation at bay. But like I said before, it's made for full-deities, not demi-gods."

Caden's brows knitted together in concern, "So what does that mean, exactly?"

Arrick held his hand out to each of us, and we took the bottles. Once we each held our own bottle, he answered, "You two are like brothers to me, so I won't sugar coat it. We've never tested it on a demigod before, so I'm not sure how effective it will be. But I know it will help since it is a radiation blocker. I just don't know if it relies on our inherent healing capabilities as deities or if it will block anyone from the radiation."

"Great, that makes me feel warm and fuzzy all over," Caden muttered, eyeing the bottle like a venomous snake. "Be honest, how likely do you think it is to work?"

Arrick shrugged helplessly, looking like he'd swallowed something bitter. He didn't seem to like the situation any better than the twins did. Or me, for that matter. After a brief pause to consider, he replied, "It will make Bekka and I completely immune from the effects of radiation for ten hours in our pseudo-mortal forms. So, assuming that it piggybacks on our ability to heal faster than humans, I'm estimating that you'll get about an hour. Give or take. And, that's taking into consideration the difference between my speed to heal versus an average human's when I'm in the mortal realm."

"By estimating, you mean guessing, don't you?" Deklan asked, cutting through to the grit of the issue.

Arrick looked over his shoulder at the domicile. He seemed uneasy, which made sense. The situation wasn't cut and dry. It was clear from the way he slid his hands over his hair and from the strain in his expression that he didn't like this level of uncertainty where his friends' safety was concerned. But then he also carried the burden of Moldize and the survival of all its people on his back. After a long pause, he sighed in resignation. "If you want to change your mind, we can go back now. I wouldn't blame you."

"Fuck that. We're not cowards," Caden snapped, then he popped the cork and drained the bottle in two large gulps.

Deklan remained silent but popped the cork on his own bottle and followed suit. When he finished, he said, "No one is turning back. This is the only way that keeps Niko and Kaleb alive."

Arrick and I followed their lead and drank. The liquid was smooth, delicious, and I could feel the effects immediately. Warmth suffused my body, and I hummed from head to toe.

Then Arrick turned toward the holographic map and pointed to the second northernmost point on it. "This is our destination. Based on the physical description of where we're going from Arabella, I believe this will drop us about twenty minutes from the site."

"I have one question," I interrupted. "Can't we just bring another bottle of this blocker and dose Caden and Deklan again after an hour?"

Arrick shook his head. "I don't want to risk it. It's potent, and they could overdose."

I looked at the brothers from the corner of my eye. Their bodies were tense and, occasionally, Caden's hand shook with an involuntary tremor. They were scared, and I didn't blame them. None of us wanted them to risk their lives on this quest, but we didn't have a choice—we were running out of time and options.

"OK then." I sighed, disappointed that nothing could ever be simple here. I cracked my knuckles in a nervous gesture. "We'll just have to make an hour work. That means we only have twenty minutes once we get to the sight to find the portal. If we don't, we turn back."

They all gave me a look like I had something in my teeth. "We are turning back if we don't find it in twenty minutes. We all agree on that, right? We can always come back when it's safe to dose you guys again."

Arrick looked from me to them, and it was the first time I saw the strain of fear on his face. He was afraid for Caden and Deklan, but the urgency of our situation weighed on him. I could tell that he didn't want to waste another day any more than I did. After a pause from all three of them that had me ready to lose my cool, Arrick said, "Let's just make sure we find it on the first trip out there."

It didn't really answer my question, but the brothers both nodded in response. Apparently, all three of them were on the same page on this one. I glared at them. "Will you two stop trying to be freaking heroes? We need you alive to access the portal. So, if we overstay our window and don't find it on our first trip out there, then we're screwed. Aside from that, I want us all to get through this with a pulse. I owe you both that much at least."

"We're not trying to be heroes," Caden said. "We're just trying to be realistic, Bekka. You've never experienced radiation, but we have. We lived further north when we were young. We've had radiation sickness before, and we were lucky we didn't die that time. But that was nothing compared to what we're about to face."

I pressed my lips together in annoyance. I opened my mouth to argue, but Caden continued before I could, "If we go out there and come back without finding that portal, it's possible that we'll die before we can go again. We don't know how well this radiation blocker will work for us. It's all a guess."

"He's right," Arrick agreed, eyes full of remorse and resolve. "We have one shot. If the blocker doesn't work as expected, then we'll need to get them into the immortal realm as soon as possible. They should heal once they're inside our borders. Though a demi-god's presence there will be a first, I expect that the immortal part of them will be enhanced once they cross into it. I wish it were different, but that's our best shot at keeping them alive. Going back after 20 minutes only increases the risk."

I bit my bottom lip and chewed over this logic. I didn't like it. Not one bit. But what choice did I have? This portal gave us hope to save all four of the Itorian men who'd witnessed my divine act. If we didn't risk Deklan and Caden's lives, then they would have to die anyway, along with Niko and Kaleb. Because that was the only other way home for Arrick and me. Aside from my powers, which I had serious concerns about trying to access again. With every attempt I made, the pain only got worse. More sinister in its intent.

Deklan, who had been silent through this exchange, eyed me shrewdly. He knew that I was working through this conundrum just as they already had. He shrugged dismissively. "We've faced worse odds before."

His body language screamed cavalier, but his eyes were full of unspoken emotion. I could tell that this bravado was for my benefit. He knew damn well the danger in what we were about to do.

I wanted to argue. I wanted to scream my frustration and let it echo off the walls of this massive cave. But instead, I dropped it. What was left to say? What could I possibly do to make this situation any better? From my perspective, we were just wasting time that we needed for the blocker to work by arguing.

At my lack of response, Arrick tapped a few holographic buttons, set our location, and then the domicile doors released. They opened upward, presenting us with a sleek black, red, and gray interior. He led us into the vehicle, and I saw a small holo display in the center between the two sets of captain's chairs that faced each other. The straps were harness style, cushioned, and comfortable. We all buckled ourselves into them, Arrick showing us the right way to do it.

"How exactly does this work?" Deklan asked, squinting at the hologram display in the center of the vehicle. "This technology is way beyond anything I've ever seen."

"Right." Arrick seemed to realize that curious mortals surrounded him. He pointed to the display, which looked like a network of tunnels that spanned over large swathes of Moldize. "This is a hologram, and it's linked into a network of speed travel tunnels. This is just the basic tech we use to operate all our major devices in Moldize. It works like a computing system via an intranet, but it's more powerful because it's enhanced with a little of our godly magic – courtesy of the Science & Technology Pillar of Power. The way we travel, though, that is from a combination of Afryel's magic and the Time & Dimensional Pillar of Power. Together, they opened dimensional tunnels using their magic, and that allows us to travel without any time passing. So, as we pass through the tunnel, time stands still."

"I'm going to pretend I understood that, in the interest of saving time," Caden said. "But one more question before we go. Why do we need a harness? How fast are we going to be going, exactly?"

"The speed of light," Arrick answered. "Don't worry, the interior of the domicile is spelled for comfort. The harnesses are just a precaution. Now, can we go? I'm sure the effects of the blocker are underway now, and I don't want to waste any more time."

In response, Caden fidgeted in his seat. Deklan looked about as comfortable as a fly in a spider's web, but they both nodded their assent.

Arrick pressed a green button on the holographic display, and it flipped from a map to an ETA, which showed a five-minutes and ten-second countdown. When the countdown hit zero, the domicile eased forward; it felt as though we were barely moving, just like in Valeria.

Five minutes later, we stood in another cavern across the world from where we'd started. The room was a mirror image of the one we just left, and I spun a quick circle. The sense of déja vu was eerie.

Wasting no time, Arrick jogged over to the hologram and powered it up. Once everything turned on, he opened all the lockboxes, grabbed a pack, and slipped it onto his shoulders. Next, he grabbed thick sunglasses and canvas jackets for each of us. He jogged back over to us. "Put these on quickly. It'll protect your eyes from the sun and your skin from the wind and sand."

We did as he asked without question, hurrying to get our clothing in place. Then he handed us each a bladder of water. We all sipped from it sparingly, and he put it back in his pack.

"This is going to get uncomfortable, but we can't stop no matter what. We push through."

"Don't worry about us," Deklan assured him, gesturing to his brother. "We don't plan to stop."

"Me either," I promised, nodding. My legs still felt rubbery from our dash through the forest, but we were only twenty minutes from the sight where we believed we would find the portal. I could make it twenty minutes.

"Good. Everyone ready?" Arrick asked, waiting for our verbal approval before he started for the exit. "We can't afford to waste any more time."

"Ready as we'll ever be," Caden replied.

I merely nodded and checked all the buttons on my jacket. Deklan gave his signature affirmative grunt, and Arrick turned, jogging down the tunnel that I knew would lead to the cavern's entrance. My legs creaked and complained, but I kept up, just as I promised I would.

As we drew closer to the mouth of the cave, the light became brighter and brighter. By the time Arrick instructed us to put our glasses on, I was already squinting. I followed Arrick's advice, and the relief was exquisite. Not five steps later, we were out of the protection of the cavern and into an explosion of light like I'd never experienced before. I slammed my eyes shut and blinked hard to adjust; the heat seeped through my jacket and into my skin, causing it to go slick with sweat. We each stood there, dumbfounded and each adjusting to the severity of the environment at our own pace.

Recovering first, Arrick asked, "Everyone OK?" The light was so bright that it cast dark shadows and made my companions look like nothing but black silhouettes. The only way I could tell it was him was his shape. He was just a little taller and slightly bigger than the brothers.

I managed a raspy, "I'm OK," my throat as dry as a desert.

Caden sucked in a few gulps of poisoned air. "I'm as good as can be expected."

Deklan gave us a curt nod. "I'm OK for now, but not getting any better. Let's move before this tonic wears off."

"Stay close," Arrick ordered, then he turned and broke into a jog. I waited until Caden and Deklan passed me. I wanted to bring up the rear so that I could keep an eye on them. Even with the blocker, I could feel the intensity of this place and the oppressiveness of the red supergiant in the sky. Burned was the perfect way to describe this place. Everything was charred to a crisp, as though the whole world had been raked over hot coals for decades.

As we jogged, I pulled my scarf over my head to protect my face from the whipping winds and the pelting sand. This was similar to what we experienced when I first entered Moldize, only it was about a hundred times more intense. All around us were old, dried trees, killed by the intensity of the sun. There was nothing underfoot but rocky dirt and sand stripped of all its nutrients. We ran past countless animal bones, sitting on ceremony like a sacrifice to the burning fire god in the sky. I felt sorry for them. They never would have known what hit them.

No more than five minutes passed before my legs felt leaden beneath me. Five minutes more, and the brothers came to an abrupt stop in front of me. I almost plowed into Deklan's back, unable to cease movement fast enough with my shaky muscles.

"Do you see those rocks?" Arrick yelled and pointed into the distance. He had to shout to be heard over the roaring wind. Deklan and Caden's shoulders heaved up and down, and I could tell that this hike had exhausted them. I watched them closely as I tried to discern how badly affected they were; they never showed any signs of tiring when we ran roughly the same distance from the Puhari camp to the cavern. How well was the blocker working? If I had to guess, I would say not as well as we'd hoped.

"I see it." Deklan dug below the layers of clothing he had on. He withdrew the journal and flipped to the map. His finger settled on the paper as he tapped the drawing and looked back at the rocky outcropping not a hundred feet ahead.

"This is it, right?" Arrick asked, leaning over to look at Arabella's drawing. I could tell he hoped that the answer was yes. We shaved off about ten minutes by running instead of walking and, if we already found it, that meant we could start searching for the portal right away.

Deklan used his hands as a visor, examining the map to discern other clues and landscape markers. The contrast between her drawings and the actuality of this place was immense. Judging by her art, this part of the world had once been full of life and dense foliage. Now everything was lifeless and dry as a bone, burned up by the sun.

After another moment of silent comparison, Deklan shouted, "I think that's the great tree." I followed his line of sight to a massive, fallen oak tree. "This is it." The excitement in the dour man's voice gave me hope that we were in the right place. Because if Deklan was hopeful, then there was a better than average chance we had found what we were looking for.

Now that we were here, I realized how anxious I was to get back to our realm and shed this clunky pseudo-mortal form. I desperately wanted to be in my true body again, the one that was impervious to things like bullets and radiation sickness.

In our excitement, we all sprinted toward the rocks and the felled tree, our feet moving faster with the destination in sight. According to the map, the doorway was located between a crevice in the rocks. Activating it was a little bit vaguer, but we would find out how that worked soon enough.

We split up, each of us checking the larger boulders and rock formations near the felled tree. I felt for the presence of godly magic, but the wind roared around me and made it difficult to concentrate. I moved from rock to rock, laying hands on each of them and closing my eyes. I felt nothing. When I finished my quadrant, I jogged over to Arrick.

"Anything?" I shouted, my voice barely audible.

He shook his head and then replied, "Nothing." Wasting no time, we both turned and jogged over to Deklan. "You find anything?"

Deklan gave a curt shake of his head.

"Hey, guys!" Caden shouted. "I feel... something! It's hard to explain."

On a rush of adrenaline, we hurried over to him. I paused, sucking in a breath of astonishment. I felt it too. There was power emanating from the crevice of rock in front of him. It was faint, but it was there just the same.

Caden turned to his brother, "Can you hear that?"

"I can," Deklan said. "It's like it's talking to us."

"Welcoming us," Caden corrected, and I imagined that his eyes were wide as saucers beneath his black goggles.

"What's it saying?" I asked, unable to sense what they did. I expected it had something to do with their family heritage.

"Take my hand," Caden demanded, holding it out to me, palm up. I did, and Caden touched his other palm to a split in the rock. Nothing happened. He knit his brows together in confusion, removed his hand from the rock, and then placed it there again—still nothing. Deklan stepped forward, touching his own hand to the rock. But again, there was no reaction from the portal.

Deklan slipped a knife out of his holder and slid it across his palm. He pressed the wound to the stones. Again, no reaction. Caden repeated the same operation, and the results held steady. The brothers could hear the portal, and Arrick and I could feel that it was here, but it wasn't working.

Deklan pulled the journal out once more and flipped through the pages. We all huddled around him to read, but there were no specific instructions on how to use the portal. All it said was that the only ones who could activate it were of Arabella's family lineage.

I looked at Arrick. "How much time do we have left?"

"Fifteen minutes. Counting all the time we spent in the caverns and on the domicile."

Frustration and panic welled up inside of me so quickly that I had to work to tamp it down. If we ran all the way back right now, we might be able to make it. I looked at the brothers, most of their bodies covered from sight, but, judging by their slow movements and the labored rise and fall of their shoulders, I knew that they couldn't manage it.

"How bad is it?" I asked, staring at the bright pink on their hands, a clear indicator of radiation sickness.

"We're fine," Deklan croaked, and the weakness in his voice spoke volumes.

"You're not fine. Take off your scarves," I demanded. They shook their heads.

"Take them off now, or I swear to the ascended, I'll take them off myself," I snarled, my voice a desperate command. I had to know what I was dealing with here. Maybe Arrick and I could support them and get them back to the domicile, but then again, maybe it was already too late. Either way, I had to know.

They each hesitated a moment, and I stepped forward, reaching for their scarves. Caden raised his hand to stop me, and his shoulders dropped in resignation. His movements were painfully slow as he pulled off his glasses and his scarf. I sucked in a horrified breath—his skin was red and blistered, his face puffy. Deklan froze as he took in Caden's appearance and then followed his brother's lead. My hands flew to my mouth, and I stepped back. I turned to Arrick, involuntary tears swimming in my eyes.

"I thought you said we had an hour?"

Arrick stared at the brothers, his body tensing into the consistency of marble. His jaw flexed. "It was a guess." He let the stoic mask slip for a split-second, and I saw just how horrified he was by the sight of his friends. He reached out and gripped Caden's shoulder, fear and anxiety now plain on his face. "How long have you been feeling the full effects?"

Caden shrugged, resting his back against the rocky portal entrance. He slid down it, exhausted and no longer worried about putting up a front for us. That single act scared me more than anything else he could have said or done.

Deklan braced his hand against the rock, his knees going weak. Slumping, he joined his brother on the ground. "It's hard to say. All I know for sure is that we don't have much time left."

Desperation, fear, and helplessness warred for dominance in my mind as I watched the life flicker out of my new friends. Deklan coughed, and blood dribbled out of his mouth. I knelt before them and felt tears slide down my cheeks.

"I'm so sorry. We should never have asked you to do this," I trembled, but the words felt empty.

Caden shook his head and replied weakly, "You didn't. We volunteered. It was the only way to save our people."

I leaned forward and cupped his ruined face in my palm. "You're a good man, Caden." I turned to Deklan. "You both are."

I looked at Arrick, who crouched beside me, looking every bit as helpless as I felt. He rose to his feet and stepped to the portal, our friends' blood streaked across the stone. He slammed his palms onto it and pushed, the chords of his neck straining with his effort. "Son of a bitch. Open!" he growled, his desperation making my heart squeeze. With one more useless kick against the immovable stone, he turned to face me. "Can you get Caden? I'll carry Deklan. We can run them back to the cavern. Maybe we can make it in time…" He trailed off as I shook my head, tears slipping down my cheeks. He ran his hands through his hair, pulling it tight in frustration as he realized the futility of our situation.

There was no way around it—they were dying. Our only shot at saving them was to get this damned portal open and fast. My eyes locked onto his as I stood my ground, resolve stiffening my spine. I knew what I had to do. When I spoke, my voice held all the command I could muster.

"Don't try to stop me."

Then, I slipped my gun out of my holster, held it to my shoulder, and pulled the trigger.

CHAPTER 18

A Painful Return

"Bekka, wait!" Arrick shouted, reaching for me as the shot ripped through my soft tissue. The agony of it pierced through my arm like a white-hot poker. I screamed and would have fallen to my knees, but Arrick's arms wrapped around my waist and held me steady. Blood dripped down my arm and off my fingers in a red river, mixing with the dirt on the ground.

I shoved out of Arrick's grip at the sudden rush of power I felt clawing its way out from inside of me. Pain exploded in my brain—the wards' punishment—and I saw red. I screamed again, fighting to stay conscious. Arrick rushed forward, trying to catch hold of me, but I stumbled backward, away from all three of them.

When he reached for me once more, I cried, "No, get back! Stay away!"

I fought through the blinding agony in my shoulder and the even worse pain in my head. I reached for the well of power that I knew sat just out of my reach. To my astonishment, it swelled, breaking through the wards in an excruciating show of strength. In response, I grabbed hold, yanked it forward, and the sharp poker in my skull stopped just as quickly as it had started.

I watched, transfixed, as a blue glow permeated my entire body in seconds. It swelled, surrounding me in a swirling cloak of power and healing the gunshot wound to my shoulder and the pulsing bruise on my face. The surge of magic hit me hard and fast, and I tried to leash it, fighting desperately to keep it contained. But before I could get it under control, it exploded around me, and the resulting shockwave hit Arrick square in the chest. It slammed him into the dried corpse of the great tree but passed right over the brothers' supine bodies.

Dimly, I heard Arrick grunt in either pain or surprise, but I couldn't afford to worry about him now.

I needed to focus because it was the same as it was before.

It was too much, too big.

I couldn't control it.

I started to panic, but then I heard Arrick shout, "You control it, Bekka. Remember, it doesn't control you! *You control it.*"

His words reminded me that I had done it before with the Puhari. So, I tamped down the panic that the magic pulled up inside of me, and I took the reins. I commanded it. The blue energy pulsed once more and then relaxed, settling around me, a wild but obedient pet. With my goal in mind, I stepped forward, closer to the portal. I could see the problem now. Niko had been right—Afryel had sealed it when he left Moldize. The magic wound itself around the door, like mystical chains.

I focused my energy, managed to contain the vibrant hum of it, but every second was a fight for mastery over myself. How did one person handle this much power? Arrick, now recovered from the blow I'd issued earlier, stood beside me. I felt his presence and turned my head to him.

He saw the anxiety in my eyes and shook his head calmly. "You can do this. Focus on what you want to do. Bend it to your will. The power belongs to you, not the other way around."

I clung to his words and forced myself to make them true. I was Caden and Deklan's last hope. This was the only shot we had to save them; I would not blow it.

With my goal in mind, I closed my eyes and focused on what I wanted to do. Turning back to the crevice, I rested my hands on it and let out a pulse of power. Afryel's magic fought back, warring against my desire. He was the one to seal it, and the portal wanted to remain that way.

I countered his power, winding my magic around the chains and commanding the portal to open. Nothing happened. I dug deeper, pulled harder and more magic swelled inside me. I gathered it, imagining it as a large well at the center of my being. When it felt so big that I couldn't contain it anymore, I unleashed it. I punched my power at the portal with everything I had.

When it connected with the metaphysical chains, the seal cracked. Light fissured through the cracks, and I kept pushing. Just when it felt like my power would rip me in two, the seal broke altogether. The shackles shattered into a million magical pieces that flew away, shining on the roaring winds.

Stunned, I turned to Arrick. I had done it. He wrapped me into his arms and twirled me in a quick circle, elation overcoming both of us. He set me down, and we stared at the shining light of the now open portal in amazement.

"You did it," he yelled, warmth and appreciation radiating off him. He tugged my hand, and we rushed over to where Deklan and Caden lay, slumped as though overcome by exhaustion.

Arrick pulled Caden from the ground and passed his unconscious body to me, settling him on my shoulder. In the presence of the open portal, I could already feel some of my immortal strength return. As a result, his weight felt light as air as I walked through the doorway and back into our realm. Arrick and Deklan followed close behind.

We set the brothers down, gently propping their backs against the wall of the hallway the portal deposited us into. I turned back to the open portal, the mortal realm still visible through a thin sheen. I reached out with my magic and willed it closed. A bright light pulsed before the door slammed shut, closing off all visibility to the human's realm.

As soon as this was done, my body vibrated, hummed, and finished its transformation. My muscles grew stronger, and my skin thicker, the effervescent light that made me a goddess returning in full force. My power still bloomed blue around me, and I watched in amazement as the brothers also began to heal—the signs of radiation sickness melted away, and the rise and fall of their chests eased.

Within seconds, there was no more blood, no more burns, and no more ragged breathing.

Arrick's supposition had been right. When they entered our realm, the godly part of them had been enhanced. The healing song had called to their demi-god's blood, and it had answered. I wore a grin so wide that it threatened to split my face in two. They were going to be OK. They each looked at their hands in amazement and then stared at me.

They blinked and shielded their eyes with their fingers. Remembering that I still glowed like a blue spotlight, I pulled my power back inside of me and forced it beneath the surface. It was now within easy reach whenever I should need it. With the full power of my godly body at my disposal once more, my creation magic felt less volatile here, and I felt more in control. I wasn't sure if this was because I had more practice or because I was back in my godly body. Probably, it was a little bit of both.

Caden stared at Arrick and me, his mouth wide in shock. Then he closed his eyes, squinting tightly. "I'm not sure if you know this, but you guys are really bright."

CHAPTER 19

The Best We Can Do

After Caden and Deklan regained all their faculties, I'd hugged them tight enough to crack a few mortal ribs. Thank goodness they were demi-gods, or else they'd have been in serious trouble. Arrick had given each of them one of those manly, back-patting hugs, beaming all the while. Though his top priority had always been the salvation of the Moldizean planet and its mortal realm, I could see some of the tension he'd carried since my incident with the Puhari release.

His friends had made it, and I could tell now just how much the idea that they might not survive this terrible ordeal had weighed on him. But as I was learning, he was the type to push forward no matter what. To keep going. To never let the true extent of his fear show. At least, not until it had passed.

Without warning, Arrick reached out and held his palm face up. Black mist bloomed from his hand, falling and settling on the ebony floor. It grew, doubling its size, and stopped when it was just a few inches taller than Arrick himself.

"Let's go," Arrick strode purposely toward it.

I recognized this as his death god's ability to translocate wherever he pleased. It was the same mist he had used to kidnap me from my sister's wedding, so I knew that no harm would come to us if we used it. Arrick stepped through the black sheet and disappeared. I made to follow but then hesitated when I caught the expressions on the brothers' faces.

They blanched, feet not moving as they stared in stupefaction at the eerily powerful blackness before us. To be fair, if you didn't know what it was, it looked like a portal straight to hell. "It's just a doorway," I explained, resting a comforting hand on Caden's shoulder. "I know it looks creepy as all hell, but I promise, it's safe." Demonstrating, I turned on my heel and walked through without delay.

Arrick waited for me on the other side, and a few seconds later, Caden and Deklan appeared. The mist evaporated as quickly as it had come, and the brothers took in the scenery around them, awestruck expressions on their faces. It was the same reaction I had when I first laid eyes on Castle Molo's grand ballroom. The size and beauty of it still had me awestruck.

Before we could explain where we were, a door burst open at the far end of the ballroom, and Erykha flew through it.

"Thank the ascended!" she shouted as she drew closer. Arrick braced himself, and she flew into his arms. "Oh Arrick, you made it back! Both of you!" To my astonishment, she finished with her son and grabbed me, pulling me into a tight hug as well. Unsure how to react, I patted her back awkwardly. She pulled away and hurried to explain. "We've been on total lockdown here. We did everything we could to try to break through the barrier to the mortal realm, but we were cut off." She shrugged helplessly, her eyes dancing with elation at our return.

Her attention flicked to the brothers, who stood just behind us. My gaze followed hers, and I took them in once more; I was amazed by their transformation and not just because they were healed—they were also different here. Their skin shone in an iridescent shimmer, and their bodies seemed larger and stronger. It was like someone had removed a dimmer switch from them, and now we saw the real deal—the demigod within the mortal.

"And who are you two, exactly?" Erykha asked, her brows crinkling together. She wasn't so much unwelcoming as she was baffled by their presence. Like me, she could see that they were not exactly human. But they also weren't bright, shiny, and immensely powerful, like we were. They were something else, something *other*.

Arrick stepped forward, "Erykha, these are our cousins. Deklan and Caden."

Damion caught up with his wife just as Arrick delivered this news. Both of their mouths dropped open in shock, and they stayed that way for longer than could possibly be comfortable. I resisted the urge to snap my fingers in front of their faces to pull them out of their stupor.

After they recovered, we filled them in on the brothers' family story as quickly as we could. We even showed them the journal, which Deklan then tucked back into his shirt for safekeeping. To say that they were stunned would be the understatement of the millennia.

"So, that means Afryel was trying to change the way his father ruled. He wanted to merge with the humans and create a better world?" Erykha asked no one in particular, chewing on a nail in thought. She turned to her husband and questioned, "Why didn't my mother or father tell us this before they ascended?"

I cut in, having thought about this a lot since we first learned the truth. "My guess is that she was traumatized. She lost a lot that day, and then she had to start all over from scratch. I can only imagine how that would feel."

They all thought about this for a moment, and then Erykha sighed in resignation. Damion put a hand on his wife's shoulder to comfort her. "Hun, I don't think we'll ever know the full truth. Not unless we were able to find Afryel."

"He probably ascended years ago," Erykha murmured as she ran her fingers through her cape of dark hair. "At least this fills in some of the gaps we've had for so long."

"I hate to interrupt the revelations here," Deklan said, his voice quiet and intense. "But don't we have bigger problems to solve right now?"

"Of course," Erykha agreed, waving her hand and shaking her head as though to clear it. "I'm sorry, you're right."

Damion gestured for us to follow him. "We can talk while we walk." He led us quickly to the opposite end of the ballroom, his gait fast and determined.

I kept up with ease and enjoyed the perks of my immortal body. Words couldn't describe how much I'd missed it. I would never take it for granted again. I would also never forget what it felt like to be mortal, an experience I was oddly grateful for now. Well, now that it was done.

"How much time do we have left?" Arrick asked. "Has Gabryel come sniffing around yet?"

When we left this palace four mortal days ago, or about nine hours in godly time, we estimated right around one single, immortal day for my grandfather to find and extract me. We also projected less than a week before the planet would become uninhabitable. That was when we expected all the water to evaporate from its surface. It was hard to say just how much the situation had changed from the mortal realm—feeling the impacts up close and personal skewed our perspective. So, I agreed with Arrick. We needed an update on the cold, hard math. The facts, as they were, would be critical to deciding our next move.

"There's been no sign of him," Damion replied. "But we have no access to any intel from Valeria. They locked down tight after the wedding. It's been impossible to track his movements."

"OK, it could be worse," Arrick replied. "He could be here already." I didn't miss the relief in the set of his shoulders as he moved.

Erykha frowned. "Unfortunately, that's the only semi-good news we have. The sun is expanding rapidly and gaining too much mass. It's happening faster than we predicted."

We picked up the pace, hurrying down the hall. We exited into a large, circular room and crossed the black marble floors as quickly as we could manage. At the far end of that room, we breezed through a door that Damion held open for us. When we crossed the threshold, my mouth fell open. It was oversized and packed with electronics and spelled gadgets. A large, circular table dominated the center of the room, and a huge hologram hovered over it, depicting all the planets in this solar system. Right now, it was focused on the star that was rapidly swelling into a supernova. If I had to pick a phrase to describe this place, I would call it a command center.

As a royal deity who'd spent time studying each Pillar of Power, I knew the science around the life stages of a star. A star became a red giant when it used up the hydrogen supply inside its core and began the thermonuclear fusion of hydrogen around the core. It went supernova when it acquired too much mass, and the core collapsed, resulting in a massive explosion. My grandpa, the sole member and leader of the Creation Pillar of Power, had spent months teaching Remi and me about the importance of keeping our solar systems in balance and what would happen if we failed in our duties.

Erykha moved toward the holo as Caden and Deklan stared, mouths agape and unable to move from the doorway. Arrick and I followed his parents deeper into the room, stepping around the brothers to give them time to process their new surroundings.

Erykha strode to the holograph and slid into a leather chair directly in front of it. She pointed at the screen and a readout of mathematical symbols I didn't understand. "As you can see, the sun has expanded substantially in the time you've been gone. We thought we had four days, but now our calculations estimate only two days before the planet becomes uninhabitable." She stared at the blood orange orb dancing in front of her and chewed on her fingernail, a nervous habit. "But, the bigger problem is that it has become increasingly unstable. We're concerned that it could explode at any time. There's just no way to tell for certain when that will happen and if it goes supernova before we do something…" She shrugged helplessly, her eyes wide with concern.

"Then there won't be anything left to save. Including us," Deklan finished from behind us.

"Exactly," Damion replied. He fixed his attention on me. "We have to act quickly, Bekka."

My belly clenched as my plans for honing my gifts and practicing them a little more dissolved into the necessity of the moment. Based on the new situation they described, we no longer had time for that. We had to act soon or risk losing our window.

"What exactly are you proposing Bekka do about this?" Caden asked, eyes fixed on the glowing orb and the small planet next to it.

"We need her to repair it," Arrick explained. Everyone fell silent for a moment as we contemplated this. Given my limited knowledge of what had to be done to fix the existing sun, I was hesitant to go that route. The only idea I had was to add more hydrogen into the core, thus providing more fuel for the sun to burn, which could stop its expansion. It seemed like a solid theory to me, but science was not my forte, and I would not risk the lives of everyone left on that planet based on a hypothesis that I couldn't test first. And as far as I knew, no one had a sun handy that I could accidentally blow up without any repercussions.

I bit my lip and thought back to that day at my sister's wedding. I had created a sun then, and it had grown rapidly, progressing through its life cycle stages, at least until my grandfather had stopped it. But, if I could do that again while someone monitored my creation, they could stop me when it hit an ideal state for the planet. That just left the conundrum of, what do we do with the old star? I rubbed my temples in frustration and looked up, realizing that the room was now silent and that everyone stared at me.

"Did I miss something?" I asked, feeling oddly uncomfortable as if I had food in my teeth or maybe toilet paper stuck to my shoe. I ran my tongue over my teeth to be sure.

"No, but you're onto something. It would be risky to mess with the balance of hydrogen in an unstable star," Erykha said. Apparently, I had been thinking out loud. *It seemed that I needed some serious time in stasis sleep,* I thought, embarrassed that I had narrated my thoughts without even realizing it.

"She's right," Damion confirmed, gesturing to the data feed pouring in from the solar readings. Numbers and equations spit out in rapid-fire on the hologram, and he squinted at them. "Based on these readings, we're past the point where we can fix it. You'll have to start from scratch." I tried to keep my face impassive. Though this was in line with my own suggestion, it was daunting to realize that this was now our only viable option.

Caden's voice pierced through my reeling brain as he mused. "You asked what to do about the old sun… Can you disintegrate it, as you did with the Puhari raiders?"

I thought about his question and tried to stay emotionally distanced from the memory as I considered. Even though I knew that those Puhari raiders had deserved what they got, it still disturbed me how easily I'd made the decision to end them. Ignoring the deeper question of what that said about me, I focused on the issue at hand. So, could I do the same thing that I did to the Puhari to the sun? As far as ideas went, it wasn't bad.

I looked down at my hand, and blue bloomed around it, swirling up my arm. My power seemed less explosive here, more under my control, probably because I wasn't in a blind panic or injured.

The only way I'd know for sure whether I could do it on command was to test it out for myself. I looked around for something I could use and spotted a half-eaten sandwich on the table. It was the only disposable, organic matter in the immediate area. So, I focused on it, and I pushed my power out of me gently. It trailed along the ground and wound around the food. I closed my eyes, concentrating. Then, I could see them. The molecules, the atoms. The very building blocks of life that made it. With a single thought, I pulled them apart. It disintegrated into nothing, and there was no sign left that it had ever existed.

When I finished, I looked up at them. "It's not exactly a sun, but I might be able to manage. The only thing is, that's not the part I'm most worried about. I'm more concerned about the actual creation. At Remi's wedding, my star had a mind of its own. I didn't exactly have control over how fast it grew or what stage of life it was in. What if I start creating it, and then I blow us all to kingdom come anyway?"

"You see the readings here?" Erykha asked, pointing to the holo. I nodded, and she continued, "We could modify this program to run an analysis on the progression of your creation, just like you suggested." Then she turned to Damion. "We could monitor it and ensure that you stop at just the right point in the star's development."

Damion nodded with enthusiasm. "Using these machines and Erykha's power, we should be able to give you a heads up. Not long. We're talking seconds, maybe a minute, to ensure accuracy. But it's still something."

"Okay, so that solves one worry. But I have another one. What happens if I can't stop?"

"You'll be able to stop," Arrick assured me. The confidence in his tone was inspiring but probably not warranted. I couldn't stop last time, so what made him so sure this time would be different?

"I don't know," I hedged. "The power and energy that it takes to create something like this—" I threw my hands out to gesture toward the swirling orange-red hologram in front of me. "You don't understand. It took on a life of its own. It drew from my energy, gained mass, and didn't exactly ask for my permission."

I looked at all of them, but they were silent. I assumed that they were all thinking about how to solve this issue. But then slowly, both Erykha's and Damion's gazes turned to Arrick and, as though controlled by the same puppeteer, their brows rose in question.

"If it comes down to it." Arrick stared at his parents, careful not to meet my eyes. "I can stop you. But that will have to be your choice."

"What do you mean you can stop me?" I asked, staring at him in surprise. "The only way you could stop me is to—" I broke off, frozen in shock. He stayed silent, waiting for his meaning to sink in, and when it did, I shivered. "You mean you'd pull my soul from my body, don't you?" My voice was small in the large room, and I felt chills run down my spine at the thought. It was the only thing that I could think of that would stop me in the throws of full power. He was a death deity, capable of manipulating the metaphysical and of collecting souls, ferrying them to the other side. In Valeria and the rest of the known multiverse, this was illegal to do to another deity and was punishable by death via the surface of the sun. So, if I couldn't stop, then I'd be damning us both to death. Because if he used his death deity powers on me, my grandpa would find out and I knew he would never let that slide, even if I had given my consent.

His eyes fixed on me, and I could see the pain in them. Of course, he already knew the risk to both of us. "Yes, that's exactly what I mean."

I stepped closer to him, putting my body into his space bubble. "Well then," I said, trying for bravery that I didn't feel. "I guess I better stop. For both our sakes."

"I guess you better," he agreed. He reached out a hand, brushed a stray lock of hair off my face, and tucked it behind my ear. His eyes bored into mine, and I felt my legs go weak under the intensity of his stare. "But for what it's worth, I know you can do this."

At least that made one of us.

He said it would be my choice. Which meant that if I lost control over my creation, I would have to decide between saving everyone with my death or letting the sun get so big that it would blow us all to pieces and kill us anyway.

In all honesty, there wasn't much of a choice here—if I intended to help, I had to accept the risks that came along with it. But even knowing this, the words still lodged in my throat, and I had to swallow hard to speak once more. "You have my permission to do what you must," I vowed, my voice and my mind carefully disconnected from emotion.

I would just have to make sure it didn't come to that because the only way that Arrick and I would make it through this alive was if I stopped when Erykha and Damion said to. So, rather than fixate on all the outcomes that could result in both of our deaths and dissolve into a puddle of fear, I decided to deal with our next problem. "There is one other thing. I can't create and disintegrate simultaneously."

Damion nodded. "You're right. Timing is the other tricky part of this plan. We'll need to move one sun into place at the exact same time that the other is disintegrated. Otherwise, the temperature fluctuation will kill everyone and everything on the planet."

"That's a pretty serious problem. But I'm guessing that you have a plan?"

"This is where our time deities' powers will come into play," Erykha explained. "You'll have two actions that have to be completed separately but that need to appear to the mortal plane as though they happened simultaneously. To combat that, we've created a time lag for the mortals' protection and a barrier for your protection while you're working."

My mind swirled with questions. "How will that work exactly?"

Erykha pulled up a map of the mortal realm and how it flowed around and through the celestial plane, shared but separate. "You will need to be in position here." She tapped at a spot on the cusp between the godly and mortal planes, close enough to the existing sun to do severe damage to any deity in that vicinity. I winced, and she gave my hand a reassuring squeeze before she explained further. "The barrier that we've built for your protection is here, between your location and the existing sun. It's also positioned to protect you from your own creation too when that time comes. Then, just beyond that spot, closer to the mortal realm, is a portal that we can tap into. From what we understand, Afryel used it for basic maintenance before he disappeared. We'll utilize that to move the sun from the immortal to the mortal realm."

Damion picked up her explanation. "So, once you're in position, we open the portal, start the time lag and raise the barrier. You'll disintegrate the old sun in the mortal plane; then, you'll create the new one in the immortal realm. We think your power will have more teeth behind it if you create the star in the godly realm rather than trying to place it in the mortal realm right away," he clarified. Then he continued, "We'll use the projected model to tell you when to stop. Once you're done, we'll tap into the portal and move the sun, as Erykha said. The only thing is, even with the time lag, the most we can give you is about 15 minutes before time snaps back. Do you think that'll be enough?"

I exhaled loudly as I thought about it. "I think so." I remembered the rapid growth of the star at the wedding and how quickly I was able to break apart the molecules of that sandwich and the Puhari raiders. Unfortunately, I would not have the opportunity to practice on anything as massive as the sun. As a result, my answer was tentative. "I guess we'll find out how long it takes for me to disintegrate a red supergiant, and then we'll have our answer."

Arrick chimed in. "If Bekka's protected by a barrier, how can she access the old star to disintegrate it and create a new one behind it? And how are we tapping into the portal to move an entire sun, exactly?"

"That's all in the timing and the composition of the barrier," Damion said, nodding and gesturing for Erykha to call something up on the holo.

When Erykha pulled up the new screen, she continued the explanation, "The barrier here won't do anything but protect Bekka from the harmful rays of the sun. So, she'll still be able to access the red giant through it and via the open portal to destroy it. Then once she's finished creating the new star, we will run an algorithm through the portal to ensure that her creation settles into exactly the right spot. Long story short, the algorithm creates a modified vacuum effect and will suck the new star through the portal and into the ideal position." She tapped the screen to show where the current red giant sat. "Easy as pie."

She called up another screen, and my eyes went blurry as I tried to read it. This had to be the algorithm that she was talking about.

"Whoa." I leaned forward and squinted at all the complex figures and numbers. "This is complicated." And way over my head. "Did you do this?" I asked Erykha.

She shrugged modestly before she nodded, "With some help from our time and dimensional deities. It's what I do."

Impressed, I thought back to a conversation I'd had with Arrick before we made it to Itoriah, in that hallway with those horrible feeds to Moldize. Arrick had mentioned that they had time deities here, but none powerful enough to go back a substantial amount of time. It explained why the lag could only buy us fifteen minutes.

It made sense, so I nodded thoughtfully. "So to recap, the first step is to set up the conditions here, barrier, and time lag. Then I disintegrate the current red supergiant from behind the barrier. Next, I create the new sun close to the portal in the immortal plane, but still behind the protective barrier. You guys run your projections and tell me when to stop. Once I stop, you deploy the algorithm, and the sun pops into the right place." It was a simplified version of the plan, but it always helped me to think of things in their simplest terms. I continued my thoughts. "Once the time lag, which I assume stops time in the Moldizean mortal realm, runs out, the new sun will be in place. Then the mortals will have a brand spanking new sun at exactly the right temperature in exactly the right spot to sustain life."

"Sounds about right to me," Arrick said. "The only part of this plan that concerns me is that fifteen-minute window. You'll have to disintegrate our current sun and build another--all within that timeline."

My fingers absently tapped against my chin. There was no way to know for sure if I could manage it, not without practicing on the real thing. But again, I couldn't just destroy an entire solar system for practice. "If it comes down to the wire and I can't make it happen, we'll…we'll just have to cross that bridge if we come to it. For now, let's stick with what we've got."

Arrick's jaw flexed, "The risk if we don't have a contingency plan is that the sun is either partially created or completely gone when time snaps back. That seems like a big gap to me."

"You're not wrong. But what other choice do we have?" I racked my brain to think of another possibility, any other option. "Is there like a revert option on that time lag? An undo button or something?" It was a long shot, but a girl could dream.

Erykha's eyes shifted to her husband, regret evident in them. "No, there isn't, but it's a risk we're going to have to take. The effect is net-net either way. Do nothing, and everyone dies. Do this and mess up, and everyone dies."

I ran fingers through my hair in frustration as I turned to Arrick. "So, I'll just have to make that 15 minutes work."

"You're all missing one key thing," Deklan said, arms crossed over his chest, calm in the face of possible doom. "What about Gabryel?"

I cursed under my breath. "He's right."

Everyone stayed silent for a few moments as we tried to figure out how to handle that wildcard. I didn't want to hurt him or do anything too drastic. He was my grandpa, and I loved him. But I also did not want him to interrupt me before I finished what I started.

"I have an idea if you're interested," Deklan said.

We all gestured for him to continue. "Caden and I can't help much here. But we can be decoys if you have two extra domiciles we can use. Then when Bekka and Arrick leave, we'll go in different directions. That way, if Gabryel shows up at an inopportune moment, he will have three domiciles to contend with instead of just one. It isn't much, but it could buy you some time."

"We have four domiciles left in the castle, all outfitted for space travel," Arrick said. "I think this is a good idea. It would force Gabryel to check each one individually, and it would reduce the odds of him picking ours first. I can show you how to operate them."

I smiled at Deklan. "I agree. It's a good plan. But you have to promise me you won't do anything to provoke him, and you definitely can't attack him. He's not someone you should mess around with. I don't think he'd hurt you, but he's going to be very angry. As far as he knows, I've been kidnapped by his sworn enemy and am being held against my will."

Caden held up his hands. "Alright, alright, you got it. We'll keep it peaceful."

Deklan grumbled an affirmative reply, and I knew it was the best I would get from him.

Erykha slapped her hand down on the table surrounding the holo. "Alright then, it sounds like we have a plan."

"How much time do you think it will take to rework that program and build that model?" Arrick asked his mom, crossing his arms over his chest in thought.

Erykha rubbed her chin as she analyzed the existing data stream. "Probably a few hours. I'll need to work out the kinks and make sure it performs as designed."

She looked away from the readout, rose from her seat, and rested a hand on my shoulder. "In the meantime, Bekka, you need to rest as much as possible, get some stasis sleep, and gather your power. Even I can see you're drained from your time in Moldize. Your light is dim."

"But I feel fine. I can stay and help."

Erykha gave a stern shake of her head, "If you don't rest and recover now, you won't have enough power to manage what needs to be done. You know our magic isn't infinite. It's like a well that needs to be replenished. You need stasis sleep to build up those reserves."

"She's right." Arrick twined his fingers into mine. "You have the hardest job out of all of us, and we need you at the top of your game. So, shower, eat and get some rest. All of that will revive your power reserves and make you stronger."

I stared down at our joined hands and resisted the urge to argue further. They all made good points. Of course, I knew that our powers weren't infinite, and I knew I'd used a substantial amount of energy punching through the portal. The problem was that I wasn't sure I could manage to rest with the nerves jumping around in my belly. But then again, I could eat, and I could definitely use a shower.

I tilted my head to look up at the god I had grown so close to and shared so much with over the last few days. I searched his eyes and thought of spending a few more hours alone with him. Ideally, with his body wrapped around mine. I wanted it more than I dared to imagine. Because who knew how this would end or what would happen next?

"You're right." What good would I be if I didn't have the strength to complete my mission? I thought of Niko and Kaleb, Mariah and Jarrod, Donny, and all the other people I'd met back on Moldize. They were all stuck on that death trap of a planet; I was their only shot at survival. "I could use all of those things."

"Good, it's decided," Erykha said, eyes locking with mine. "Let us do our part now, and you rest."

I looked around the room at all the gods and demigods who surrounded me. We were a team, and I was supremely grateful for them. Caden and Deklan had done nothing but help me since the day I met them in Itoriah. Erykha and Damion had planned most of this mission on pure optimism and faith that they would get the help they needed. Then there was Arrick. He would be there to help me through this, no matter what happened.

"OK. But come get me as soon as you're ready. And don't forget, we aren't just worried about the sun. Keep an eye out for my grandfather too. If he gets here before we finish—" I broke off and shuddered, letting them imagine the rest.

"Of course," Damion assured me. "We'll let you know immediately if his status changes." With a firm grip on my hand, Arrick led me out a different door than our original entrance. He then guided me down another hall that looked exactly the same as all the other halls. This place was easily the most confusing building I had ever been inside.

As we strode down the hall, we made a few turns and then ended up back at the room where I had awoken on that first day here. Arrick opened the door for me, and I walked inside. I let out a deep breath as I looked around at all the comforts and furnishings, so grateful to be back where things like mattresses and warm, running water were the norm. I would never take them for granted again.

Inside the room, Arrick wrapped his arms around me and pulled me in close. "Everything is going to be OK," he whispered, his mouth close to my ear. I wasn't sure if he said the words for my benefit or his own. But it was clear from the way that he held me, just a little too tightly, that he was worried.

If I had to guess, I imagined he was most concerned about what would happen if he had to stop me mid-creation. As I turned my cheek into his chest, I tried to picture how I would feel if the roles were reversed. Could I kill him if it meant saving every mortal in Moldize? The truth was that I didn't know. Mistaking my silence for fear, Arrick murmured, "Don't worry, I'll be with you every step of the way."

I sighed into his chest. "I know you will."

"Good." He kissed the top of my head. "I'll see you in a few hours then?"

Despite the butterflies in my belly and the chills that crept up my spine at his nearness, I managed to comprehend his words. "Wait," I blurted, turning my cheek into his chest to peer up at him. "You're leaving?"

"Well, we're not fake married anymore, and we have sufficient blankets for warmth. So you can have the room to yourself, and you can have your privacy. I thought you might want that. Might want space." He trailed off, his eyes searching mine, trying to read my emotions.

"Do you want to leave?" I tried to keep my voice even. I didn't want the neediness I felt to show. I wanted him to think of me as strong and independent. But the reality was, I needed the distraction, the company, and the comfort his presence would offer.

"I want whatever you want. I don't want to pressure you, Bekka. Or force you to spend time with me when you'd rather not." Where was he getting this stuff? When had I ever made him feel like I wanted space from him?

"So, you want to stay if I want you to?" I asked, making sure that I interpreted him correctly. He nodded, and I breathed a sigh of relief. "In that case, please don't go. Or at least, come back after you change and shower. Because I gotta be honest, you stink." I furrowed my brow. "We both do." To be fair, it was not our fault. We still wore the clothes from the battle, and they were coated in an array of grime.

His chest moved in a quiet laugh, and still holding me against him, he leaned down to kiss me. When our lips touched, the kiss was filled with raw need. He deepened it, and when we broke apart, my body yearned for more, begged for it. But he stepped away and ran a hand through his shaggy hair, the chestnut strands shining in the light of the room.

"I'm going to get that shower, change, and find some food. I also need to see to Deklan and Caden. But I'll be back as soon as I can. I promise." He kissed my palm, and then he turned away from me.

He started to walk away, but I stopped him. "Oh, one more thing!"

He turned back to face me. "What, miss me already?" he teased, the lopsided grin he bestowed upon me making my knees wobble.

"You have a very high opinion of yourself, you know that?"

His grin flashed wider, a thousand-kilowatt smile. I rolled my eyes and remembered the little girl I had met upon my arrival. "Where's Lilja?" He had promised me that I would see her again, but there had been no sign of her since that first introduction.

"My parents evacuated her the day you arrived in Moldize, along with all of the other deities," Arrick said.

"So, she's safe then?" I felt a surprising level of relief.

"Very," he assured me. "No matter what happens with this sun, she'll be okay."

"Good," I breathed, my shoulders relaxing with his words.

His gaze was measured and approving. "Now I'm gonna go so that I can get back here sooner. But, first, do you have any special requests for food?"

I thought about his question. As far as I was concerned, it was a serious one since it could be my last meal, ascended forbid. Then as I settled on the answer, a smile bloomed across my lips.

CHAPTER 20

Missing Out

We sat on my bed in clean clothes, on clean sheets, with clean bodies and wet hair, eating the nectar of the gods. Or as I liked to call them, tacos. They were introduced to me by this awesome deity from another universe, and became an instant classic in the Valerian immortal realm. We even introduced it to the mortals there. Talk about crossing multi-verse cultural boundaries to spread deliciousness.

Now that we were back in the godly realm and my mind was settled, I found that it kept drifting back to the scene with Niko and Lorus. Whenever I thought of the expression on Niko's face when we stumbled upon him, my entire body broke out in chills. "Have you thought about Niko at all?" I asked, setting down my half-eaten taco and wiping my hands on a napkin. I couldn't help but feel partially responsible for whatever had snapped in him that made him do what he did.

Arrick shrugged and asked, "You mean with Lorus?" He set his food down, too, and watched me, waiting for me to elaborate.

I nodded gravely. "Do you think he's OK? He seemed… I don't know… disturbed?" I wasn't sure how else to describe it.

"I hope so. What he did to Lorus…" Arrick shook his head. "Things like that leave a mark on a person's soul. I think it's going to take him a long time to make peace with that. He may never move past it. But for his family's sake, I hope he does."

Chewing on a lip, I asked, "Do you think we're the reason he snapped?" I remembered the compassion and intelligence that had once tempered Niko's more dangerous edges. The last time I saw him, those two components of his personality were gone. It begged the question, would they return?

Arrick shook his head, "Niko has always been on the edge. It's what made him a great leader for Itoriah. But I think when his home was destroyed, and his people were killed, it broke something inside him."

I thought about this, turned back to my plate, and picked up the taco again. I forced myself to finish the last few bites and tried to think about something other than Niko. In an effort to accomplish that feat, I changed the subject, "So, what will your parents think about us spending time alone in my room, sleeping together?"

I could tell that Arrick was as happy with the change in topic as I was. He grinned. "If they notice, which I doubt they will, I think they would be happy for me."

"Happy about the idea of possible premarital relations?" I opened my mouth into a perfect "o" and tried my best to look aghast. I didn't look aghast often, so I hoped that I got it right.

He finished the last of his taco and then shook his head in amusement. "Things aren't the same here as they are in Valeria. Relations, as you call them, are a choice between two people. They are not bound by marriage."

"Really?" I asked, scrunching up my nose in thought. I fell back on my pillow and stared at the ceiling.

"Really." He moved our empty plates onto the bedside table and then leaned back to lay beside me. I snuggled closer to him, and he put an arm around me. "My parents aren't even married. They're just... together." He shrugged his broad shoulders as though unable to explain further. It surprised me to hear that the ruling deities of this universe weren't married and that they had no contract that dictated the terms of their relationship. All royal marriages in the Twelve Realms were arranged and contracted with prenuptial agreements that protected what each party "got" out of the arrangement. That wasn't to say that love matches didn't exist. It was just that love usually came later.

"You make it sound so easy." I sighed, knowing that my own parents would not be excited about whatever was happening between the two of us. "Why do you think your parents would be pleased if they knew?"

"Well, I don't normally date the goddesses here on Moldize. So, I think they would just be happy to see me with someone, period," he answered, giving me a teasing wink. I elbowed his ribs, and he pretended it hurt for my benefit. He was such a gem like that. He paused, chewing on his lower lip as though debating whether he wanted to tell me something. He opened his mouth, stopped himself, and let out a long sigh, remaining silent.

I rolled onto my side to face him. "What is it?"

When he replied, he was careful not to make eye contact with me. "I want to tell you something, but I'm afraid you might take it the wrong way."

I'd never seen him quite so nervous before.

Anxiety jumped in my belly. "Well, now I'm curious."

After another long pause, he shook his head. "Never mind."

I narrowed my eyes. "Uh-uh, no way. You're not getting out of this that easily. I don't know if you've figured this out about me yet, but I'm relentless. I will pester you until you cave. And if you're wondering, no, I will not tire out and give up. I don't have that in me."

"Are you saying that I'm doomed to be hounded for all eternity until you get your way?"

"Yes." I arched a brow for emphasis. "So now that we're on the same page, please, continue your thought."

When I stayed silent, waiting for him to continue, his features shifted, and he grew serious. "What I was going to say is that I know that we haven't known each other for long, but I like this." He rubbed my arm to demonstrate what he meant. "The truth is, I've liked you for a while. Even before you ever came here."

He paused and visibly braced for my reaction. My brows knit together in thought, and then his meaning clicked into place. My grin spread wide, and I pointed an accusing finger at him, "Oh my gods, you are such a creeper. You liked me when you were stalking me!"

He glowered at me, "For the last time, I was not stalking you! We were doing surveillance!" His expression showed amusement intertwined with irritation. "It was a mission to save the planet."

"Sure it was, Mr. Creepy," I teased.

He leveled a finger at me and squinted one eye, "See? This is exactly why I didn't want to tell you."

I threw my head back and laughed, the levity of this moment a breath of fresh air and just what I needed to get my mind off the heaviness of my responsibilities. I stopped after a few moments and offered him the olive branch I was always going to give him. I just couldn't resist the urge to give him a hard time first.

"Well, I'm glad you did. And for what it's worth, I like this too."

His shoulders seemed to relax with my assurance that we were on the same page.

We sat in silence for a while, and I contemplated just how complicated this would get after our mission, as he put it, was over. It wasn't like I was going to abandon my family and stay in Moldize indefinitely. I was pretty sure that Arrick felt the same about Valeria. Besides, he would never be welcomed there, even if he wanted to leave with me. This meant that we literally had an entire universe standing between us with no way to communicate if things stayed as they were now.

I gnawed on my lip as a darker thought entered my mind. *When my grandpa shows up here, I know I can convince him not to disintegrate Moldize into dust.* But I didn't have any delusions about him suddenly reconciling with the deities here, especially after Arrick had kidnapped me. Convincing him to do that would take time and would require proof, of which I had nothing concrete. There was only my own personal experience here, which I seriously doubted that he would consider an unbiased perspective. Even if he did believe me, it would be a long road until relations were healed and we opened up a line of communication or travel between our worlds.

Arrick broke the silence, "You know I'll find a way back through to see you, right? If you want me to, I mean."

I considered his offer and understood what he meant. He would find a chink in the armor of Valeria's protections, just as he had when he kidnapped me. My body hummed with our closeness, and I peered up at him from beneath my lashes, "I want you to."

Arrick rolled to face me, wrapped his arms around my waist, and covered my lips with his. My toes curled, and my heart sighed. He lit up every part of me, so I breathed him in like he was a drug. No one had ever made me feel so alive before, and I reveled in the feel of every inch of his body against mine. I didn't know if this electricity between us was real or if the direness of our situation caused it. But at that moment, I didn't care. All I knew was that I wanted more. Twisting my fingers into his hair, I deepened the kiss.

Our hands roamed freely, touching, and exploring. He trailed his fingers down my braid, brushing them over my neck and down the length of my spine. I shivered, dragged my hands down his back, and slipped them under his shirt. Desperate for the feel of his skin against me, I pushed the fabric up and pulled it over his head. Running my fingertips down the rungs of his sculpted abs, I was reminded again of the warrior's body beneath the godly polish. He had spent so much time with his people and done more than any immortal I knew to help them. To save them from a fate he found unconscionable.

Pulling back, I cupped his face in my hands and looked at him. His hooded eyes were filled with desire and passion, and I knew that mine were a mirror image. Before I could second guess myself, I breathed, my voice soft and husky. "I want to be with you."

I'd had some time to think it over and, if things went wrong tomorrow, I wanted to do just one thing for myself. Before I came here, I had lived my life to please my family and to support my people. And I knew that when I went home, my life would be given over in service to Valeria. As a result, I would have little say in the details of it. So instead, I would do this one thing for myself. I would make sure that my first time was with someone I chose, with someone who meant something to me. No matter what happened tomorrow or the day after, I knew that I wouldn't regret it.

"You're sure?" Arrick asked, brushing a finger over my swollen lips. In answer, I sat up and slid my shirt over my head, tossing it to the side. My breasts were bare, exposed, and his eyes went dark with desire.

"I'm sure," I answered, and then I leaned down to kiss him, fastening my teeth to his bottom lip. He growled with pleasure, rolled me onto my back, and did a thorough job showing me just how much I had been missing out on all this time.

CHAPTER 21

Hidden Meanings

I woke to voices, and my eyes popped open. I reached for the sheet to cover my naked body. I must have kicked it off in my sleep. When I got the fabric settled around me, I noticed that Arrick was gone from the bed and at the door, talking in low voices with Erykha. I heard the door click shut and saw him walking toward me as I sat up in bed. He wore black pajama bottoms and carried coffee. I let the grin spread wide across my face as I appreciated the very delightful fact that he was shirtless.

"Go time?" I asked, reaching for the mug and taking a glorious sip.

He nodded and settled in next to me, "They're finished with the model, and they're ready for us. Also…" Arrick rubbed the back of his neck as he hesitated.

"What's wrong?" I asked, belly jumping.

"Gabryel's here."

"What?!" I vaulted from the bed and spilled coffee all over the white sheets. I stood, chest heaving, naked as the day I was born. Oddly, I didn't mind this time. "What do you mean he's here?"

"Don't worry," Arrick reassured me, gently pulling the half-full mug from my shaking hands. "He hasn't broken through our protections yet, but he's figured out we're the ones who took you. We need to hurry."

When I blew out a semi-relieved breath, he handed my cup back to me. "I'll finish this quick then." I took a few more hurried sips and then set it on the night table beside the bed. I scurried over to the armoire full of clothes and picked something that seemed appropriate for the day. But then, what did one wear when one planned to create a star, destroy another, and save a planet from extinction? The answer, as it turned out, was a hoodie, jeans, and slip-on sneakers. I would not take any chances that I would trip on some loose shoelaces, and that would be what caused the destruction of Moldize. Once I was dressed, I pulled my hair into a tight braid and wrapped it into a bun, pinning it in place.

I turned to face Arrick and nodded decidedly. "I'm ready." Coincidentally, he was wearing the same thing— hoody, jeans, and sneakers. I grinned despite the grim situation. "What is this? Now that we've slept together, you're trying to get all coupley and matchy-matchy with me?"

"I'm sorry, but did you say coupley?" he asked, all innocence and surprise. "I thought this was a casual thing. You know, no attachments, just sex."

I threw a pillow at his face, and he caught it easily. I was under no illusions that last night meant that we were together now, but I certainly didn't qualify it as casual sex. Laughing, he gathered me into his arms and settled his hands around my waist. "I'm just kidding. I think we both know that last night was anything but casual." His eyes darkened, and my breath caught in my throat at the intensity of his gaze. He grazed his thumb over my cheek. "When all of this is over, we have a lot to figure out. But for right now, for today, I just want you to know that I've got your back."

The words caused my heart to throb as I realized that this could be the last day I would ever get to see him. What if he never found a way through the protections in Valeria? Hell, what if I died? What if we both died? I remembered that conversation about what he could do if I couldn't stop myself and shivered.

After a short moment to compose myself, I looked up into his preternatural, green eyes. So unusual and so very gorgeous. "I've got yours too, you know."

In response, he kissed me, trailing his fingers along my neck and up to my cheek.

When we broke away, my body felt loose and limber. I was as ready as I would ever be for what needed to be done. "We should go. We don't have a lot of time."

Arrick released me and opened the door to let me walk through first. "Don't worry, Bekka, we'll get through this."

I heard his words, tried to make them feel real. Tried to accept that there was a chance that they weren't. If I blew us to kingdom come today, at least I could die knowing that I gave up everything to help real people, good people, live and thrive on a planet that had been through so much pain and suffering.

As we hurried down the halls of the palace hand-in-hand, I tried not to let my mind wander to the gloomy. I worked to keep a level head and held my power close. I could feel it simmering within me, and I knew it was stronger from the stasis sleep and maybe even the sex. Who knew that would help? But the question was, would it be strong enough? Would I be fast enough?

When we entered the command center, Erykha and Damion were sitting around the hologram. Deklan and Caden were there too, but they stood closer to the edges of the room. They looked ready to play their part, and I inclined my head in greeting.

Erykha gestured to a table along the back wall. "There are pastries there if you're hungry. You'll want to eat quickly. We don't have much time left before Gabryel's upon us."

I grabbed one filled with cream cheese from a tray and devoured it, savoring every delicious bite. As I did, I wondered if this was really the breakfast of champions. Shouldn't I have a more balanced meal before attempting to save an entire solar system? Meh, sugar, and carbs were probably good enough. At the very least, I would get a nice energy rush.

As I ate and drank a second cup of coffee, Erykha and Damion gave us the rundown. "OK, we've laid out the timeline," Erykha said, tapping a few keys on a keyboard as the hologram shifted from a solar analysis to a precise schedule. "We decided it would be better not to delay. So, we've already erected the barrier here." She indicated the point we discussed yesterday. "It will take you approximately five minutes to get to its border using one of our domiciles. We'll need to make sure that we are in communication through the entire mission."

Arrick and I nodded our ascent just before Damion picked up her explanation. "When you arrive, we'll start the countdown and initiate the time lag. This part needs to be very precise. You'll need to know exactly how much time you have left at any given moment, and you must start working immediately. No delays. Got it?"

"Understood," Arrick agreed.

"We won't delay," I promised.

Damion continued. "The brothers will already be out there, acting as decoys. But there's no guarantee that it will work as planned. So, the faster you can start, the better."

Before we could say more, Erykha cut in. "Bekka, your only focus is that sun and then the new one you're going to build. Arrick will keep in contact with us, giving us updates on your progress. He will also take care of the countdown. Don't waste any of your energy worrying about us doing our part. Just focus on yours, and we promise, ours is taken care of."

"You got it," I said. "I'll let Arrick take point on communication, and I'll just focus on what I need to do."

"Good, we start in approximately ten minutes," Damion said, nodding at the clock. Ten minutes from now was 1:56 in the afternoon. *What an arbitrary time for such an immense task,* I thought, staring at the numbers on the holo.

Erykha handed me a backpack. "It's full of supplies. Water and food, mostly. Stay hydrated, and don't let yourself get too hungry. You'll need this to recover afterward. Your reserves will be depleted."

I swallowed nervously and took the pack.

Arrick grasped my hand, and I turned my attention to him. "It's time."

At this, Erykha reached for me and pulled me into a bone-crushing hug. Then she whispered in my ear, "Good luck, Bekka. Don't forget, you were made for this."

I pulled away, guts roiling with nerves. She smiled warmly at me and cupped my cheeks, eyes full of certainty, and then she turned to her son. They embraced, the hug firm as she told him how much she loved him.

Damion hugged me too and then offered me a quick and easy, "See you soon." He did the same to his son, unable to accept anything but a positive outcome. It was nice to know that one of us was a pure optimist.

Caden and Deklan hung back, waiting for the family farewells to conclude. We broke away from Erykha and Damion and approached them. They would be accompanying us to the domiciles, and then we would go our separate ways from there. "Are you guys ready?" I asked.

"I think the bigger question is, are you?" I could see the concern in Caden's eyes. Affection warmed me, and I reached up and wrapped him in a hug.

"Ready as I'll ever be," I murmured just loud enough for both brothers to hear me. When I pulled away, I stood back, overcome with emotion. We had been through so much together. They had saved me from a terrible fate in the battle at Itoriah. Then they had been willing to give their lives to help us get back here, to save their friends. Eyes filling with tears, I blinked hard to stop them. "I can't remember if I ever thanked you both for what you did for me."

"Which time?" Deklan asked, his mouth twitching into a grin. "You attracted more trouble than an untrained scavenger with a crossbow."

I let out an involuntary laugh and pressed my hand over my mouth to stifle it. "For all of them. I owe you both."

Arrick reached out a hand to each of them, and they clasped forearms in that way guys do. "We all owe you. Thank you."

Once we said our goodbyes, a sleek door slid open. Across the hall, another door opened, and Caden and Deklan stepped into it. I waved at them one last time as Arrick led me into what turned out to be an elevator. He pressed a button labeled "Domicile," and the door slid shut with a smooth whoosh, Caden, and Deklan's faces disappearing from view. As we ascended, my nerves began to jitter. Or maybe it was all that coffee and sugar.

I reminded myself that I was a badass creation deity. I told myself that I was made for this. I reassured myself that I had done everything I planned to do today before. After I finished my mantra, the elevator doors slid open. I followed Arrick out and into a short airlock made of thick plastic tubing. Outside was pitch black, and I marveled, realizing that we had just been transported into a space station. For all his talk about a lack of upgrades since Afryel's departure, this was first-rate godly technology. It spoke to Erykha's talents as a goddess of physics, despite the lack of other high-powered deities here to help her.

Looking ahead, I saw a domicile, this one outfitted for space travel. Approaching the end of the airlock, Arrick keyed into an electronic pad and a seal formed around the vehicle's door. I heard air rushing into the room, though it was still closed off to us. Then the door slid open in time with the domicile, and we walked inside.

The spacecraft was luxurious, outfitted in two-tone white and black leather seats and a large hologram station in the center of the room. Inside, there was a cozy lounge area and a bedroom with two plush looking cots. There was enough space for at least ten people to sit comfortably in the main room. I slipped into a leather seat near the center of the lounge.

Arrick claimed what was obviously a captain's chair. He unlocked the holo and silently keyed in the destination coordinates Erykha and Damion gave us. When he finished, I felt the airlock detach and the forward rush of momentum as we took off into space. The holo displayed our position on the map, along with two other dots that represented Caden and Deklan's decoy domiciles. They were positioned on either side of us, rapidly approaching the sun, but from different angles. They would be safely away from the creation but in a position close enough that it would throw my grandpa off our trail, should he break through the Moldizean protections before I finished my task.

I watched through small, slot windows as we hurtled through the vast darkness. Time counted down on the hologram as Arrick queued up the communication line and ran through checks with Erykha and Damion. I stayed silent, trying to center myself. To prepare for the massive undertaking I was about to attempt. Anxiety rocketed through me, and I did the best I could to quell my rising fear. I could do this, I assured myself, falling back on what I knew to be true. I was made to do this. It had been prophesied. It was my destiny.

After five minutes passed and the clock hit zero, Arrick moved his hands along the hologram, and the domicile slowed gradually. We spun slowly, the walls descending all around us. What had once been a closed-off room with tiny windows was now an open, glass-like bubble, with no obstruction to our view whatsoever. As we spun, a planet came into focus outside. It was tan and ruddy, and I realized that this dry, sad-looking place was the

Moldizean mortal home-world. Only the southern hemisphere retained any greenery.

Then we spun a little further, and I saw the giant, glowing orb of the sun. It was massive and pure, molten fire. It looked close enough to reach out and touch. But it was an optical illusion due to the enormity of the star. It was breathtaking.

We were nearly in place now, and Arrick spoke into the communication device. "Bekka and I are approaching our position. Command center, do you read us?"

"Loud and clear," Erykha responded. "Keep your mics set to send and receive. If we lose you, we'll start with the emergency protocol to restore the connection."

"Mics are adjusted," Arrick confirmed. "We'll confirm once we are ready to start the delay. Is there a status update on Gabryel?"

A pause before Damion said, "We don't have much longer. He's almost through. You need to hurry."

Without any preamble, Arrick turned to me. "Bekka, are we a go?"

I stood near the window and stared at the massive star in mute amazement. I flicked my eyes to him and then back outside. I felt the well of power deep inside of me and that tug of destiny once more. I was *She Who Was Sent*, and I accepted my fate. I took comfort in that fact. I understood that there was power in it. A calm settled into my bones, a confidence in my own ability that drove me forward. I could do this. Not only that, I was meant to do this. I let out a breath and shook out my hands. "I'm ready. Start the delay."

On the holo, a timer appeared with a readout of fifteen minutes that immediately began counting down. "The time delay is in place, and the model is queued. You're on," Damion said.

With his confirmation, I closed my eyes, seeking my power. Finding it, I pulled it out from deep inside of me and let it grow. As the blue light swirled around me, I focused harder and grabbed for more. Believing that I gathered enough for the first part of my task, I concentrated on the massive, glowing star before me. Gaze fixed on it, I took in steady breaths, trying to stay calm in the face of the overwhelming surge of magic inside of me. I clamped down the familiar panic at the sensation of wielding too much power. I was getting used to it by now. Plus, it was easier to control in my immortal form. After all, this body was made for it.

After one more breath, I pushed my power out and toward the existing sun. It shot from the domicile, a stream of blue, speeding through space. When it reached the star, it wound around it like a constrictor snake. Just like with the Puhari raiders, I closed my eyes and concentrated. I continued to twist my magic around it, and then I pierced through it. That was when I saw them. The building blocks that comprised the burning mass of fire. All its molecules and atoms were laid bare to me now, a patchwork puzzle.

I was surprised by how simple it was for me to tap into something this gigantic. When I had it all organized in my mind, I let out a long breath and pulled it apart at the seams. Once I was finished, I opened my eyes and watched as my will was done.

The sun hummed and roared, bright and glowing for a moment. Then it expanded, its glow dying as its fire went out, and it disintegrated into nothing. All that remained was total darkness in its wake. I wiped the sweat from my brow and realized that the task had taken more energy than I'd realized.

Dimly, I registered Arrick say, "Five minutes down, ten minutes remaining."

Erykha's voice rang out through the domicile. "Arrick, she needs to hurry. Gabryel's through. He's here!"

I could hear the desperation in her voice, and my nerves skittered.

"I see something," Caden shouted. "Holy Sh—" His line cut to static. Anxiety spiked inside me, but I couldn't worry about Caden right now. I didn't think my grandpa would kill him, and I needed to do what I came here to do and quick or else every mortal on Moldize would die when the time delay snapped back.

Hurrying, I re-focused my thoughts on creating what I had at my sister's wedding. Only this time, I wanted it to be outside of the room we were in, and on the other side of the protective barrier. So, I thrust my power out, gliding it smoothly through the walls of the domicile, and landing it in the exact place we'd determined. I kept drawing, pulling, shooting it out, and letting it amass. The glowing orb of it doubled in size, then tripled and quadrupled until it was about the size of three of our domiciles stacked together. I dragged in gulps of air as sweat slithered down my back from all the energy I was expending.

An explosion of sound ripped my attention away from the task at hand. Cutting my power off, I whirled around and saw blue light crackling around the far wall of the domicile. It spread, growing into the size of a doorway. Wind whipped around us as my grandfather walked through. His long, white hair flew around his face, his power enveloping him like a cloak. The strength of his magic left the room tangy with energy, and the air hummed around us. My heart pounded in my ears as the very thing I had dreaded from the moment I had agreed to help the Moldizeans came to fruition. My grandpa was here. He would stop me, maybe even kill Arrick. My throat closed in panic.

His eyes locked onto me, and I saw a moment of utter and complete relief flash over his expression before Arrick stepped between us. Gabryel's lips pulled back in a snarl, and he was no longer the grandfather I knew so well, the one I loved beyond measure. This was the warrior god. The Peacekeeper of Twelve Realms, and he took shit from no one.

His voice was filled with rage when he spoke. "Arrick, I should have known it was you. Death deities are always rotten to the core. Just like your grandfather was."

My brows rose in surprise. I had no idea that my grandpa knew who or what Arrick was, especially not by sight alone. I was equally stunned to hear him mention Arrick's predecessor, his malicious grandfather.

"So tell me, what made you think that you could cross into my world and kidnap my granddaughter without any consequences?"

My frantic gaze flipped between Arrick and my grandfather. Though this had been what I feared most all along, seeing it unfold in front of me was so much worse than I'd ever imagined.

Arrick never took his eyes off my grandpa even as he spoke to me. "Bekka, don't stop. We can't afford to waste any time." Before I could open my mouth to reply, black mist swirled in front of Arrick, creating a shield between my grandpa and us. "We only have four minutes left," Arrick yelled, frantic. "That's not enough time to sway him to our side and finish the job."

I looked at the shield, and panic rose inside me. "Please, Arrick, you can't hurt him."

"I won't. You have my word. But this won't hold him long."

Nodding, I turned back to the sun and shot my power out once more. The star grew, and I could hear frantic shouts as flashes of blue light erupted within Arrick's shield. Arrick and I were a mirror of each other, standing braced as we unleashed our power.

Loud booms rumbled from the other side of the barrier, but Arrick held fast. He weathered the barrage of attacks and managed to keep his makeshift shield intact. A few more seconds passed, and I could hear him groaning under the strain of his effort. In response, I pushed harder, working as fast as I could and pumping my magic into the core of the sun. After a few seconds, it doubled in size.

We continued like this for at least another minute. Arrick's grunts and growls of effort sang in the back of my mind like a muffled chorus as I poured my focus into my task. I could see the star's growth accelerating. We only needed another minute, and we'd be done.

But just as the sun neared the size of the planet it would serve, Arrick dropped to one knee, a cry of agony ripping through his throat. "Bekka! I can't hold it any longer. I'll keep my promise. Just keep going!" Arrick shouted.

I had a moment to look over my shoulder and watch as he closed his fists and his misty shield evaporated. My grandpa stood on the other side, blue light crackling all around him as his shoulders heaved.

He looked furious.

He reached out his hand and shot out a blast of power, aimed right at Arrick's heart, who blocked and dodged, using his warrior's body to evade and to play defense. Gabryel lunged, and Arrick parried again, keeping him busy with a dangerous game of cat and mouse.

My gut wrenched at the sight of my grandfather trying to kill Arrick, and I yelled, "Stop, please! Stop! Both of you stop!" But neither god listened to me. Either that or they couldn't hear me over the roar and boom of their magic.

I moved, starting to shift away from my task in a desperate attempt to stop the melee before me. To explain everything to my grandfather.

To make him stop.

But Arrick saw me and shouted, "No! Don't!" Another flash of blue and Arrick deflected it, rolling on the floor and getting up running. He yelled, desperation licking his words, "Keep going. Two minutes, Bekka! They all die in two minutes if you stop! Don't worry about me! Focus on them!"

My heart racing, I looked from the two gods I cared for, battling each other in what seemed like a deathmatch, and then back to the sun. I hesitated for just a second longer before I made my decision. I turned back to the burgeoning sun and doubled down once again, pushing even more power out. The sun grew steadily, but even I could see it was too slow. I'd taken too much time deciding what to do about Arrick and my grandfather. Now, I would need every last second of the time I had left.

I worked as fast as I could on the sun, keeping the battle in my peripheral vision, terrified of either possible outcome. I found that no amount of worry or terror could have prepared me for the gut-wrenching agony that filled me when my grandfather's magic finally hit home.

It blasted Arrick across the side of his face, slicing deep into his flesh and sending him sprawling. He skidded to a halt a few feet away from me, his body limp as a doll's. I squeezed my eyes shut as fresh tears sprang into them.

I knew it was an unfair fight.

Arrick had given me his word that he wouldn't harm my grandfather, and as a result, he had been forced to fight with one hand tied behind his back. *Why can't I stop fucking everything up?* I thought as I saw the god that made my heart beat faster and stomach swim with butterflies, lying on the floor. Blood trickled down the side of his face from the large gash, and I watched in mute horror as my grandfather advanced on him.

Before I even registered my decision, I twisted my body so that one hand was outstretched into the domicile and the other toward the sun. Without thinking, with one hand I erected a barrier of magic, just as Arrick had before, and with the other, I continued to feed my power to the sun. My grandpa's shock was complete as he ran straight into the wall of my power.

As I looked into his eyes, I could see that he hadn't understood until now. This was my choice.

"You can't hurt him," I cried, my eyes wild with fear as my grandfather took me in. I wasn't sure if Arrick was dead or alive, but I couldn't risk letting my grandpa near him right now. Not when I didn't have time to explain.

Not when I needed to see this done.

"Bekka, what are you doing?" my grandpa shouted, his voice muffled beyond the barrier. "You don't understand. You need to stop! It's too dangerous!" He hammered on my barrier with his power and his fists. Despite his protestations, I continued to pump my magic in both directions, one to uphold the shield and one to build the sun.

Sweat dripped down my brow, sliding down my cheeks, and I felt the familiar well of power inside of me draining faster than I could have imagined. Concern wove through my thoughts, but I ignored it.

I kept going.

When the sun grew to double the size of the planet it served, clearly visible through the window, my arms and legs shook. The quaking was soft at first, a small vibration. But it quickly gave way to violent, painful shudders. My body convulsed, and I let out a quiet moan, sinking to my knees.

"Bekka, please!" my grandpa screamed, his voice reedy with terror. "Let me through! You can't do this! You won't survive it!" I ignored his plea and his warning. I kept going, my magic still flowing out of me like water. My mind grew fuzzy. I was vaguely aware of Arrick's presence beside me. He was on his knees next to me, and I registered with dim relief that he was not dead after all.

He was shouting something. Maybe yelling my name? His hands gripped my shoulders, and he shook me, trying to get my attention. But I couldn't focus on him, couldn't hear past the roaring in my ears. All I knew was that I had to keep going. I had to save everyone, even if it meant I burned myself out in the process.

As Arrick had said earlier, he would save them at all costs.

As my power drained, I realized that I was willing to pay any price, too. If it meant that Mariah and Jarrod, Donny, Niko, and Kaleb got another chance at life, I would do whatever it took.

Then without warning, the star's growth stagnated, my barrier dropped, and my power guttered, fizzling to a halt. Tears sprang into my eyes, and I knew it was still too soon. The sun was too small to support Moldize. But I had nothing left to give.

With the barrier down, my grandpa rushed inside and slid to his knees next to Arrick in front of me.

Arrick turned terrified eyes on him and said, "She wouldn't stop. I tried to make her, but she wouldn't stop."

I looked from Arrick's beautiful face to my powerful grandfather. My grandpa's face was ashen with horror at what I'd done to myself, and his eyes were wide. "Bekka, why didn't you stop? I tried to warn you. The prophecy, it was too dangerous to let it play out."

Despite my dazed condition, I understood his meaning—this was why they had kept it from me all along. They were worried it would kill me. I looked down at my hand, and the light that made me a goddess, my celestial essence, was dull and nearly non-existent. I was burned out, and yet, it still hadn't been enough to accomplish my task. I turned my head to look at the timer. Just over one minute remained.

Had so much really happened in such little time?

I looked at Arrick. His face was coated in blood, and I felt a pang of guilt. *My fault,* I thought. "I'm sorry I couldn't do it," I whispered, my voice weakening as I heard the call to ascend like a song in my blood.

He stroked my hair, "No, I'm sorry. I should never have brought you here."

I shook my head, "I'm glad you did. I wanted to save them. They deserve a better life than the one they were dealt." I saw as my grandpa's eyes registered surprise. He looked from me to Arrick, and I thought that maybe he understood at last. Really understood.

The song to leave this plane of existence grew louder in my heart, and it felt so damn good. I wanted to reach out and grab onto it, riding it like a wave into the next oblivion.

"Give her to me," my grandpa urged, holding out his hands. Arrick looked at him and hesitated. "If you want any chance at saving her, then give her to me right now."

Arrick did as he was told, and my grandpa looked down at me and smiled sadly, "I'm sorry we didn't tell you, and I'm sorry I screwed this up. But don't waste any time once I'm finished." His voice was so distant, and I was floating away. He leaned down and pressed his hand to my heart and his forehead to mine. He whispered, "I love you, Bekka, and I trust that you'll use this well."

Then he pushed his power directly into my body.

I convulsed under the pressure of it, the strength of it.

At the first burst of it, my senses returned, and I realized what he was doing—I knew what his plan to save me was. I thrashed, trying to break away, not wanting any part of what he was offering me. I shouted and bucked, kicking my feet, but he held fast.

"Don't let him do this!" I wailed, trying to focus on Arrick. "It was only supposed to be me. Stop him, please!" Soggy tears rolled down my cheeks as his power kept flowing into me. The stronger I got, the harder I fought, but it was no use. He had made up his mind, and there was not a damn thing I could do to stop him. Because, a god can only gift his power to another deity once.

And once he does, he ceases to exist.

The only reason he could do it at all was because we were both creators. Like calls to like, after all.

As the final burst of his power flooded into me and his body started to fade, my grandpa whispered in my ear, "Finish what you started."

My heart shattered in my chest as my grandpa dematerialized entirely, his body turning into a million sparkling lights that slowly disappeared.

Anger and grief washed through me, but I remembered his last words.

His final request of me.

Finish what I started.

So, I rose to my feet and looked to the clock. Ten seconds left. I reached out and punched as much power out of me as I could manage.

The molten sphere grew, magic flowing around it. We were so close. It was almost done. I pushed with everything

I could, and at the two-second mark, Erykha shouted through the comm device, "Stop!"

Effortlessly, I cut off the flow of our combined power. I stared at the glowing orb in the sky in a combination of amazement and sorrow.

Shouts of excitement and congratulations erupted from the comms, everyone but Arrick and me oblivious to what had just transpired with my grandpa. I heard Caden and Deklan's voices flow through, and I felt a pang of relief that they were safe, but I couldn't find it in my heart to celebrate with them.

Instead, I sunk to my knees and gave into my grief entirely.

"Why?" I moaned, keening as I sobbed. "Why did he do it? It was just supposed to be me." Arrick kneeled next to me and wrapped his arms around me. I let him, the need to feel anchored onto this world overwhelming.

Arrick waited a long time until my wails had died into quiet tears before he whispered, "He did it because he loved you." We stayed like that for a long time, until I burned out all the emotion inside of me.

I was raw and ragged by the time we finally rose to our feet. I stared out the window at the sun and the planet floating in the distance. I knew that I would soon be forced to come to terms with the fact that Gabryel, my grandpa, the protector and the ruler of our multiverse, was gone.

Why hadn't he just let me die? No one would have missed me, except a handful of those closest to me. But the rest of the multiverse would have been safe.

But now, the 900 years of peace that my grandpa had achieved would be threatened. Everyone he kept in check through the force of his power and his leadership would challenge *me*. I would not be able to just go home and continue with my old life. I would be forced to take up the

Peacekeeper's mantle, or else watch the construct of our peaceful multiverse come crumbling down.

Arrick stood beside me and rested a hand on my shoulder, "I'm so sorry," he whispered, "I never imagined it would come to this. I thought—"

"It wasn't your fault," I interrupted, but found that I had no other words of comfort to offer. My emotions were still too close to the surface, and I knew that I would lash out if I said more. So instead, I stared out the window, mute as the weight of truth hit me.

I was *She Who Was Sent*, but it seemed there was more to the prophecy than met the eye. My power curled inside of me, now merged with my grandfather's. I could feel both distinct essences there and knew what the truth of the prophecy was.

I was the most powerful creation deity ever to exist.

But not because I was created that way.

Instead, I had been forged from tragedy and from the joining of both my power and my grandpa's. And as I turned and stared into Arrick's eyes, I whispered, "I'm afraid."

He brushed a loose lock of hair off my cheek and looked into my eyes, "Of what?"

"Of what comes next," I answered, looking down at my hands. When I looked back up at him, I saw understanding and regret in the lines of his face.

"I know. But like I promised before, I've got your back. Always." He reached out to squeeze my hand. "We all do."

My breath shuddered, and despite his reassurance, I still felt the weight of responsibility settle onto my shoulders. I looked out the window one last time, at the glowing sun I had created, at the planet I had saved, and wondered if it was worth it. I found that I would not know the answer to that question until a long time from now when the full ramification of today's events played out in their entirety.

But what I did know for certain was that nothing would ever be the same again.

EPILOGUE

The Nefarals

She sat, lounging by her family's pool in the Bicaidian immortal realm and popping juicy grapes into her mouth. *If I had to name a painting after this moment, I would call it 'Goddess in Repose,'* she thought, biting down into a particularly tender morsel. *Or maybe a more apt name would be 'Goddess Just Released from Prison,'* she mused.

She was a Nefaral—a goddess with gifts deemed unsavory by the great and powerful council. The Nefaric Pillar of Power, and all its members, had been under tight restrictions since Gabryel had taken the helm as Peacekeeper of the Twelve Realms. Since then, the glory days of her predecessors had been systematically and carefully destroyed.

In their modern, Peacekeeper's world, all Nefarals were required to register their powers and only used them under heavily regulated circumstances. The more powerful Nefarals, like her, were implanted with governing chips that suppressed their magic as soon as they came of age.

Despite this, she would sometimes fantasize about carving the governor chip from her neck and releasing all that magic roiling inside of her, just dying to get out. But she hadn't dared to attempt it, at least not when Gabryel was alive. A slow, feral smile bloomed across her red-coated lips at what she knew to be true.

The Peacekeeper was dead.

She had felt his life force depart this dimension not an hour earlier—a shockwave had rippled through the ether-sphere, making her magic dance with delight at his departure. She surmised that he must have met an untimely demise because he had been still relatively young by godly standards. This was all fine by her, though.

In fact, it was better than fine.

This was the chance she had yearned for since she came into her powers over 100 years ago on her 18th birthday.

"What are you smiling about?" a deep, male voice asked from just outside their family's white, stone mansion. Cactus plants with vivid red, orange, and pink blooms lined the walkway that led to her lounger, and the owner of the male voice strode down that path. His gait was predatory and swaggering, as befitted someone with his substantial power.

"Can't you feel it?" she asked as he drew closer, inhaling the statically charged atmosphere around her. It was as though she were alive for the first time since her powers materialized, just before that damned chip had been embedded in her neck.

"Feel what?" he asked, the sharp lines of his face morphing into a mask of curiosity. He took a seat on the lounger next to her and planted his forearms on his knees, surveying her. For someone with his abilities, it seemed to her that he should have figured it out already. But instead of chastising him for being so thick, she decided to ride on this high just a little longer and humor him. So, she dropped her sleek, toned legs off the lounge chair and faced him.

Her canines gleamed sharp in the sunlight as she said, "Our time has come."

ACKNOWLEDGEMENTS

Diary of a Deity - The Burning has truly been a labor of love. There were a lot of people along the way who helped make this book possible. So, without further adieu, I want to give a big thank you to my editor, Melissa Bourbon, who gave me amazing feedback and inspiration. This book wouldn't be what it is today without her insight, guidance, and encouragement.

Another big thank you to Leoneh Charmell, who believed in this story from the first moment she read it and who encouraged me to publish it. Without her guidance, I know that I never would have gotten it all done. So thank you!

Special thanks to Elvins Acurero and Leoneh Charmell for their amazing artwork on the cover and for bringing my world to life.

Also, thank you to my parents, sister and the friends who read through my initial versions of this story and gave me the encouragement I needed to go further with it. You have no idea how much your belief in me pushed me to be better and to finish this story.

Last but not least, thank you to my critique partner, Tamara, who pushed me to deliver my best work throughout the entire novel.

So again, to everyone who supported me through this process and continues to support me today. You are all amazing and I am so grateful to you all.

ABOUT THE AUTHOR

Loryn Moore lives in Northern California with her husband and two young sons. She and her husband are avid DIYers, backyard gardeners, proud chicken owners, and recreational soccer players. Her eldest son is in non-stop motion and keeping up with him proves ever more challenging as his ability to sprint like the wind grows with each passing day. Her youngest is an infant and his epic smiles are the absolute highlight of her day, every single day. These three men are the loves of her life, and her inspiration in all that she does.

Loryn knew that she loved writing by the time she hit sixth grade. She took a poetry class that year and enjoyed every second of it. This led into a passion for reading, which further spurred her passion for writing. The place she cultivated a large part of her acumen was with friends in high school, passing long, funny notes between classes. They would always try to one-up each other with ridiculous stories that they would fabricate over any mundane detail they could find. It always left them with aching bellies and stitches in their sides from laughing so hard.

By the time college hit, she switched her major four times. Business, Journalism, Creative Writing and then back to Business, which stuck. But she continued to take creative writing workshops all through her coursework. This was where she wrote her first book. And to be blunt. It sucked.

But she kept at it, writing a new story that allowed her to stick to her strengths. A mere eighty drafts later and she had come up with her debut novel. She learned that writing is a labor of love and that characters do the damnedest things, constantly destroying the author's carefully crafted plotlines. But to her, that's what makes characters so real. They all have minds of their own.

VISIT Loryn's Website at www.LorynMoore.com

Follow Loryn on Facebook @LorynMooreAuthor

https://www.facebook.com/Loryn-Moore-Author-105941031361188/

Follow Loryn on Instagram @LorynMooreAuthor

https://www.instagram.com/lorynmooreauthor/

OTHER BOOKS BY LORYN MOORE

Diary of a Deity Series
- *The Burning is Loryn's debut novel and the first book in a trilogy, but she has much more in planned for 2021.*

- The Rising (Book 2) - Coming December 2021

Jenna Torrence Series
- Jenna Torrence Book 1 - Coming Early 2022